WARTIME COMES TO WEST INDIA DOCK ROAD

RENITA D'SILVA

Boldwood

First published in Great Britain in 2025 by Boldwood Books Ltd.

Copyright © Renita D'Silva, 2025

Cover Design by JD Smith Design Ltd

Cover Images: Shutterstock and [Magdalena Russocka] Trevillion Images

A CIP catalogue record for this book is available from the British Library.

Paperback ISBN 978-1-83617-276-5

Large Print ISBN 978-1-83617-275-8

Hardback ISBN 978-1-83617-274-1

Ebook ISBN 978-1-83617-277-2

Kindle ISBN 978-1-83617-278-9

Audio CD ISBN 978-1-83617-269-7

MP3 CD ISBN 978-1-83617-270-3

Digital audio download ISBN 978-1-83617-272-7

This book is printed on certified sustainable paper. Boldwood Books is dedicated to putting sustainability at the heart of our business. For more information please visit https://www.boldwoodbooks.com/about-us/sustainability/

Boldwood Books Ltd, 23 Bowerdean Street, London, SW6 3TN

www.boldwoodbooks.com

For the educators and mentors who provided such wonderful grounding and set such an amazing example through their selfless caring and kindness.
Truly blessed to have been taught by you, Ms Thecla Pereira, Sister Hildegard, Reverend Father Valerian Mendonca and Reverend Father William Gonsalves, amongst others.

PROLOGUE
PADDY

Paddy dreams of home. Ballinacurra, County Cork. Ireland.

Lush, rain-bejewelled fields stretching as far as the eye can see. Long, lazy summer days spent playing with the other village children, mud fights on the riverbank, hide and seek and make believe in the harbour, the exotic perfumes of distant lands wafting on the ships coming in to dock.

Perhaps that was when he decided he wanted to leave, jump on one of those ships and see where they took him.

For he was a dreamer, was Paddy. He longed to see the world and what it had to offer. He had never been happy staying in one place, even one as safe and contained and comfortably familiar as Ballinacurra.

'Restless feet and restless heart,' his mammy always said, shaking her head sadly. 'You were born squirming. Wanting to escape from the get-go.'

He is jolted from his homesick musings laced navy with regret by a high-pitched keening. Scarily familiar. The sound of his nightmares.

On and on it goes, loud and insistent, screaming danger.

And now, instead of the sparkly, emerald, peaceful and welcome, although ache-inducing visions of his homeland, other gory images, ones he's tried and failed to forget, assault him with remorseless persistence. His friends and fellow infantrymen, lying bloodied and limbless in foreign soil, eyes open yet unseeing, faces frozen in painful grimaces. Some gravely wounded, their life force draining onto enemy ground as opposed to the beloved earth of home, colouring it the deep crimson of what might have been, with their last breath calling out to their mothers, their wives, their lovers, their children.

No.

No, no, no.

Soft arms around him. The perfume of roses and love. His mother's scent. Reminiscent of childhood and comfort.

A gentle voice crooning, 'Shh, it's all right.'

It is *not* all right; he doesn't deserve this. To be held. To be cradled in gentle arms like he is someone precious, a calm voice providing consolation.

He had not done the same for his fellows. Provided them the solace they sought as life left them, so violently, too soon. He should have held them, pretended to be their mother, their wife, their daughter, their son, their love. Whoever they sought with their last breath.

But he was terrified. Traumatised.

It is no excuse.

No, it was not. For he had turned tail and run, afraid and also relieved that his life had been spared. That he was free to live one more day. Taking deep breaths of gunpowder, blood, suffering and agony-stained, ice-splattered foreign air, poisoned with the cries of dying souls, smoke and burning flesh.

'I am a coward. I don't deserve this, Moira. I don't.'

'You do, Da. You do.'

'I should have stayed. I should have consoled my fellows. Died with them.'

'You came back for us. For me.'

'Moira? Is that you?'

'It's Charity, Da.'

'My Charity. My bubba.'

'Yes. Your Charity.'

'That sound... The war... I thought it ended. I thought we won. That we are safe...'

'It's just air raid sirens, Da. You *are* safe. We all are.'

'Moira?'

'She's all right. She's here, right next to you, see.'

'My boys? Your brothers?'

'They are here too.'

'Da, we are safe,' he hears. His boys.

He is being rocked, comforted in his daughter's arms. When did the tables turn and it became her, his child, soothing him?

You are pathetic.

He tries to shut his ears to the sirens.

But they pierce through regardless.

He shuts his eyes tight but the images keep on coming, a revolving kaleidoscope of guilt.

His penance. The only way he can do justice to the dead he abandoned.

By remembering them. By always carrying them with him.

He thought he was leaving them behind.

But they never went away.

His mammy used to complain that he had dreams too big for sense. 'You want *everything*.'

'And why not?' Paddy would ask.

'Don't be cheeky now.'

But he *was* cheeky. And determined with it. He had worked all hours at any job going and once he earned enough, he had jumped on the boat to England.

He hadn't reckoned with homesickness. A physical ache throbbing in his heart, keeping time with its beat. *Ballinacurra. Ballinacurra.* He had wanted to experience everything. But now he was in England, all he wanted was the certainty of home. But he couldn't go back with nothing to show for it.

And so he stayed. Even though he was miserable.

And then...

He met Moira. Beautiful Moira, who was also missing home so much that she had turned to God, hoping He would cure it.

'But instead,' she would whisper to him during their first heady days together, the happiest days of his life, in her sweet voice that brought to mind the morning mist draping the hills behind his childhood home, 'He sent you.'

They rented a room on West India Dock Road. For the docks reminded Paddy in some small way of his hometown. And, what was more, they housed a thriving Irish community, their speech carrying the rhythm and cadences of home.

They worked hard, he and Moira, and they made plans for the future. With Moira, at West India Docks, restless Paddy was finally ready to put down roots.

So when the tall house came up for sale on West India Dock Road, he and Moira scraped together the deposit for it.

There were always sailors at the docks looking for a place to stay and so, with far too much space for the two of them in the house, they lived in the room next to the kitchen and rented out the rest.

Thus began the Paddy O'Kelly Boarding and Lodging house.

'It should be the Paddy and Moira O'Kelly Boarding and Lodging house,' he'd said to his wife and she'd laughed, that infectious giggle that he thought of as angel song, a host of divinity celebrating, and said, 'It is a mouthful so it is, Paddy. Leave it be.'

Mammy, would you look at me now?

And then...

He can't quite remember which came first: the best thing to happen to him after Moira, or the worst. Charity, beautiful, bonny Charity. Or the war of 1914, the war they said would end all wars.

Paddy, young and idealistic and fired up by patriotism, wanted to do his bit. For his country and his fledgeling family. And so he signed up.

He signed up and now...

Here it is again.

Screeching, screaming hell.

'It's all right, Da. We're safe,' his daughter says in her calm voice, so like Moira's.

For a brief moment, in his mind's eye, he sees the hills behind his childhood home in Ballinacurra, shrouded in a lace of morning mist, enchanted and ethereal.

Then it shatters into a thousand pieces, the beautiful memory, momentarily soothing, shot through by the relentless screeching which splinters his heart, his sense, his rationality.

You don't deserve to be soothed, they cry, his dead comrades.

I don't.

'It's all right, Da.' His daughter's tender arms, her gentle kindness.

It is too much.

It is not all right. He's brought children into a world sundering apart once again.

Nothing is all right.

Nothing.

I want to go home, Paddy thinks even as he clutches his daughter's hand for dear life until the keening stops and there is a blessed breath of peace, sweet as his beloved Moira's kiss.

PART I

1

CHARITY

Charity pegs laundry to the line. The air that brushes her face, although carrying a hint of smoke from last night's air raid, is fresh and frisky in the unseasonal autumn sunshine. It is at odds with the general mood of the residents of West India Dock Road, which, despite their best efforts at being cheerful and standing up to Hitler and keeping calm and carrying on, is gloomy.

For when the war started, everyone assumed that the Jerries would be seen off in a matter of days. Then it became weeks, then months.

And now it is more than a year since the war started and the outlook is not good.

It is cold but sunny, and Charity decided to chance it, dry the clothes outdoors. The sprinkling of morning frost they woke up to has been chased away by honeyed sunshine, making even the rubble, all that is left of Number 57, which took a hit during the relentless air raids they've been experiencing, glow and sparkle like treasure. Thankfully, Mrs Devlin, whose house it was, was spared as she was taking shelter in the Underground station along with the other residents of West India Dock Road. But all of her precious mementoes and keepsakes by which she remembered her sons and husband whom she had lost in the first war went up in smoke.

'They were priceless,' she sobbed. 'Irreplaceable.'

'Edna,' Mrs Kerridge soothed. 'You carry your loved ones here.' She placed a gentle hand on Mrs Devlin's heart. 'They are always with you.'

The matrons of West India Dock Road, kind-hearted but everyone knew, not to be messed with, had taken charge, sending the housing officer packing.

'No, our Edna will not bed down at the school until you find somewhere for her to stay. She already has somewhere. She is staying with me,' Mrs Neville declared firmly. Even though she had no teeth at all (nobody knew why; Charity's youngest brother Paddy maintained resolutely that it was because she was a witch and witches had no need for teeth when they had spells and could brew potions), she could get her point across very clearly indeed when she chose to.

'Rather Mrs Devlin than us.' Charity's brothers shuddered.

But despite Charity's brothers' reservations, the arrangement has worked very well indeed. Both women were lonely, Charity knows, and would have gone to their graves without admitting it. But now they have company, they are thriving.

'Mrs Neville looks less like a witch now,' Paddy mused in wonder, 'but Mrs Devlin is looking more like one.'

As always, Charity's thoughts drift to her brothers and her worries with regard to them. Since the incessant and continued air raids, she has broached the subject, over and over, of sending them out of London to safety. But they are adamant that they want to stay right here, at the boarding and lodging house started by their parents, which Charity has been managing since both Da and Mammy took ill.

'This is our home,' they insist. 'We are not going anywhere, Charity.'

Fergus, who has just turned fifteen, left school last year and is apprenticing at the shipbuilders' down at the docks.

Charity worries about Paddy and Connor's education. At ten and eleven respectively, they need the structure school lends to their day, not to mention the learning. But educating children has, understandably, taken a hit since the war, what with teachers signing up and children being evacuated and school buildings requisitioned to house all those displaced by the air raids.

Charity shakes her head to clear it. Ah well, what will be will be. They are here, all together, and making the best of the circumstances. And truth be told, she would miss her brothers something terrible and worry about them if they did evacuate. She does not know how those mothers and sisters and daughters and wives deal with their loved ones at war. She sees them bravely smiling and carrying on even though they are worrying every minute of every day, hoping for the best while dreading the worst.

'Charity, I have a confession to make.' Paddy (the youngest of the O'Kelly siblings, given his father's name for by the time he came along, neither of Charity's parents had either the energy or the inclination to think up something new) had come to Charity looking very glum indeed just after the war started.

'What is it, my love?' Charity asked, setting her pencil down; she had been trying to do the dreaded accounts and was glad of a break from them. She squatted down to Paddy's eye level and gathered him in her arms; he still was young enough to let her do so. He smelled as he always did of dirt and mischief and that sweet scent that was uniquely him, and she breathed in deeply of it, even as she felt a skein of anxiety knot her spine. For the scrunched up face and the frown lines between his eyes were very unusual for her happy-go-lucky brother.

'I have not been saying my prayers like the nuns said I should every night before bed. Is this why the war started?' He looked so upset, tears sparking in his eyes.

Her heart went out to him, even as gently she kissed his worry lines away.

'No, my love. God sees your heart and I promise he has forgiven you for not saying your prayers. Shall I tell you a secret? I forget often too.'

'But the war...'

'You knew the war was coming, didn't you? We all did. The papers were full of it, weren't they?'

'But it started the week I didn't pray,' Paddy said, but his tears had stopped now and the frown lines had disappeared from his face.

'It started because Germany invaded Poland on September first, my love. And Britain couldn't sit back and do nothing. We can't let one country take over another any time they feel like it now, can we?'

And now, Paddy smiled, that full-beamed glow that lit him up, and Charity's heart swelled and she hugged him tighter. How she loved this child.

But then his brow furrowed again. 'Charity,' his voice a whisper against her chest. 'Are we going to die?'

'Well, we all will, one day when we're old and grey, but not now, don't you worry,' she said firmly, keeping her fingers crossed even as she prayed in her head, *Please God, let it be so, where my brothers are concerned.* She held her brother at arm's length and looked into his eyes. 'Paddy, you know that all the able-bodied men in this street and all over the country have signed up to fight, don't you?'

He nodded solemnly.

'They will win this war and will not allow you or any of us to die.' She kept her gaze steady, hoping her eyes did not convey her fear, her worries, even as she continued to cross her fingers behind her back.

'But *they* might die.'

'They might and they know this. They are bravely defending us, even at the cost of their own lives. And we all will be doing our bit here, Paddy, all right?'

He nodded but still looked worried. 'Fergus says he will fight too.'

'Well, he's too young so don't you worry, my love.'

Paddy nodded again, gravely. Then he threw his arms around Charity, planted a kiss on her cheek and was gone.

Charity had sighed, stood up and returned to doing the accounts but her heart was not in it.

Now more than a year into the war, she keeps a continued eye on her brothers, talks to them, is upfront with them and repeatedly asks them to come to her with anything that might be worrying them, 'At any time, day or night, boys.'

'We know, Charity,' they say, sighing.

But Paddy, and indeed all of Charity's brothers, seem to have accepted, in the way of children, their changed lives, the rationing and lack of food, the constant danger and continued uncertainty, and, recently, the nightly air raids, the fragile precariousness of their existence and for this, Charity is grateful.

Charity waves to Mrs Boon and Mrs Ross, from the tenements opposite, who are also pegging their washing on the line, taking advantage of this sudden and rare blessing of sun.

Mrs Ross looks beaten – she has already lost her daughter, who had joined the Women's Auxiliary Air Force, to the war – she was one of the first on the street to receive the dreaded telegram.

'She wasn't even in active combat. She was working at one of the military installations on the home front.' Mrs Ross had cried, her face pale as fog with shock and upset.

And she hasn't heard from her son since the Battle of Dunkirk.

Charity shivers even though she's wrapped up warm. When the Belgian army surrendered to the Germans at Dunkirk, British troops were rushed in, among them, good men from in and around these docks. The Germans won and several British destroyers and ships were sunk and bombed, and thousands of men lost their lives. A major evacuation process ensued to rescue the British divisions stranded behind defensive lines.

It was precarious and involved, with many dying on the beaches at Dunkirk and others being captured, but some of the men from around the docks have, thankfully, made it back, looking lost and tired, hollow-faced and haunted-eyed but appearing relieved to be home.

'Hundreds of civilian vessels – from fishing smacks and cockle boats to lifeboats and sailing barges, trawlers, passenger ferries, and yachts – answered the Royal Navy's call for help and crossed the English Channel. They sailed from Ramsgate all the way to Dunkirk,' Mr Stone had said.

Mr Stone and his friend and chess opponent, Mr Brown, were veterans of the first war, but too old to sign up for this one, although of course, like everyone else on the street, they were doing their bit to help out on the home front. They read the papers each morning and relayed the news to the diners in Divya's curry house – Charity, her brothers and lodgers, and everyone else in the street (sadly depleted now with the able-bodied men at war), and then some – for everyone loved Divya's food.

'Their mission...' Mr Brown had begun.

'Whose?' Mrs Neville asked through a mouthful of Divya's Indian-style spiced porridge, which was also Charity's favourite.

Charity savoured the warming kick of spices as she listened to the conversation. Her brothers too were agog even as they tucked into their food with a gusto they had never shown for anything Charity, not a good cook at the best of times, prepared. Thank God for Divya and her curry house, where Charity, her brothers and her lodgers took all of their meals.

'The civilian vessels who volunteered to rescue the men stranded in Dunkirk,' Mr Brown said patiently.

'Ah, go on.' Mrs Neville nodded regally, although the porridge coating her toothless gums spoiled the effect a tad.

'Their mission was to pick up the soldiers from the beaches and ferry them to larger ships. But they faced several challenges.'

'They would do,' Mrs Murphy said gravely.

Mrs Neville shot her a look that could start a war. She hated the fact that Mrs Murphy had beat her to the title of oldest woman in the street by a whisker.

'She's lying,' Mrs Neville said of Mrs Murphy often. 'How can she be eighty-five when she has all her own teeth?'

'Those thousands of tiny civilian boats crossing the English Channel to rescue our men battled air attacks, German artillery and mines, U-Boats, E-Boats, and "friendly fire".

Those brave civilian sailors who volunteered to help our stranded at Dunkirk rescued not only our men but also French and other Allied soldiers,' Mr Brown said, sniffing, his eyes sparkling, no doubt recalling his own war, and Mr Stone reached across and patted his arm.

'There's no need to get so emotional just because I've checkmated you – again,' Mr Stone declared.

'Never mind, Mr Brown, here's your porridge. Tuck in,' Divya said, placing a steaming bowl in front of Mr Brown, who liked his porridge plain: 'no fancy Indian spices for me, not with porridge, thank you.'

'Now then, *I* am the reigning champion, winning against you so often that I've stopped keeping tabs, as God and everyone in here is my witness,' declared Mr Brown grandly.

'Don't bring God into it,' Mrs Kerridge admonished sharply and Mr Brown, looking suitably chastised, turned his attention to food.

'And as for the chess,' Mrs Kerridge continued, 'you're each just as bad as the other.'

Mr Brown snorted and Mr Stone huffed but they kept their peace knowing they didn't have a chance of winning a war of words or even fists for that matter against Mrs Kerridge.

'She would send Hitler packing, she would,' Mr Stone grumbled, sighing with great feeling, out of Mrs Kerridge's earshot.

When Mrs Kerridge heard this – news travelled fast in this street and if it was not meant for someone's ears, that only meant it reached them faster – she preened. 'That's what my eldest says, that Britain is missing a trick and that if us ladies of the East End went to war, we would bring victory in two weeks, if that.'

Divya caught Charity's eye and smiled.

Divya is Charity's best friend. Charity cannot believe she's known her for only a couple of years; it feels like forever. And what's more, Charity's brothers love her too.

Divya had come to England as a nanny to a family who reneged on their promise to book a passage back to India for her once they had found an English nanny to take over from Divya. Divya, alone and abandoned in England, had, serendipitously, fainted in front of the Ursuline nuns' convent in Forest Gate. The nuns are like family to Charity. Her mammy, Moira, was a novice nun before falling in love with Paddy and leaving the order. The nuns stayed in touch and visit often, with goodies for the boys and Charity and soup and anecdotes for Moira and Paddy.

Their visits are highly anticipated by Moira, Paddy and their children alike. Charity's mammy and da are always happier when the nuns have been to visit. They sit with Charity's parents and regale them with stories of 'home'. Ireland.

When Divya fainted in front of the Ursuline convent, the nuns had cared for Divya until she regained her strength. Then, they had directed Divya to the lodging house that Charity ran and luckily, Charity had a room to offer Divya.

And that was it; they became fast friends. Divya, who is brilliant at cooking, had taken over the kitchen at the lodging house and when the entirety of the East End turned up to sample her food, Charity's friend Jack Devine had helped Divya lease the vacant house opposite Charity's to start her own curry house. It has been thriving ever since, even, especially now there's war, as Divya is a dab hand at concocting delicacies with very few ingredients given the dearth of food.

Since the beginning of September, London has been bombed every night, the East End taking the biggest hits. Wapping has been wrecked, she's heard – not that they are any better. The factories along the docks are targeted, sugar, butter and molasses leaking into the Thames, lending it an oily sheen, the scent of fire and smoke and charred spices and burning sugar.

Many women have received the dreaded telegrams and Charity, Divya, Mrs Kerridge and the other matrons from West India Dock Road have tried to comfort them the best they can. But what can they say, really? And all the while they are thinking, *We might be in the same situation soon.*

The mothers, sisters, daughters, wives who have lost their loved ones are hollow-eyed as they sip the chicory tea the ladies of West India Dock Road have brewed for them, using their sugar rations that they had been hoarding for a special occasion to make it nice and sweet: the least they can do, even if the women cannot taste or appreciate it.

And then there are the men who have been taken prisoners of war by Germany, and others who they are still waiting on for news of, their very own Jack Devine among them.

Jack, Charity's childhood friend, whom her brothers look up to and try to emulate. Jack, kind, helpful, who was the one who gave her the idea of making the basement of the lodging house her parents' room so that in the event of war, there was no need to disturb them, for it would work as a shelter. Charity thanks Jack in her head every night, when the air raid sirens go off and her father, Paddy, with his trauma from the first war, panics and acts out, and is in no condition to be moved. And even if he could be cajoled into going to a public shelter, Charity's bedridden mother, Moira, is too ill and weak to be moved anyway.

Jack is sweet on Divya, who has found her calling in running the curry house.

'She has the knack of making something out of nothing,

that gel,' Mrs Neville declares often, speaking for the street. 'She manages to prepare delicious meals even during these times of lack, don't ask me 'ow.'

Charity's brothers, always fussy eaters, love Divya's food and will eat anything she makes, for which Charity is grateful.

When Jack signed up, Divya had promised to write to Jack regularly and she has honoured that promise, keeping Jack up to date on the news of the street. If there's anything the neighbours want to tell Jack, they convey it through Divya. 'Only cheerful news, mind, as he has enough to be worrying about,' Divya said, and everyone on the street nodded assent.

Jack is a kind man, a good man and, Charity thinks often, would be perfect for her best friend, but Divya's heart is otherwise engaged. She loves Raghu, a lascar, who is also on the frontlines, somewhere in France but Divya doesn't have an address for him to write to and Charity knows that this breaks her friend's heart.

When the intimation about the Germans winning at Dunkirk, and that troops were being evacuated from the city, came through, everyone on West India Dock Road, along with the rest of the country, had waited on tenterhooks for news of their loved ones.

And then, slowly, the telegrams began arriving, and letters, with more grim news every day.

'My eldest has written,' Mrs Kerridge cried, bright joy in her voice, like the taste of cake. 'He's alive, thank the Lord.' She made the sign of the cross, even as she hugged the letter to her chest. 'For a moment there, I thought...' She sniffed, took a breath, and said briskly, 'He's on his way home.' Mrs Kerridge made the sign of the cross again. 'But there are others still stranded, he writes. I hope they all get out.'

Mrs Kerridge's eldest did make his way back. Thin to the point of emaciation and looking so much older than his years.

'He was unrecognisable, coated in grime when he arrived, even his eyes unfamiliar, no longer sparkling with that irrepressible twinkle, the hint of laughter,' Mrs Kerridge relayed to Charity and the other women of West India Dock Road when they asked after him. 'He sleeps for much of the time. He doesn't speak about what he has endured, although I can guess from the heaviness in his eyes, the shadows stealing the light from them. He does not want to go out. "All I need is to be here, Ma, at home," he says.' Mrs Kerridge sighed deeply. 'But at least he's back.'

For there has been no news from her younger two and she is, understandably, worried beyond belief, although she tries to buck up everyone on the street, bless her.

Divya, meanwhile, has been worrying about both Jack and Raghu.

Raghu, she has no means of contacting.

Jack does respond to her letters but since Dunkirk, there has been no communication from him, so everyone on the street is worried as they all care for Jack.

Now, Charity sees the postmistress, Mrs Jennings (who took over the reins when the previous postman signed up; she is so kind and gentle, especially when someone on the street receives the dreaded telegram, her eyes shining with empathy), make her way down the street.

Please let there be no telegrams today, Charity prays.

Across the road, she sees Mrs Boon also watch the postmistress's progress with fearful eyes. Mrs Ross alternates between fear and hope, both flashing upon her face. Much as she is waiting to hear from her son, she is worried it will be the wrong kind of news.

'Not knowing is, in many ways, better. At least this way, I can tell myself I will hear from him in due course. I can cling to the hope that he's all right, just not able to write,' she said to Charity, blowing her nose, eyes sparkling with pain and anxiety.

Each morning, when Mrs Jennings makes her rounds, Mrs Ross worries that this might be the day she receives the terrible news that she has lost her son too, Charity knows.

This is one of the sides to war that Charity just cannot get used to. The grim news, how a sheet of paper has the ability to devastate lives, forever changing their course.

Charity, Mrs Boon and Mrs Ross watch the postmistress linger at each of the tenements.

Her expression is impassive as she walks from door to door, depositing letters, Mrs Ross's expression clearing when she has no letters, which means she has another day of hope.

And now Mrs Jennings is at Divya's Curry House.

Charity waits with bated breath and she sees Mrs Boon and Mrs Ross doing the same.

Is the postmistress going to go inside?

Mrs Jennings pauses at the doorstep to the curry house.

They all crane to try and read her expression.

Mrs Boon opens her mouth and Charity knows she's going to call to her, ask if there's any news.

But before she can, Mrs Jennings opens the door to the curry house and steps inside.

Mrs Boon, Mrs Ross and Charity exchange glances, worry and anticipation, Mrs Ross no doubt thinking of the day the postmistress had stopped off at hers with the horrid telegram about her daughter.

Is today when they will hear from Jack? Or is it bad news, the worst?

2

DIVYA

September 14, 1940

Dear Jack,

I am writing to you as I promised to when you went away to war.

I am writing to you although I confess, you have me worried.

I am writing to you even though I do not know how you are.

For until recently, you have always replied.

But I write to you in the hope that you are receiving my letters, that you are well, that one day, soon, I will hear from you.

Sometimes, weeks go by before I receive your letters and then I get two at once. I hope this is the case now too. Although I must admit that it has been a fair few weeks since your last communication. There has never been such a long gap between your letters.

We think of you and all of us here at West India Dock

Road miss you. Especially Fergus, Connor and Paddy. You are their hero. To hear them talk would be to think that you are single-handedly defending us against the Huns. It's always Mr Devine this and Mr Devine that.

I don't think you know just how much of an impression you have made on all of our lives – just how much you are missed. I wish I could show you and I will attempt to do just that here.

Your letters are a cause for celebration for the whole street.

When one of your letters arrives, Mr Brown pops his head out of the curry house and shouts up and down the street in his booming voice resonating with the rich and haunting music of the land of his birth, 'Letter from Jack Devine!'

And within moments, all who are around drop their chores and collect in the curry house.

The last time everyone gathered to hear your news, Mrs O'Riley must have been in the middle of eating lunch, for she smelled strongly of the fish paste sandwiches she favours and everyone inched very slightly away from her, trying not to make it obvious, but failing.

'Why are you all acting as if I've caught the plague?' she asked, sounding wounded. When she opened her mouth, of course, the smell was much worse and the others were trying not to flinch.

Mrs Ross, kind-hearted soul that she is, went up to Mrs O'Riley and gave her a hug. 'Ach, it's not you, hen. There's some water here and we're all trying to steer clear of it, that's all.'

The water was from Mrs Nolan's hands dripping suds. She must have been washing the dishes, for she had arrived in her pinny, hair tied back in a scarf, trailing wet droplets everywhere, earning dismayed tuts from Mrs Boon and Mrs Kerridge.

Mrs Neville, of course, not one to mince her words, grumbled, 'I nearly slipped on the puddles you caused there, Poll. You've messed up Miss Ram's clean floor something terrible.'

Mrs Nolan blushed, mumbling apologies, her complexion matching her red hair – although it's now mostly silvery grey. She worries about her husband constantly. He was one of the soldiers stranded at Dunkirk, rescued by the civilian sailors who volunteered with the Royal Navy. He arrived back home safe and sound, physically. But the war, well, it's changed him much like the first war did Paddy Senior.

Most likely my mention of Dunkirk and the Royal Navy above will be crossed out by the censors as will this, but I want to say it anyway as it's been on my mind.

I think you must have been one of the soldiers at Dunkirk, reading between the (crossed out) lines of your letters when they used to come regularly. Here's hoping you too will be home soon.

Anyway, back to my tale. Poor Mrs Nolan was looking mortified about dripping water on her way in.

'Don't worry about it,' I said, fetching the mop and scrubbing the floor before taking the tea orders.

'I will be glad of real tea instead of the chicory one we are forced to drink at home because of rationing,' Mrs Porter said, sighing.

Chicory? I hear you ask.

Needs must, Jack. Wartime rationing, as you know from my letters.

So everyone makes do and we have (mostly, and some more so than others) grown used to it.

Coffee is not rationed but it is scarce. In any case, most in the street prefer tea. I remember how much you would enjoy my Indian version of tea, spiced with cardamom, cinnamon and ginger. Those were the days, eh?

The other day, Mrs Porter told us about how she stores coffee at home alongside a small collection of tinned goods, peaches, sardines, peas and the like, which she keeps adding to, she said, in the event of an invasion. Mrs Porter, who always goes against anything Mrs O'Riley says, snapped icily at her to not be so gloomy, that we were going to win the war. 'Yes, but there is no harm in being prepared,' Mrs O'Riley shot back.

Mrs Neville, sensing that things were about to get heated, intervened, complaining about the cost of meat, how dear it was and how she bulked her mince up with oats to make it go further. You can't hardly tell the difference, she said.

Mrs Devlin, who is currently stopping at Mrs Neville's because her house was bombed, disagreed. 'All you taste is Bovril and oats with the merest hint of mince.'

Mrs Neville turned quite pink with outrage which caused Mrs Devlin to backtrack hastily and declare how much she loved Mrs Neville's cooking.

'Is that why you find every excuse to eat at the curry house, eh, Edna?' Mrs Neville asked, but the sharpness was gone from her voice and she was smiling.

('It's not a smile, it is a witch's smirk,' Paddy maintains. 'Be careful, she can cast a spell on you any time,' he has warned, eyes wide as dinner plates.)

Thankfully, restaurants are not subject to rationing as of yet, which is a blessing as much of the street comes to the curry house for their meals.

Mr Barney, who came into the curry house quite out of breath, looking relieved when he realised I hadn't started reading your letter out to everyone, flat-out refused to drink tea, spiced or otherwise...

'I'd rather have ale.' He grinned cheekily.

'It's not even gone ten in the morning,' Mrs Barney said tightly. 'It will be the death of you, mark my words. You already have a cough that you cannot shake.'

On cue, Mr Barney started coughing. His wife, despite her disapproval, slapped his back, perhaps a little too vigorously, until the coughing fit passed.

'It's from the smoke I inhaled, woman, when the pub was on fire,' Mr Barney said, when he had stopped wheezing. 'And we are at war, if you didn't notice. The Jerries might take me long before the ale does.'

Mrs Kerridge glared at him. 'We are all living through it every day. No need to bring it up.'

The public house is up and running again; I don't think I've mentioned this before.

People need sustenance, and morale boosting, something to take their mind off their woes, Mr Barney maintains, and he religiously opens up the public house every day at the dot of noon. The only problem, Mr Barney complains, is that he can't find help, with all the young 'uns having signed up. And so, Mrs Barney has stepped in.

'It's not the same, gel,' he complained to me the other day, when he nipped into the curry house for breakfast. 'She puts a dampener on proceedings, summat.'

'What he means,' Mrs Barney yelled from where she was seated near the window with the other women of West India

Dock Road, 'is that I don't let him drink as much as he'd like. And I'm not above stopping serving patrons when they've had one too many either.'

Mrs Kerridge pronounced firmly that that was as it should be and the other women nodded.

'What's more,' Mrs Barney said, encouraged by her companions' approval, 'I don't care for vulgar talk or fruity language. Certain standards must be maintained, even in a public house.'

The other women cheered.

'Eyes and ears everywhere, that woman,' Mr Barney muttered, face morose as he gulped his glass of water and winced, no doubt wishing it was a tankard of ale.

Nevertheless, the public house does brisk business – people needing an outlet from what they see, experience and live through, day on day. The windows dark with blackout curtains once smoggy dusk settles, sounds of desperate jollity mingling with the pungent aroma of hops. When the sirens sound, as they do, every night, the patrons of the public house stagger outside, joining the other residents of the street seeking shelter from the air raids. And soon enough, the now familiar roar of enemy planes flying overhead, loud thuds as falling bombs find targets, the crash of splintering glass, the patter of falling bricks and the pounding smack of crumbling walls, the fiery doom of smoke and ash...

Ah, I didn't mean to talk about the raids. My letters to you help me as much as anything to make sense of these dark times we find ourselves living through. Setting my thoughts and the events of the day down to you in letter form is therapeutic. Trying to find happy snippets of news to tell you helps take my mind away from the sadness we *encounter daily. But don't get me wrong, there are also many good things happening, so much to celebrate.*

Everyone on the street chips in and does their bit. All the women, including myself, have signed up for the Women's Voluntary Service. We do what we can, when we can: helping with the evacuation of children, organising and maintaining public air raid shelters and clearing up after an air raid – often heartbreaking but sometimes very rewarding. Yesterday morning, I rescued a puppy from the rubble; he was alive just about and although we feared he might have been hurt, within minutes, he was bounding around and giving our dusty feet an enthusiastic lick.

Some of us work as ambulance attendants; we have been trained in first aid. We care for people whose homes were bombed and find them clothing and essentials. We impose blackout restrictions (Mrs Kerridge is very good at this). We inspect gas masks and make sure sandbags are in place outside large buildings. Mrs Porter runs a mobile canteen service during air raids and for troops arriving at railway stations and at the port.

And, when we cannot get out and about, we use any time we might have spare to make bandages and knit and sew clothing, scarves, vests, hats, gloves and pyjamas for soldiers. This is what the women of West India Dock Road do when they congregate here at the curry house, even while listening to your letters. We're always keeping busy; no minute is wasted.

These letters to you help boost my morale, as I said. And there is another advantage: my English is improving daily. I have been using the dictionary Paddy lent me – can you tell? I try to use at least five new words that I have learned in every letter to you. It seems the dictionary was gifted by the Ursuline nuns to Charity when she started school, then passed down to Fergus and from him to Connor, then Paddy and now I am the proud owner of it. (Paddy was very happy to give it to me. 'Finally,' he said. 'I'm handing something down. Usually, I'm the one who has to take hand-me-downs from everyone else!' He sounded quite fed up.)

Anyway, I was telling you about what happened when your last letter arrived; oh, it feels like such a long time ago. Here's hoping a letter from you is even now making its way to us.

Once I'd dried the floor, I served the drinks with snacks: potato scones and apple fritters – I'm having to come up with innovative ways to make the most of available produce. Although, as I said already, restaurants are not subject to rationing, food is scarce and expensive with it.

Mrs Neville grumbled that she was sick of potatoes and nothing else. Nevertheless she took a generous bite of her potato scone and her face lit up. She turned to me and smiled. 'Oh, but you make even the humble potato taste delicious.'

Excuse my boasting but it warmed my heart, even as Paddy took my hand and whispered urgently, 'Miss Ram, she has been doing this a lot recently, I've observed. I think she plans to try her witchy ways with you next.' He was so earnest that I hid my laughter behind a cough.

'These scones are to die for,' Mrs Neville continued through a busy mouthful.

'Do you have to bring death into it, Gracie?' Mrs Murphy complained.

Mrs O'Riley reached for another apple fritter and Mrs Kerridge sniffed loudly, turning away. She is perpetually *upset that Mrs O'Riley eats double the amount she does but while she herself is heavyset, Mrs O'Riley somehow manages to stay thin as a vine.*

In any case, once everyone had settled down to eat and listen, I read out your letter to them, words cut out by censors notwithstanding.

Although I must admit that over the months of our correspondence, you have become a dab hand at writing letters that are almost censor proof; each letter arrives with less crossing out. Myself and all here at West India Dock Road are eagerly awaiting your next one.

I know you have seen some action, that it must be difficult and soul-destroying, that writing letters must be the last thing on your mind. If so, that's fine, as long as you are well.

Mr Brown, Mr Stone, Charity, Fergus, Connor and Paddy and their mammy and da, Mr and Mrs Rosenbaum, Mr Lee, Mrs Kerridge, Mrs Neville, Mrs Murphy, Mrs Nolan, Mrs Boon, Mrs Ross, Mrs O'Riley, Mrs Porter, Mrs Devlin, Mr and Mrs Barney and the other stalwarts of West India Dock Road send their love.

Mrs Murphy said to tell you that she's praying for you daily, and even though the church was bombed, Father O'Donnell is still conducting mass as per usual. In any case, she said, God listens to prayers whether it is at church or at the shrine she has at home, so not to worry. You are being looked after by Him. She said I have to write this down word for word, so here it is. Mrs Murphy's prayers are with you.

Now for some of our news from the street.

Mr Stone and Mr Brown are still at the chess, when not occupied by their duties as civil defence workers, each insisting that they have won the most games against the other.

Mr Rosenbaum (also a civil defence worker) is still very much a spectator, tutting when they make what he thinks is an obvious mistake, much to their annoyance. He refuses to take part as he says that will start a war more grim than the one currently taking place for he will beat them both hands down.

'If you keep saying that and continue with your tutting when I make a move, I won't be held responsible for my actions,' Mr Stone growled at Mr Rosenbaum yesterday morning, tired and moody from being up all night because of the air raid and fed up with Mr Rosenbaum's interference. 'It's very bad for the concentration for one thing, and that is apart from—'

'Concentration, what concentration? Anyone who was concentrating wouldn't make such a simple beginner's mistake,' Mr Rosenbaum interjected.

'I'll give you beginner's mistake,' Mr Stone cried.

Fergus, Connor and Paddy had to wade in and hold the old men apart.

Fast friends despite being sworn chess opponents, Mr Stone and Mr Brown united against Mr Rosenbaum in their outrage.

'War, he says. We'll give you war right now if you keep insisting you'll beat us and pointing out supposed mistakes when you haven't played a single game. For all we know, you don't know how to play at all,' Mr Brown boomed.

'Of course I do. My wife will tell you. Esther, come here. Now where has she got to? Not sweeping the stoop again. A wasted effort for when there's a bit of wind, it throws the dust right back upon it,' Mr Rosenbaum exploded.

'At least she's doing something. All you do is pick holes at everyone else's actions,' Mr Stone snapped.

It is a good thing Fergus has suddenly shot up and is now taller than me (easily done) and almost a head taller than Charity too, although still a beanpole as ever, no matter how much I try with my curries to fatten him up. He's a proper young man now. I bet you wouldn't recognise him if you were to bump into him in the street. Or perhaps you would, for Charity says he is the image of their da when he was younger.

In any case, Fergus held the men back, Connor and Paddy dancing around them, excited at this development in the usually peaceful curry house.

The news was up and down the street in minutes that Mr Rosenbaum, Mr Brown and Mr Stone had nearly come to blows. Esther Rosenbaum marched into the curry house in her pinny and clutching her broom, the other matrons of West India Dock Road right on her heels, having abandoned whatever they were doing, not wanting to miss out on any more of the drama.

Mrs Rosenbaum looked thoroughly fed up with her husband.

'What is it with you getting all het up about such silly things when our people are dying in droves and I don't know the fate of my sister?' she hissed at her husband and he looked suitably chastised.

That evening, old Mr Lee, ever the peacemaker, decided that the air needed clearing.

'They friend. It not right they fighting. World sad enough already,' he said to me, when he came into the curry house bearing his potent Chinese liquor, baijiu.

Mr Lee is green fingered, as you know. There is no plant that does not thrive when subjected to his gentle and loving ministrations and nothing he cannot grow. So although he's busy with his shop, in whatever spare time he can carve out, he grows vegetables and fruit for the war effort to supplement rationing, and this, within his small living quarters above his shop and the tiny plot of garden outside.

Mr Brown and Mr Stone stubbornly refused to sit at the same table as Mr Rosenbaum but Mr Lee was unmoving in his insistence that they'd only have a shot of his liquor if Mr Rosenbaum was allowed to join the table too.

They very reluctantly agreed, refusing to acknowledge Mr Rosenbaum or even look in his direction when he made his way to their table.

Needless to say all this was great gossip fodder for the women of the street who had brought their chores into the curry house and got on with them while also avidly watching the goings on and drinking tea and snacking on the pakoras and carrot cake I had prepared.

But of course one shot of baijiu in and the men were great friends again, laughing and chatting together, animosity nowhere in evidence.

The matrons sighed; they had hoped for more.

Mr Lee, Mr Rosenbaum, Mr Stone and Mr Brown stayed at the curry house late into the evening, long after everyone else had had supper and left. With the blackout curtains drawn, drinking and reminiscing, all rivalries and irritations were a thing of the past.

This morning though, it was a different story. They were all very much the worse for wear and grumpy with each other, the camaraderie of the previous evening quite forgotten.

This letter has gone on longer than I expected. I love writing to you, even if I worry about you, where you are, why you haven't replied, if you are all right. Safe. I, along with everyone else on the street, sincerely hope so.

I write to you of an evening, once everyone has left, with the blackout curtains drawn, kitchen wiped clean but the faint scent of spices lingering even so, sitting at the table where you told me you had signed up for war and asked me if I would write to you, the lamp flickering, golden light spilling onto the page, shadows dancing all around, one ear tuned for the sirens which will surely come.

(I am striking out that last bit; I start writing to you and I find myself pouring out my thoughts and before I know it, I say something that I didn't mean to. I try to keep these letters to you jolly. You don't need more gloom when you're facing death every day. Once I'm done, I'll give this letter the once over and cross out any sentences that lower the mood and any that give too much away – save the censors a job.)

When I collate (a new word I picked up from the dictionary; I like the sound of it) all the news of the street to relate to you, I realise afresh how lucky I am to be here, doing what I love, cooking for the street, part of a community that bands together, even, especially in the worst of times. There is such comfort in that.

Ah, now here's a heartwarming story for you to end this letter with.

Mr Lee told me that his friend, Mr Wu's house was bombed over in Stepney.

'What's heartwarming about that?' I hear you ask.

It's coming, I promise.

Mr Wu and his family were thankfully spared as they were in the shelter.

Afterwards, they went to the rest centre, the local school which had been appropriated for the purpose. It was in mayhem, for several streets had been bombed and several families rendered homeless. Everyone clamouring for attention while more families kept arriving, babies wailing, parents anxious. All distressed from suddenly finding themselves destitute, tired from having spent the night on the Underground platform and afterwards, having to walk away from the smouldering ruins of their homes to the rest centre, passing more bombed-out buildings along the way. Beaten, scarred, upset, dejected people.

Mr Wu, who is a good musician, spied a battered piano in the corner of the school hall and he quietly went over and began to play.

Gradually, the room calmed down.

Someone brought an accordion which he had taken down to the Tube station to entertain people sheltering there while overhead the German death machines dropped their deadly cargo.

'It was the only thing that escaped the bombing. That and these clothes on my back,' he told Mr Wu later.

In any case, while Mr Wu played the piano, this other man provided accompaniment on his accordion, someone else sang and somehow, they created a festive atmosphere amidst all that pain and loss.

'This is for those who were not lucky enough,' the accordion player said, leading Mr Wu in a well-known hymn.

They played and sang and prayed and Mr Wu swore that the pigeons nesting in the rafters of the school building cooed in accompaniment and amidst the human voices, Mr Wu, who Mr Lee said is not normally fanciful, thought he heard angels joining in. Their prayers that day went straight to heaven, Mr Wu told Mr Lee with tears in his eyes.

So that is it from me.

Do write back, won't you, please, just to let us all know you are safe?

All of us here on West India Dock Road send our very best wishes and all our love,

Divya, on behalf of the residents of West India Dock Road

3

DIVYA

September 14, 1940

Dearest Raghu,

Here I am writing to you again. Writing into the ether.

One more letter I will not send, for I do not know where to send it.

In my letters to Jack (which do make their way to him as he, unlike you, has given me an address to write to), I save all the good and happy news of the street and to you, Raghu, I bare my soul, although of course, you will not see it.

I hope you are safe. I pray you are well.

For that's all I can do. Pray for you. Write to you: the equivalent of talking to you in my head.

I hate you for signing up for war and not leaving me a forwarding address.

But I love you more.

Why, Raghu? Why did you do it? Why couldn't I at least write to you?

In the one letter I have from you, which you sent when you joined up, without letting me know where you were going to be posted, you said you weren't good enough for me. That you wanted, want, for me to live my life without you in it, in your opinion, dragging me down.

I understand why you feel the way you do, especially after seeing the way lascars are treated here, like second-class citizens.

You might feel you are not good enough for me, but what gave you the right to decide what I want on my behalf?

In my opinion, being a lascar is a very important job. You lascars were responsible for the smooth running of the ships travelling to and from the colonies before they were all requisitioned for war purposes. You made sure the voyages were calm with no hiccups.

You helped me so much on my voyage to England. From rescuing me when I got lost on my way to my cabin to smiling at me whenever you saw me after, you steadied me. I was flailing after losing my parents, I was scared to be journeying from India across the world and you were a familiar face, my anchor, like the peepal tree in my child-hood village that I would shelter under when I was feeling worried or upset. And then, as I was leaving the ship, you called me your friend. It meant the world to me, although good girl that I was, I didn't tell you so. I even refused to shake your hand, as I recall. Oh, but life is short, I under-stand now. I should have taken your hand then. I should have held on and not let go.

Raghu, for me, you are perfect. You are kind, you are good. You work hard. You understand me. You touch my heart. *When you are with me, I feel complete. I have never felt that with anyone else.*

I want you, nobody else.

Raghu, why, when there is death all around us, with the world at war, when life is so very precarious, are you denying me contact with you?

All I have of you are a few choice memories. Cooking together side by side, hands touching occasionally, sending jolts of connection through me, my body wanting more.

One kiss. When it felt like our souls melded. But you pulled away, too soon.

I have replayed that kiss so many times.

Will I get the chance to experience another?

I cling to that belief. For I have nothing else. Nothing tangible from you except...

I have your letter that you wrote asking me to forget you. It is too fragile now to rest against my heart so it nestles under my pillow alongside all the letters I have written to you since you left, except when the air raid siren sounds. Then, it comes with me, tucked securely next to my heart.

These letters I write to you... some are angry. Some loving.

In this one... I feel like ranting. I am grieving.

For Munnoo died.

I am devastated. I know, with the war, men with their whole lives ahead of them are dying. And that is heartbreaking. But this is too.

I grieve for those men dying before they've really lived, their entire, very brief experience of adult life: war, pain, destruction, death. And I grieve for Munnoo.

I liked the man. He was the one who lent me a helping

hand when I first arrived at West India Dock Road and stumbled upon the cobbles; do you remember me telling you? He was a real character, one of a kind. A nameless orphan plucked from the streets of India by an English Lord, christened Munnoo and brought to England. Dressing like nobility (he was buried in his suit) and speaking 'posh' like the king. After his master's death, he would have liked to work for nobility – that's all he knew to do, after all – but they were having none of it. He would have been a misfit had he travelled back to India. He would have been a misfit here too, but Eastenders are warm as their posh counterparts are not and they accepted him into their fold, fondly putting up with his eccentricities.

I miss him. Munnoo. The way he would think before speaking, making sure his every word carried weight. His quiet dignity. His gentlemanly ways. That smile that lit him up from the inside even as he got weaker and weaker from his illness for which he refused to see the doctor, claiming he didn't hold with medicine. We think it was nothing to do with medicine and all to do with the fact that he couldn't afford the doctor. But he was very proud and repeatedly refused the loan offered by his friend Mr Benjamin Juma (one of Charity's lodgers – you remember him, don't you? He too signed up and left a few weeks after you did). Munnoo knew there was no way he could repay Mr Juma. Mr Juma tried to tell him that he didn't need the money back but Munnoo was having none of it.

The last time Munnoo was here, at the curry house, both he and his suit looked the worse for wear, worn and fragile.

Everyone in the curry house – the matrons of West India Dock Road, Charity, her brothers and lodgers, Mr Brown, Mr Stone, Mr Lee and Mr Rosenbaum – exchanged worried *looks. Munnoo appeared very wan and was wheezing something terrible.*

Mrs Kerridge (once again) recommended Dr Barrett. 'He is a good man; you will like him.' He also doesn't charge much for his services, but she tactfully kept that to herself.

Nevertheless, 'No thank you, my dear. I have a healthy Indian disrespect for doctors,' Munnoo declared. The sentence sounded odd, spoken in his posh accent.

Kind Mr Lee intervened, challenging Munnoo to a game of cards, which he lost on purpose. Nobody in their right mind will play cards with Mr Lee, not if they want to be beaten soundly.

In any case, Mr Lee shook hands with Munnoo and tried to give him money. 'You win, I lose. You must take.'

Munnoo saw right through it. 'I am no charity case,' he growled and turned away from Mr Lee.

But when he left here, having eaten barely anything, he shook hands with Mr Lee, telling him he was a good man. Mr Lee, not to be deterred, tried to give Munnoo his 'winnings' again.

'I don't want them but thank you all the same,' Munnoo said, inclining his head regally, the effect spoiled by his wheezing, one hand on his chest as he tried to collect his breath, Mr Lee trying not to look alarmed.

And do you know, Munnoo didn't have much to his name, yet still he deposited a coin or two in the jar I have by the till for people to pay as much as they see fit; the times being as they are, I no longer put prices on what I serve. People give as much as they can, when and if they can.

Charity wrote to Mr Juma to tell him about Munnoo's passing. She dithered as to whether she should but did so in the end. You see, when writing to those of you at the battlefront, we try to be as positive as possible; after all, you see such loss. You go out to fight with your life in your hands each morning not knowing if this is the day you will not make it back. (I, on the other hand, pour my heart to you for I know these letters are not going anywhere. Yet still I cling on to the stubborn hope that perhaps one day, we will meet and I will give you this huge pile of letters that contain my heart, everything I've experienced since you've been gone, my hopes and fears, my pain and heartache and missing. I write in the hope that one day, you will read them.)

I picture Mr Juma, surrounded by death and devastation – the East End with its quirks, its mishmash of businesses and people, open-hearted for the most part, must seem so very far away – opening Charity's letter and shedding a few tears for the man who was his friend.

We all attended the funeral in our mourning best. It was at the local church. Munnoo must have been born Hindu but he didn't know either his parents or his own name, if he had one. He always maintained, 'I was given a name and a life by my master.' He adopted his master's beliefs and was a staunch Christian, praying regularly and attending church when he could, right until the very end.

The church, which has been bombed but nevertheless still holds regular services, was packed. Munnoo had amassed a lot of friends during his time here. It seemed as if the entirety of the East End – those not away at war, that is – had turned up to pay their respects. The Ursuline nuns were there too. 'Oh, we knew Munnoo very well,' they said. 'He would attend mass at our church sometimes.'

They used to bring him fruit and Irish soup, just as they did for Charity's parents, and as they were nuns, Munnoo would take it whereas he would have refused it from anyone else.

The nuns attended the funeral mass after their visit to Charity, her brothers and her parents at the boarding house.

The nuns also, bless them, dropped in on me and brought some vegetables they'd grown in the convent gardens for me.

'Look at you, our girl, you're thriving,' they said, beaming, eyes glowing. 'Didn't we say you'd find your community here?'

I served them some of the carrot halva and spiced potato cakes that I had made.

'These are like boxty,' they exulted of the potato cakes. 'But with more spices,' they coughed, turning quite red and taking great big gulps of the masala tea I had also served, flavoured with cardamom and cinnamon.

Mr Lee cried openly at the funeral, which was a more sombre affair than usual. Father O'Donnell conducted the service among the bombed-out ruins of the church with gravity and ceremony. It was a reflection of our times. The nuns' voices raised in song reverberating hauntingly among the smashed tiles and piles of rubble. The wind howling through the gaping holes in the burnt bricks, smashed glass casting rainbows on the casket when the sun shone through.

Birds flying overhead, dark silhouettes against a jagged section of smoggy sky, visible through the broken roof. In a few hours, as dusk descended, German planes would do the same, raining their deathly cargo, making light of darkness, deceptively bright firework orange.

Do you believe in the afterlife? We never talked about this, did we?

I don't know if there is an afterlife, but I quite like the Christians' idea of heaven.

I think my ma and baba are somewhere up there watching over me and I think your ma is too, watching over you. She will make sure you come to no harm. She will deliver you safely to me; that is my hope.

At Munnoo's funeral, as we said goodbye to him, I hoped and prayed that there was a heaven or something like it. I prayed that Munnoo would be reunited there with the one man he loved and was loyal to all his life: his only family. His master. The way his eyes would glow when he spoke of him. 'I was fated to be one of the beggar boys, fighting for scraps, living and dying on Indian streets, but my master saw something in me. He rescued me, gave me a life I hadn't even dreamed of. What I am, everything I am, I owe to him.'

Raghu, I first met you when I was on my way to a new life in England.

Then I met you again here in West India Dock Road and with that curry competition, everything changed once more.

I know one thing. Our time on Earth is short enough as it is and I want to spend whatever time I have with you.

I will stop before my tears make a mess of this.

I am in a maudlin mood today, my love.

I will go to bed now and dream of you until the sirens jolt me awake.

Be safe and come back to me.

Yours, always,

Divya

4

CHARITY

Charity has just come back into the lodging house and is preparing to go over the accounts: a joyless task but it must be done. Every month, she worries about whether this will be the month they will have to shut down. She prays to Jesus, Mary and Joseph and all the saints and also keeps her fingers crossed for good measure that she will be able to keep this boarding and lodging house that her parents started with such hope and promise soon after they were married, going for another few weeks.

There are bigger problems of course, what with the war. The numbers of lodgers staying at Charity's are at an all-time low, since she started keeping records after taking over the management of the business when it became obvious her father couldn't. Her mother couldn't either, what with her health being too fragile.

But Charity's worries about the lodging house pale in light of the persistent nightly bombing of the East End. Each morning, the residents of West India Dock Road emerge from shelters and Tube stations, yawning from broken nights, stretching their backs from tiredness, their bodies cramped from being cooped up and falling asleep in whatever small corner of the shelter or station they managed to carve out for themselves and give thanks that their home, a small flat in a run-down, cold and leaky tenement though it might be, is still standing and that they are alive, even as they set about helping those who have not been as lucky, in whatever way they can.

Charity and no doubt everyone in the East End carries with them the fear that tomorrow is not certain. The lodging house might be bombed at any time. But while it is still standing, Charity wants to keep it going although it is becoming harder to do so as the war drags on.

'It doesn't help that you are too kind for your own good, gel, and accept every sailor who cannot afford to board at the other lodging houses. You do not charge them what they owe but instead, you take what they can afford to pay. You really must insist that they pay upfront,' Mrs Kerridge remonstrates sternly, shaking her head. 'If they cannot pay, then you must turn them away, heartbreaking though it is. But you don't do that, do you?' Mrs Kerridge huffs. 'No, you take whatever gifts they give in lieu of money, which is why your lodging house is overrun with knick-knacks from every part of the world, gathering dust, but not enough actual paying clientele. You must harden your heart, my dear. You are running a business here.'

'We have managed so far, Mrs Kerridge, and hopefully, we will manage for a few more months,' Charity says, with more conviction in her voice than she feels.

Now, she sighs as she pulls out the book of accounts, knowing, given that it has been another month with very few rooms occupied, that it will be a dire affair.

Part of her is also dwelling on the postmistress going into Divya's Curry House.

Should she go over and see what that was about?

Stop procrastinating and get to it, she chides herself sternly and she has just started poring over the revenue for the month – almost non-existent – when Divya bursts through the door, waving a letter at Charity.

'It's Jack.' Charity's friend's eyes are wide and bloodshot. 'He's been taken prisoner.'

Charity's heart falls. *No. Not our Jack.*

Her next thought, *How will I tell the boys?*

Her dismay must show on her face for Divya says, 'But he's alive, Charity. He can write to us. That's something.'

Charity throws her arms around Divya and buries her head in her friend's neck, smelling spices and comfort.

'Yes,' she whispers. 'That's something.'

'What's something?' The boys are suddenly there beside Charity and Divya.

Charity is struck dumb, looking at her brothers' sweet faces, mischief and adventure and innocence. Their innocence makes her heart ache for it is gradually being eroded by war, replaced by a heaviness, their eyes bearing expressions too old for their years.

'Charity, what is it?' Fergus asks, Connor and Paddy looking mutely at her.

She cannot reply so it is Divya who steps up.

'Tell everyone on the street to gather in the curry house, please, boys. I have some news.'

'About Mr Devine?' Paddy asks.

'None other,' Divya says, smiling gently at Paddy.

'Is he all right?'

'I'll tell you all in a minute, along with everyone else; what do you say?' Divya says brightly.

'It's not good news then,' Connor, who never speaks if he

can help it, preferring that his brothers do it for him, says. He only talks if he thinks it is important. Now his voice is heavy, weighted down with distress.

'No, it can't be, not our Mr Devine,' Paddy cries, while Fergus is quiet, his attention fixed upon the letter in Divya's hand, all the while chewing his lower lip, which he does when he's upset.

'Boys...' Charity begins, although she has no idea what to say next.

Thankfully, she is interrupted.

'We saw Miss Ram run across to you in a hurry holding up a letter and knew it was momentous news.' It is Mrs Kerridge, busily wiping her hands on her pinny while looking askance at Divya.

The news, as is the way in this street, has broken already.

She is fast followed by the other ladies of West India Dock Road and a bemused-looking Mr Brown, Mr Stone, Mr Rosenbaum and Mr Lee.

'It's Jack,' Divya says, her cheeks flushed, voice breathless. 'He's written to me.'

'At last! Hooray!' The cheer resonates through the street.

Only Charity's brothers are quiet, subdued like Charity herself, when usually they would be dancing up and down the street helping spread the word even further than it has already. They know there's a 'but' coming.

'The lad survived Dunkirk. Good for him,' Mr Stone says in his foreman's voice.

There are more cheers. The street exuberantly celebrates every small bit of good news, given joy has been in short supply recently.

'He has been taken a prisoner of war,' Divya says gravely and the cheers die down.

Paddy comes up to Charity and slips his small hand through hers. She squeezes it, even as her heart breaks to see the worry crowding his and her other brothers' eyes, the same expression reflected on the faces of everyone currently spilling out the small hallway of the lodging house and into the street.

'But he says he's fine. He's given me his new address so I can write and tell him you are all sending him love and asking after him,' Divya says, her voice wavering slightly.

'Tell him to come 'ome in one piece, mind,' Mrs Neville clucks. 'We want to see the boy. 'E's a ray of sunshine in the street so 'e is. 'E always gave me a hand with anything at 'ome that needed doing – no chore too much for 'im. I miss that.'

'I will tell him, Mrs Neville,' Divya promises.

'I can help you with anything that needs doing, Mrs Neville,' Fergus offers.

Beside Charity, her younger two brothers recoil, Paddy hissing, 'What are you doing. Fergus, don't you know she's a witch?'

But Charity is too overwhelmed to chastise Paddy. She could kiss Fergus, if he would let her, her heart blooming with pride. He's turned out all right, has Fergus.

Mrs Neville agrees, for she beams widely at him, displaying those toothless gums, making Paddy flinch and surreptitiously inch closer to Charity. 'You're a good 'un, son. I might just take you up on it.'

'Any time, Mrs Neville,' Fergus says.

'And now, come on over to the curry house for tea and some fruit scones and onion bhajis,' Divya says. 'And I will read you Jack's letter in full.'

'Now you're talking.' Mrs Kerridge smiles.

But in the shadows crowding Mrs Kerridge's eyes, Charity knows she is worrying if her younger two boys, whom she's not heard from, have met the same fate as Jack. And if they have, she must be wondering, why haven't they written to her. Is no word from them good news or...?

Charity asks her brothers to stay back for a bit.

'That's a good thing you did there, Fergus,' she says.

Fergus nods, trying to appear nonchalant but the tips of his ears turn pink like they do when he is pleased.

'But, Fergus, Mrs Neville! She's a witch, she is!' Paddy is outraged.

'There's no such thing as witches,' Fergus says.

Paddy's face falls and he looks at his brother with an expression of pure betrayal.

Connor is looking from one brother to the other, not sure whom to believe.

Paddy however is firm. He crosses his arms and says, mutinously, 'Well, don't come to us when she casts a spell on you.'

Fergus smiles and ruffles his hair. 'Too right, squirt, I won't.' But his voice is fond.

'Now, boys,' Charity says. 'You heard Divya. Jack is fine. There's nothing to worry about.'

'But the Germans have captured him!' Paddy cries, indignant. 'How can he be fine?'

'They're letting him write home; that's a good sign, isn't it? Look, he will be fine, I promise.'

'You can't promise that, Charity,' Paddy says and Charity's heart breaks at the certainty in her youngest brother's voice. There was a time when her brothers believed she could fix anything, when they took her promises at face value.

Not any more.

War has changed that too.

'Yes, you're right, I can't,' she says softly. 'But we must

believe that he will be okay. He wants us to. It is the only way he can go on and we can too.'

Her brothers, knowing that she's now telling the truth, nod agreement.

Paddy throws his arms around Charity. 'Don't be sad. Like you said, he will be fine. I will pray for him. The nuns said God listens to the prayers of children.'

'You do that.' She smiles shakily. 'Come now, let's go to Divya's and hear what Jack has to say, shall we?'

* * *

The residents of West India Dock Road try to put on a brave face but secretly they agonise about their loved ones, the country, the world, smiling even when they feel like crying.

Divya worries, Charity knows, about her beau Raghu's fate. She has no way of contacting him and so she thinks the worst even though she says to Charity, often enough, 'If something happened to him, I would know, I am sure,' her voice fierce with defiant hope as she adds, 'Right now, my heart tells me he is all right.'

And both Charity and Divya understand, like the rest of the street, that while Jack's letters might be cheery, he will not let on as to what he is enduring, and they hope and pray that it is not too much to bear.

This is what war has done to them: made them dissemble and smile and cheer and applaud, while they carry worry around like an extra limb.

5

DIVYA

September 20, 1940

Dear Jack,

Oh, it was such a blessing to receive your letter! The whole street rejoiced.

How are you, my friend?

I know you can't tell us much but we all hope that the Jerries are treating you all right.

We are very grateful for any news from you and here's hoping your letters continue until you are freed which will be very soon, we pray.

You said in your letter that you love hearing the goings on over here. That it brings your beloved East End alive for you.

On that note, here's all the news from home.

This morning, when I went over to Mrs Kerridge's table – she was with Mrs Neville, Mrs Devlin and Mrs Boon – with tea and ginger and honey biscuits, Mrs Kerridge lowered her voice to a confidential whisper. 'I dropped in at Poll's earlier, to see how she is doing. She worries about her old man something terrible as you know,' Mrs Kerridge said. 'Bless her, she insisted I had one of the biscuits she'd baked. She's a gem, is our Poll, but goodness, she can't hardly bake to save her life. I took a biscuit just to be polite. Hard as stone, my dear. I nearly lost a tooth!'

'Mind you don't end up like me, Vera,' Mrs Neville cackled, showing off her toothless gums, caked with biscuit crumbs.

Over at the next table, Mrs Porter, Mrs O'Riley, Mrs Murphy and Mrs Rosenbaum were discussing rationing.

Mrs O'Riley asked if the others had tried Marmite biscuits while helping herself to another one of my ginger and honey ones.

Mrs Porter, who always goes against anything Mrs O'Riley says, made a face. 'No, and I wouldn't want to. I mix dried egg powder with water and fry it for when I'm peckish. It's better than you'd think.'

'I caught some children eating Oxo cubes and munching on sticks of rhubarb, in place of sweets the other day, the poor dears.' Mrs Murphy said, sighing. 'I asked them where they'd got the rhubarb from; you know how difficult it is to get anything fresh these days.'

'Tell me about it; the queue at the greengrocers' is a mile long no matter what time of day you get there. And of course, the later you leave it, the less there is of anything,' Mrs Porter grumbled.

Mrs O'Riley wanted to know where the young ones had got their rhubarb from.

'They confessed that they'd stolen it from the trenches dug by the Home Guard where they're growing fruit and *vegetables to make up for the lack. I promised I'd keep their secret,' Mrs Murphy said.*

'This is 'ow you keep their secret is it: by announcing it to the whole street?' Mrs Neville cackled from the next table.

'Mind yer own,' Mrs Murphy grumbled, downing her tea in one gulp.

'Well, aren't we lucky we have the curry house in this time of rationing?' Mrs Rosenbaum said, smiling at me as I topped up their teas and placed a fresh plate of biscuits before them.

Every time I cook, I think of you and what you said when we set up the curry house: 'Divya, Indian food will lend itself nicely to rationing. We will need your restaurant and your food during the war.'

That has proved prophetic. You are so wise; have I told you that before? But I must admit that it is a challenge thinking up recipes and making ingredients stretch as there is a lack of food items, and those that you do get are very dear indeed.

Just like everyone in the street awaits your letters eagerly, so too the women of West India Dock Road long for letters from their sons and husbands and brothers who've signed up.

I know Charity is glad the boys aren't old enough, although Fergus, at barely fifteen, is agitating to do just that.

'I want to do proper war work, at the frontlines,' he cried yesterday when he brought it up yet again at supper here at the curry house.

And once again, Charity said, 'Not on your nelly, my boy. In any case, your apprenticeship at the shipbuilders' is war work. Ships are needed for the country's defence. And when not doing that, you are volunteering with the Boy Scouts. You barely have a minute to yourself. If that is not war work, I don't know what is!'

Fergus scowled and muttered that he was a man now and wanted to fight like one.

Everyone in the curry house tutted and shook their heads while Charity endeavoured to explain that the work Fergus was doing with the Scouts was important, necessary. Vital.

Fergus protested grumpily that it was hardly life and death work, his arms crossed, face mutinous.

To which Mr Stone listed all the ways in which the Scouts made a difference to people's lives: rescuing those caught up in air raids by working alongside civil defence workers, as well as acting as air raid wardens, firefighters, fire watchers and stretcher bearers during the air raids. Scouts helped build air raid shelters, Mr Stone added. They delivered important messages back and forth, while working as police messengers. They painted white lines on the edges of roads, thus helping with visibility during blackouts.

'That is a matter of life and death, so it is,' Mrs Devlin, who had just come into the curry house, alongside Mrs Neville, said. 'Myself and Gracie here are blind as bats every night when we come out of the house when the air raid siren sounds. If it weren't for those white lines, pointing out where the pavement dips into the road, we would trip and fall, and would die in the stampede to the Tube station.'

'But—' Fergus began.

Mr Stone did not let him finish, stating how Scouts also helped convert land for food production as part of the Dig for Victory campaign.

'And we collect wastepaper and scrap metal to raise funds for the war effort,' Paddy chimed in.

Fergus shoved him with his elbow while glaring at him. 'Whose side are you on, squirt?'

'I was just saying.' Paddy frowned, rubbing his arm where Fergus had shoved him.

Connor looked from one brother to the other fearfully, and finally at Charity, wanting his big sister to intervene, which she did, declaring that the Scouts also helped evacuate children to safety, adding that if only her brothers would agree to it—

'We don't want to be evacuated, Charity,' Paddy cut in sternly, hands on hips. 'This is our home, and we will stay right here.'

Charity sighed. Then turning to Fergus, she earnestly reiterated that he was making a difference, that what he was doing here at the home front was just as important as fighting abroad.

'No it's not,' Fergus cried, voice cracking. 'Our men are being taken prisoner, Charity. They are dying. They need more to step up and take their place.'

'They need more men. You're not a man yet, Fergus.' Charity cried.

'I'm man enough,' he yelled and stormed out, leaving his pilau rice, which he loves, half-eaten.

Charity stared after him, and then sighed loudly, wringing her hands in upset.

I put my arms around her.

She did not look up, but mumbled, 'If Jack talked to him, he'd listen. Fergus looks up to him. Could you ask him to write something to this effect in his next letter, please Divya?'

So there it is, Jack. Fergus is going through a phase, pushing boundaries as he grows into a man, that's what the matrons say, but in any case, would you please pen a message to him, using your famous Devine charm, asking him to wait until he's older and not to worry his sister so? Thank you kindly.

Oh, I meant to tell you about Mrs Neville and Mrs Murphy nearly coming to blows in the Underground station where we were sheltering from the air raid last night.

Mrs Neville accused Mrs Murphy of snoring, to which Mrs Murphy retorted that Mrs Neville passed wind something terrible, but had she uttered one word of complaint?

You should have heard the laughter; I swear the entire Tube station rocked with it.

Even Mrs Nolan, whose face is permanently creased in worry, sported a rare smile. It was like a gift. Mrs Murphy nudged Mrs Neville, who was shooting her dark looks, and pointed to Mrs Nolan. Mrs Neville harrumphed and tried to edge away from Mrs Murphy but in this she was foiled as the platform was packed.

Mrs Nolan, the poor dear, has a job and a half convincing her husband to come into the Tube station. We try to help but he doesn't like it; he gets upset when there are lots of people crowding him and it takes an age just getting him underground. When finally, he has made it down the steps, he shuts his ears and keens, frightening the children and making the babies, who had just nodded off to sleep in their mothers' arms, startle awake and start wailing.

And that's not all. There was another kerfuffle last night, if you can believe it.

Mrs Smith from East India Dock Road brought her girls soaking wet into the Underground station.

Mrs Boon sniffed that it was damp enough already without Mrs Smith and her daughters making it ten times worse.

'I was washing the girls in the tin bath when the siren sounded. What could I do?' Mrs Smith sighed, rubbing her belly where another little bubba is growing. 'In all the hubbub, I quite forgot to grab a towel.'

Mrs Rosenbaum, who always comes prepared, shared her own.

'Is there anything you don't have in that bag of yours, Esther?' Mrs Kerridge tutted fondly.

The other ladies wondered why Mrs Rosenbaum had brought a towel down here.

Mrs Rosenbaum blushed and mumbled that it served as a blanket. She is quite shy and doesn't like it when she is the centre of attention. She prefers to unobtrusively go about her business.

The ladies appeared puzzled for Mrs Rosenbaum had a blanket in her bag too, alongside the towel she had lent Mrs Smith and her girls. 'You never know when it might become of use,' Mrs Rosenbaum said.

In any case, Mrs Smith's girls, who were shivering, their teeth chattering, were grateful for the towel.

And not only that: Mrs Rosenbaum shared her matzo crackers with them too. After that, the girls did not leave Mrs Rosenbaum's side.

The planes hovered overhead. Phut, phut, phut. We heard them dropping their lethal cargo, the buildings shaking.

And then...

There was a loud bang and one of the men cried out loudly.

We all turned, afraid that somehow the bomb had fallen inside the Tube station.

But it wasn't that.

It turned out Billy Gibson had fallen asleep and rolled off the edge of the platform and onto the tracks and bumped his nose. The blood!

Good job Mrs Kerridge always makes sure to have her first aid kit with her; yes, she even brings it to the Underground.

'You gave us quite the scare, young man,' she admonished sternly as she was mopping him up.

'What a to-do about nothing,' Mrs Neville clucked. 'You would think he was bombed to see the blood.'

'Don't fall asleep too close to the edge of the platform next time, young Billy, eh?' Mr Stone said.

Billy, although exempt from signing up for medical reasons, is nevertheless part of the Home Guard, doing his bit. He clutched his nose – patched up thanks to Mrs Kerridge – with bloodstained fingers and grinned. 'I thought I'd be safe here.'

Billy's ma sighed, grumbling that she couldn't take him anywhere.

'The whole point of taking shelter here is to escape getting beat up, lad,' Mr Barney hollered.

When the air raid siren sounds each night, I grab whatever snacks are at hand; I make sure to have some ready for the Tube station. People get ever so hungry when there is danger overhead, I've found.

Everyone is now a dab hand at rushing to the Underground station, some, like Mrs Rosenbaum, more prepared than others. They bring their knitting and their half-eaten dinner, their bedding and their treasures just in *case when they go back up again, their house is no longer there.*

These treasures I've found are not jewellery or money, but keepsakes. Photographs and letters from loves no longer here, to remember them by.

Mrs Boon brings photographs of her pa and brother, whom she lost to the first war, and her ma whom she lost to pneumonia soon after that war ended. Their likenesses are faded and worn, bearing the marks of Mrs Boon's fingers, where she has gently traced them.

The other night, she showed me a packet of letters, these too read so often that they are falling apart, fragile and infinitely precious. They were from her love, she told me, eyes sparkling.

'Mr Boon?' I asked.

'Oh no. He doesn't have a romantic bone in his body. These are from Tom. My first love. We were engaged. We were to be married when he came back from fighting in the Great War.' She sighed deeply and tucked the letters next to her chest.

She didn't have to say any more. I read it all in her shining eyes, the wistful regret there, the pain, still fresh, made all the more so by the current war no doubt, despite the years that had passed.

Old men regale children, misty eyed, with their exploits in the first war.

'You didn't wade into enemy frontlines single-handed and unarmed, taking the Huns out with your fists. Stop giving those young 'uns the wrong idea,' old Mrs Alleyne from East India Dock Road admonished her husband the other night.

'How would you know what I did and didn't do, woman?' Mr Alleyne sniffed. 'You weren't there. I was.'

And he went right back to telling the children of his, it must be noted, alarmingly brave, some might even say foolish, experiences of war; it was a wonder he had made it out alive when he was but one man taking on a whole army of very well armed Germans, while his wife rolled her eyes beside him.

Mrs Kerridge told us about her friend in Limehouse, whose house, sadly, was one of the casualties of the air raids.

'Not a brick left upright or untouched by fire, Pam said,' Mrs Kerridge told us, her eyes moist. 'Nevertheless, she, her husband and kids picked their way through broken crockery and the wreckage of their belongings to try and salvage what they could.' Mrs Kerridge paused. 'But her husband said they needed to get to the rest centre. That he'd come back for whatever had not escaped the fire.'

All of us agreed that that made perfect sense.

'But he came back to find that they had been looted. Nothing that wasn't damaged beyond repair was left.' Mrs Kerridge sighed.

'That's shocking, that is,' Mrs Ross cried.

'Human nature, my dear,' Mrs Kerridge said, sadly. 'People are desperate, run ragged by this war that is going on longer than we expected and is showing no signs of stopping.' She shook her head. 'It brings out the best in most but also the worst in some of us.'

Some of the musically gifted, or, more to the point, those who fancy themselves as such, sing, often tunelessly, until Mrs Neville screeches for them to, 'Stop that noise at once. It's worse than the bombing overhead. Some of us *are trying to get a shut eye, and it is giving us nightmares. Can't you hear the babies wailing in protest?'*

'The babies are wailing in protest of Mrs Neville's screeching,' Mr Barney muttered under his breath.

'What's that?' Mrs Neville turned her beady eye on him. 'You have something to say, Mr Barney?'

'Not at all, Mrs Neville,' Mr Barney said.

'Funny that. I would have sworn you mumbled something just then,' she said, staring evilly at him.

I would have sworn he shrunk two inches, Jack, and I wondered if Paddy was right and Mrs Neville was a witch after all.

Hope in the midst of war.

We all cling on to hope.

I hope that they release you and that you will come home soon.

I pray for it and so does everyone.

We are keeping our fingers crossed for you.

Hark, can you hear our prayers floating up and through the bombed-out roof of the church, straight to heaven? Yes, I too go to church when I get a minute; we need faith at times like this. I pray to the Hindu gods and goddesses and also to Jesus, Mary, Joseph and all the saints. Surely someone up there will heed our prayers?

Take care, Jack.

Until next time.

Divya and all here at West India Dock Road

6

DIVYA

September 20, 1940

Dearest Raghu,

How are you, my love? I hope, I wish, I pray that you are all right. Well, as all right as can be in the midst of war.

I cannot begin to imagine what you must be experiencing over there. Here too we are feeling the effects of war. The air is rent with rubble and smoke and the dregs of ruins. Thankfully, most of us on West India Dock Road have been spared – so far – but other Eastenders, not so much.

For the first few months after war was declared, it was calm here. But then, oh it started and how.

I will never forget that first experience of the bombing we have been enduring, night after night...

7 September. Late afternoon. I had served tea with milk barfi and coffee cake and spiced potato drops.

Mr Stone and Mr Brown were playing chess with Mr Rosenbaum and Mr Lee looking on, and the matrons of the street were knitting while they ate and drank and gossiped *and set the world to rights, when suddenly, the sky darkened.*

We all looked at each other, surprised. It had been sunny a moment ago.

'A storm, perhaps,' Mr Brown said but his voice lacked conviction.

And then came the sound, ominous and rumbling, a gradually building roar.

We learned later that it was the menacing clamour of thousands of enemy aircraft flying towards London. And then... the air raid sirens sounded, loud and urgent, making our hearts pound with adrenaline and fear.

Even as we grabbed our gas masks and rushed to the Underground station and Mr Brown, Mr Stone and Mr Rosenbaum to attend to their duties as civil defence workers, we heard the enemy planes flying overhead and the thud thud crump of bombs dropping.

And then we saw the orange flares arching up to the sky – the docks were aflame. The noise was deafening, the heat scorching us even as we ran. We were bombed continuously, through the evening and into the night.

The whole of the East End was on fire, the entire docklands ablaze.

Afterwards, we found out that hundreds of bombs fell on the docks. The fires then attracted a second wave of aircraft with high-explosive bombs. In a short time, the docks were a mass of flames, molten sugar, burning liquor and hot tar. Mr Brown told us later that hundreds of rats poured out of the warehouses.

I must admit, Raghu, I thought I was going to die, that we all were. And in that moment, I was grateful for my life so far; I had lost so much but I had gained more. A commu-

nity on West India Dock Road. My own curry house doing what I loved: feeding people. Friends for life in Charity, her brothers, Jack, Mr Lee and all the others.

And I had experienced love with you.

Since then, we've been bombed every single night.

Even the Anderson shelters are not safe.

'It appears a bomb fell down the ventilation shaft of a shelter in Bethnal Green – many were killed and several more injured,' Mrs Kerridge told us the other day, eyes bloodshot.

This is why we prefer taking refuge in the underground Tube station. It's not only that the shelters are damp and cold; that is only one reason.

Hospitals have been bombed but the medical staff keep on working, regardless, showing astounding bravery, Mrs Boon tells us, courtesy of her niece, who is a nurse.

And of course, we all do our bit.

Civil defence workers, our very own Mr Brown, Mr Rosenbaum and Mr Stone among them as I said, help rescue people trapped in bombed-out buildings, finding them temporary shelter and food.

Mrs Porter bravely operates her mobile canteen distributing food to those injured and caught up in the raids and the volunteers helping people, despite the threat of bombs.

And we, the Women's Voluntary Service, help with the clear up.

It is heartbreaking seeing all that pain. The savage and ruthless destruction. The scorching brand of smoke. Trenches and rubble and holes where buildings used to be. Orphaned children. The senseless loss of loved ones.

We've learned to live with it.

'It's as if we've gone back in time,' Mr Brown says.

'Food shortages, rationing, wounded soldiers and civilian casualties – it's a different war and yet still the same horrific toll.'

'Except that now we are getting on and are not as sprightly as we used to be,' Mr Stone says with a sigh.

'Speak for yourself,' snaps Mr Brown. 'I'm plenty spry enough.'

'I never imagined we'd experience two wars,' Mrs Neville clucks. 'I would have thought we'd learn from the last one.'

'It's the mothers I feel for.' Charity is pensive. 'They lost brothers and fathers in the last war and now...' She doesn't continue but I know she is thinking of Mrs Ross, who lost her daughter to this terrible war, and who doesn't know the whereabouts of her son. And, like the rest of us, Charity is brooding about what is next, what is to come, what new trials are in store for us all.

Charity constantly worries about her brothers: whether she should send them away, evacuate them to the country, where they will be relatively safer. But they are adamant they will not go.

'Please, boys, it's for your own good,' she pleaded yesterday when they were here in the curry house having supper.

'How is it for our own good when we will be away from everyone we love?' Fergus was mutinous. 'Look at Mammy and Da, missing Ireland and yearning for it several years on. We are not going to be like them. Hitler and you are not doing this to us,' Fergus yelled and stormed out.

Charity had tears in her eyes. 'I hate that he said Hitler and me in the same breath,' she cried.

'That's what's upsetting you?' I said.

And she gave me a weak smile.

I worry about Charity. Her da is bad as ever, the air raid sirens bringing to the fore the trauma he suffered in the last war. She has her hands full managing him and keeping the lodging house running during these extraordinary times. She is looking run-down, that girl. I wish there was something I could do.

Even Buckingham Palace is not safe. I don't know if you heard but five German bombs were dropped on the palace, destroying the chapel. The bombs also hit the palace gates and the Victoria Memorial. Four palace staff members were injured, and one died. The king and queen, thankfully, were unharmed. And do you know what Queen Elizabeth said? She said, 'I'm glad we've been bombed. Now I feel we can look the East End in the face.' When we heard that on the wireless, we all cheered.

Dinners are left uneaten, clothes dishevelled, everyone bringing with them whatever they can when the sirens announce yet another raid. We gather in the Tube station, knitting, eating, singing, snoring while waiting for the all-clear.

And in our dreams, the constant, threatening rumble of the Luftwaffe, the thud crump crash of falling bombs, orange flares and barrage balloons. The stench of fire and burning flesh.

Ships, as you warned, have been requisitioned for war purposes. The river is patrolled by firefighting boats which are often on fire themselves.

I hope you come back from the war. I pray for it. I hope that you were one of the lucky ones in Dunkirk. If you were there, that is. I keep expecting you to get shore leave and come home.

I wait for your knock on the kitchen door. I long to see your smiling face, twinkling eyes, for you to say, 'Hi, Divya. I'm back, missed me?'

I imagine it and fantasise about it, although I know it will not happen as you have decided we are not meant to be together, that you are not good enough for me.

I wish I had a moment with you to convince you otherwise.

Raghu, when we kissed, that one precious kiss, what did that tell you? For me, it felt right, like we belonged. I felt complete. I am sure you felt the same.

Life is short. People are dying. Please come to me, my love.

Love is all that is important, I have realised, and we were lucky enough to find it in each other. So why are we denying ourselves?

This is my dream. That you will come back to me, safe and sound, and I will hand over these letters to you then. I will say, 'See, I missed you. I love you. I have been waiting for you, writing to you. You can't just instruct me to love someone else; love cannot be made to order, a heart cannot be instructed. It does what it does. It loves who it loves and in my case, it's you.'

I hope that when you do read these letters, you will be back here with me, so it won't matter if they are doom and gloom. What I am describing here will be in the past, the danger long gone, both of us having lived through it and come out the other side.

Of course I wish every day that there was a means of me actually posting these letters to you – then I would cut out all the grim bits – but I don't know where you are. And so I write these and keep them here for you, and they wait, like me, for your arrival one day.

You will come, won't you? Do. Please. I wish this every day. You know where I am.

I hope, fiercely, that you are fine.

I go to sleep worrying about you. I dream of you and wake up thinking of you, my pillow wet.

I love you so much, you are always in my thoughts so surely, my heart would tell me if something had happened to you?

Forget me, you wrote blithely in your one and only letter to me.

Have you forgotten me?

Will I see you again? Give you these letters? Touch you? Cook with you? Hold you? Kiss you?

Or was that too-brief kiss fated to be our only one?

No. I will believe that I will see you again.

It is the only way I can go on.

In every letter I write to Jack, I am tempted to ask him if he knows where you are.

But you don't want me to contact you; you made that clear. For my sake, you said. But Raghu, don't you know that my love for you transcends everything else? I don't care if I am ostracised as you think I will be if I associate with you. I don't even care if I lose this business that I love – as long as I have you.

I will not ask Jack about your whereabouts. Not least because I have my pride.

I will wait until you see sense. And you will, won't you?

I hope that, by my sheer yearning and loving and wanting, I will spirit you back into my arms.

But then I think of all those mothers and sisters and wives and daughters who are waiting for their men to come home, who also have hearts suffused with longing and wanting.

Who dread that telegram that arrives every so often and then we see them with swollen eyes and defeated faces. They stand stiff and unyielding in our arms when we try to offer comfort.

We understand.

For ours is not the embrace they want.

And the arms they want will never be around them again for they are lying with all the other casualties of this horrible war in some battlefield in France.

I'm sorry, this has become grim.

I love you.

I will stop here otherwise this paper is in danger of becoming a salty mush.

Yours,

Divya

7

CHARITY

Another sunny day. Another load of washing.

Their world might be sundering apart brick by brick, war intent on destroying them, but as long as they are spared the bombs, life goes on and dirty laundry piles up with depressing predictability.

Charity shakes her head to keep her musing at bay and pegs the washing to the line, taking advantage of the sunshine while it lasts. Weeds are having a field day, she notes, pushing through cracks in the paving, sunny yellow, hopeful mauve and bushy white, giving absolutely no heed to the fact that the world is at war, the scent of smoke hanging in the air which is thick with grit in addition to the ever-present smog.

She sighs as she clips Fergus's overalls to the line; he is already outgrowing them, although he's barely had them a couple of months, if that. He's had yet another growth spurt and now his ankles are exposed when he wears the overalls. Thank goodness that he's the oldest of her younger brothers, and they can be passed on to Connor and then from him to Paddy.

Paddy, who is joy, innocence and mischief.

Paddy, who complains, hands on hips, face scrunched in a frown, 'Why do I always get hand-me-downs? From *both* Fergus and Connor?'

Paddy, whom she has essentially brought up on her own and who, like his brothers, owns her heart.

Thank God for her brothers, she thinks again, even though she fondly likes to complain that three younger brothers are more curse than blessing.

She picks up Fergus's shirt from the basket, breathing in deep of the freshly washed scent, a luxury given the boys' predilection to get everything dirty in a couple of minutes, even as she mentally goes over the list of chores she has yet to do.

'Yoohoo, Charity, it's Friday. Why don't you and Miss Ram across the road take the evening off and go to the pictures?' calls Mrs Kerridge.

Charity sighs.

'Ah, if only – I have a list of things to do a mile long,' she grumbles.

'You're young, Charity. The men are away at war. Go on off to the pictures. Live a little.'

Charity smiles at Mrs Kerridge and gives a small nod. The older woman means well.

But as soon as Mrs Kerridge's considerable back is turned, Charity droops.

She wishes that just once, she could be carefree, not have anything more on her plate than going to the pictures of a Friday evening.

You are being ungrateful. There is a war on. You have three wonderful brothers, who are safe, for now. Your parents are alive.

You have a business which is, if not thriving, then at least limping along.

She agrees with the voice of her conscience. Yet... she is weary.

Her shoulders slump from the burden she carries, the constant worry. Her father is worse now there are air raids every single night, the East End receiving battering after battering.

It is getting to them all.

Mr Stone and Mr Brown play chess with trembling hands over at the curry house, their faces drawn from the lack of sleep.

'It's the sirens. They give me nightmares.' Mr Brown sighs.

'My da too,' she says, seeing the same haunted look in the old men's eyes that is in her father's, when she tries in vain to comfort him.

What did they suffer in the previous war?

And the men out there fighting this war, what are they facing? Some, Mrs Ross's son and Mrs Kerridge's younger two among them, are still unaccounted for.

And Jack Devine, her childhood friend, loved by all in the street, a prisoner of war.

Please, let him not have to endure more than he can bear, she prays.

Thank goodness her brothers are not old enough to fight.

She knows that Jack being taken prisoner of war has hit her brothers hard. They look up to Jack.

Her brothers might give the impression of being devil-may-care, but they are gentle, sensitive, kind souls. She is very proud of the young men they are growing into.

Fergus, however, is impatient, and can't grow up fast enough.

'I want to sign up,' he'd declared again this morning.

'There's an age limit for a reason. When you're of age, you can sign up,' Charity had said, even as her entire being shied away from the grim possibility of her little brother, innocent, gangly, kind-hearted Fergus, who didn't have an aggressive bone in his body, going to war.

'You don't understand, Charity,' he had shot at her. 'They need people. Young men like me. Those who signed up have been taken prisoner, like Jack, or are dead.' His eyes flashing with fervour, shadowed with pain. Intense like she had never heard him.

She tried to get through to him. 'Exactly, Fergus, do you hear what you're saying? They've been taken prisoner or are dead. *Dead.*' She sniffed, pushing away the tears that threatened. 'Your life has hardly begun.'

'And do *you* hear yourself, Charity? It's *my* life to do with what I want. And I want to sign up.'

'Enough, Fergus,' she barked. 'For the hundredth time, you are not old enough.'

'I am tall. I look like a man. People mistake me for someone older, ask why I'm not at the front, doing my bit for the country.' Fergus was chewing his lower lip in upset.

Charity softened. After his recent growth spurt, he now towered over her. His voice had broken and with the moustache and beard he was cultivating, he did look older than his fifteen years. 'You tell them that you are doing your bit, here on the home front,' she said gently. 'And that when you are of age, you will sign up.'

'I can just lie about my age and sign up now,' Fergus said.

She was tired. She had barely slept since the air raids began weeks ago. Every night, she held Da as he wailed and cowered in the shelter in the basement that Jack had fashioned for them before he left, with the help of the lodgers, while Mammy said the rosary silently in the bed opposite and her brothers slept on blankets on the floor, long since used to their father's cries and the sirens clamouring above and the enemy planes dropping their deadly cargo – and she wondered if this was it. *Please let us all go together, at once,* she prayed, even as she mused whether her mother was praying for the same thing.

Oh, but she was weary. From the sleepless nights. The worry. The long days packed with never-ending chores.

She didn't want hassle from Fergus too. 'Age limits are there for a reason,' she snapped, patience exhausted. 'You cannot lie and sign up.'

'Who says?' Fergus, never one to give up, parried.

'I do,' she cried.

'You're not my mammy,' he yelled.

That hurt and so she lashed out, losing it, finally. 'Well I'm glad I'm not, you ungrateful sod.'

Connor and Paddy gasped, looking at her with wide-eyed accusation.

'I'm sorry, I didn't mean...' she called but Fergus was gone, banging the door behind him so hard that it felt like the whole building shook, Connor and Paddy flinching.

Now she feels guilty. Regret bitter in her mouth. She will make it up to him later.

She holds his shirt, breathing deep of the freshly washed scent, so unlike Fergus, who smells of teenage boy: sweat and hormones.

But the fresh smell is overpowered by the stink wafting from the street. The reek of fish.

Ah, men taking cured fish to the port. They nod at her, smiling.

The newspaper boy saunters past on their heels, wrinkling

his nose at the foul odour, while calling out the day's headlines in a nasal voice: 'Nazis deprive Jews of possessions.'

'What do we want with more bad news, off ye go,' Charity hears Mrs Neville grumble.

See, you are lucky. Be grateful for what you have, her conscience hectors.

I am grateful. But...

She does not have time to finish the thought for Connor is beside her, suddenly, looking worried. Connor, her brother who rarely speaks but is always smiling, even during the recent challenging days, now appears distressed. Paddy, beside him, is in tears. Fergus, who should be with them, is missing. (He collects them from school after his stint at the docks and they all go together to the Scout Hut to see what needs doing; this is where they should be right now.)

'What's happened?' she asks, clutching Fergus's shirt to her chest as if her life depends on it. 'What's wrong?'

For the boys look so upset.

Her heart beating nineteen to the dozen.

Jesus, Mary and Joseph, please let my brother be all right. I'm sorry I was ungrateful, complaining about my lot in life. Please let him be all right.

Connor opens his mouth but nothing comes. Tears shiver on his lashes.

'What is it?' she asks again.

'Fergus is gone. He's run away to join the army,' cries Paddy even as Connor bursts into tears and throws his arms around his big sister.

8

CHARITY

'What do you mean, Fergus is gone?' Charity asks, unable to process it.

Has she heard wrong? But she knows that isn't the case given Paddy and Connor's tears.

'You...' Paddy hiccups through his sobs. 'You said he couldn't join. He said he would. He has run away to do just that.' And, looking at her with wide, terrified eyes, mirroring the fear that is making Charity's heart pound faster than a steam train. 'Is he going to France, Charity? Is he going to die?'

'Shh... It's all right, Paddy. He won't die.' With difficulty, Charity modulates her voice to sound normal but even so, it trembles slightly, hitching on the terrible word 'die' and she notes that Connor sees right through her for he looks even more upset.

But Paddy's sobs decrease slightly in intensity, even as he cries, 'I told him, don't go, you might die. And he said... he said...'

Paddy chokes up again and Charity holds him close even as

she thinks, *Wait until I get my hands on you, Fergus. How dare you scare your younger brothers so?*

'He said,' Paddy cries, voice stumbling over his words, 'that we might die here too, and at least there he will be making a difference, being useful.'

Her heart jumps urgently with fear and worry. *What foolishness is this, Fergus?*

'They won't let him sign up. He's too young.' But even as she says so, she thinks of how tall Fergus is, how with the facial hair he is proudly cultivating, he looks older than his age. 'Whatever happens, not a word to Da and Mammy, you understand?' Charity says.

Paddy and Connor nod soundlessly. They look lost without their big brother beside them, gazing up at her with identical apprehensive expressions, wide and worried.

They need you to take charge.

She takes a deep breath but it does nothing for the fear that is ambushing her.

Please, God, please let the men at the signing office see through him, my brother, realise that he's not as old as he says he is.

But Fergus can be very convincing and his ability to lie with a straight face is second to none. Goodness knows even she, who prides herself as being able to see through every trick her brothers use, has been fooled more than once.

And will the recruiting officers, who want every able body going, look too closely at someone – a fit young man – who's clearly eager to fight for his country?

Charity closes her eyes as she thinks of her father in his bed, who has never been the same since he came back from war.

Alongside the terror, she experiences a hot flare of anger. She is so enervatingly tired, to her very bones, caring for her father, taking on the responsibility he cannot. And Fergus... He's seen his father suffer and yet... he does this?

Without even realising she's doing it, Charity takes her younger two brothers' small hands in hers and crosses the road to Divya's Curry House.

She wants her friend's counsel, her gentle smile, her kindness, her warmth, all delivered with a cup of cinnamon and cardamom infused tea, although of course she doesn't have time for tea right now.

Divya will know what to do, won't she? And even if she doesn't, someone at the curry house will be able to set Charity's thundering heart, her agonised worrying, at rest, surely?

The curry house is busy as always, scented with spices and warmth, buzzing with conversation and life. Far from appeasing Charity, it somehow intensifies her fear.

'There you are, Charity,' Mrs Kerridge calls, her mouth full of cake, which Divya is somehow managing to bake despite the shortage of sugar and butter.

'I use cheat ingredients,' Divya says, eyes twinkling, when asked for her secret. 'You don't want to know.'

'But it still manages to taste exquisite,' they all marvel.

Mrs Kerridge must read something in Charity's expression, for she swallows her mouthful and says, 'Whatever's the matter, love?'

But Charity, her mouth filling with salt, appears to have lost her voice.

Divya comes out of the kitchen, wiping her hands on her apron, her face alight, as it always is, at the sight of Charity and her brothers. 'Fergus is gone.' Paddy bursts out, his lower lip and voice trembling in preparation for fresh tears.

'Gone?'

The entire curry house is silent as they wait for Charity or

Paddy – nobody expects Connor to start talking, for he very rarely does – to expand upon this declaration.

'Run away,' Paddy cries, and Charity's heart breaks afresh for her youngest brother's voice collapses on a sob of distress. She squeezes his hand which is in hers, so small and sweaty and fragile and beloved.

'What?' Divya asks, appearing shocked, even as Mr Brown booms, 'Run away where?'

'To sign up to fight in the war. Charity says he won't die but I don't believe her.'

And at this, Paddy gives in to the tears he's been holding back, and Mrs Kerridge gathers him in her voluminous, sweat and talc scented arms.

'Ah now, what's this, eh?' she croons.

Connor sticks to Charity, clinging to his sister as if he wants to meld into her, like he used to do as a much younger boy.

Divya comes up to Charity and takes her arm. She pulls out two chairs and sits Charity and Connor down.

And looking into her friend's anxious face, mirroring her own apprehension and worry, Charity finally finds her voice, through the knot of panic holding her heart ransom, robbing her of breath. She lets out a great big sigh, tasting of salt and angst, and admits to her friend, 'As you can see, Divya, we're in a bit of a pickle.'

9

CHARITY

Charity rushes to the signing up office, barely noticing the sandbags outside large buildings, the barrage balloons dotting the sky, the rubble and the holes where tenements should be, the dust and smoke choking her throat, the scent of fire and devastation. Those whose houses have been bombed overnight salvage what they can and trudge wearily to the rest centres. Children play in the debris and women dodge expertly past as they make their way to the market with their ration books, wondering what shortages they will face today and how they can get around it and still dish up a decent(ish) meal.

A clutch of women walk past Charity and she hears one say to the others, sighing deeply, 'The children are asking for cake. You know, my dear, I've quite forgotten what a proper cake, rich and sweet with sugar and margarine, tastes like. Today for pudding, I'm making banana cream out of boiled parsnips and banana essence.'

Charity thinks of Divya, eyes glinting merrily as she tapped her nose and told everyone in the curry house that she used cheat ingredients to bake her delicious cakes.

Charity has left her youngest two brothers with Divya and is on her way to find Fergus.

Even if the officers at the registration office have let Fergus join, she will tell them his real age.

She will deal with his anger and frustration.

She will explain to him, once more and in great detail, sparing nothing this time, why he has to wait. *Believe me, Fergus,* she will say, *I don't want to stop you doing what you want to do. And if fighting for the country is what you want then you must do it. It is a very noble thing, Fergus. But at present, you're not old enough to endure the horrors you will no doubt see. Our da was an adult when he went to war and look at him. He's been permanently scarred by what he went through. You with the invincibility and optimism of youth think you will be exempt. I hope so, I do, my love. But please bide your time. Just a little longer. You can do good here too, serve the country at the home front. You can join the Home Guard if you think being in the Boy Scouts is not enough. Anything at all. Just not this.*

We all lost Da, the man he was once. We didn't know him then, Fergus, but Mammy would tell me about him, the man she fell in love with. She said he was the life and soul of the street, full of joy and laughter. It was like she was telling me about a stranger, this man she described, so gentle, kind, and witty with it. He was always smiling, she said, and when she spoke of him, her eyes glowed and she looked young, like the girl she must have been when she met Da. It is a shame that we only know him as an ill, grumpy, tormented man. But he was so much more than that, Fergus. I gather, from what Mammy has told me, that he was like you are now. A wonderful, easy-going, happy, loving, idealistic soul.

I haven't told you, Fergus, how much I love it when you creep up on me and surprise me with a hug. I bat you away, but secretly, I love it. I love the way your eyes twinkle when you tell a joke; you take care to keep a straight face but the twinkle gives it away. And I love how gentle you are with your siblings, how kind, although you grumble that you are never rid of them. You say that and yet you shorten your strides to match Paddy's, you include him in your games and even allow him to win every so often. You read Connor perfectly, divining what he does not, cannot, say. You indulge your younger brothers and I love that about you. You help out anyone in the street who needs a hand; Divya said that you have come to her aid more times than she can count. You are wonderful and I am so very proud of you, my love. I'm sorry I don't tell you this often enough.

Fergus, I am being selfish, I know, but I am not ready yet to lose you. I'm not prepared for you to lose your joy in life and living, your naivety, your innocence. You may think you are all grown-up but you are still a child at heart, and I like that. I like that you stubbornly persist in believing that everything will turn out for the best even in the face of evidence to the contrary. You may think you are ready but I am not ready yet for you to experience the horrors of war and become a jaded, beaten, wounded husk of a man.

You are still a boy. You have yet some living to do, before you grow up and grow cynical and cold. I hope you never do but with this war we are living through, I know it is asking for too much.

We have been lucky so far. We have our family intact – well, Mammy and Da as much as can be expected. But please, Fergus, can we remain so a little longer?

I have brought you up, largely on my own since you were a wee babe. I don't want to give you up to the ruthless machine that is war. Not just yet, my love, not just yet.

Even as she walks – runs is more like it – to the recruitment office, Charity is keeping her fingers crossed and sending prayers up to heaven.

Please God, Jesus, Mary, Joseph, all the saints, please let it not be too late...

Charity allows the sob she has been holding back to escape her, sniffing and wiping her nose with the back of her hand – she came unprepared, she has nothing with her but prayers – even as she thinks back to the terrible time when Da finally lost it and she had to take over the reins...

10

CHARITY

Charity was fourteen, looking forward to leaving school and obtaining an apprenticeship at the sugar factory, Tate and Lyle's, when her da lost it.

Afterwards, Charity realised that it was just a matter of time; it would have happened sooner or later.

But at the time, she was a child and naive with it, hoping, even given her father's volatility, that he would get better, and soon, so she could get on with her life.

Her da had been unpredictable since he returned from the war. Intact physically except for a limp occasioned by a bad hip and scars here and there on his body. But fragile mentally.

And that delicate mental balance tipped over, one too many memories taking charge, destroying what little hold Da had on sanity, the summer Charity turned fourteen, putting a break on her dreams, marking the end of the life she had imagined for herself.

Charity had always fancied being part of the workforce at the sugar factory. Imagine being surrounded by and working with all that sugar! Whenever she passed the factory, she would breathe in deep of the nectary, sickly sweet scent.

She knew, for Mammy had told her often enough, that before he went to war, her da's dream had been for their lodging house to be passed down through generations of O'Kellys.

But there was Fergus for that, when he was old enough. Until then, her father could manage surely, despite his behaviour getting more and more erratic so they had lost all the regulars Mammy had cultivated during the war.

Mammy ran the boarding house she and Da had started together on her own when Da was away fighting in the Great War, managing despite the rationing and the lack, the high turnover because of lodgers leaving to sign up; that's what she told Charity during her lucid moments. Charity was too young to remember Mammy's reign. But she did recall sitting under the table in the dining area, the smell of porridge and toast, marvelling at the size and hairiness of feet, giant toes poking out of holey socks. She remembered being passed from one rugged hand to another. The tickle of bushy beards making her giggle. Their laughter, these giants who hefted her so effortlessly, that started as a rumble in their stomachs and exploded out of their mouth in sour, gurgly reverberations.

But then Da came back and he was, according to Mammy, whispering in secret to Charity when she was laid up ill after Fergus was born, not the man he had been when he went away.

Mammy had Fergus and it did for her back. She was bedridden for months, with Charity doing all the housework, looking after the baby, and helping her mammy to and from the outhouse, even though she was little herself.

But then Mammy got pregnant again.

After Connor was born, Mammy was in even worse straits than before, and she was bedridden for longer, Charity once again picking up the pieces, for Mammy was too proud to ask for help, which the women of the street would have gladly given.

And then once again, when she was finally able to get up and about, Mammy fell pregnant.

And this time, she could not recover.

After the birth of baby Paddy, her body gave up. She was never the same again.

In the meantime, Da went from bad to worse and the sailors, even those desperate for lodging, went to other boarding houses, which did not do much for Da's temper.

Charity, meanwhile, was doing all the housework, and looking after her brothers, plus helping her mother with her ablutions, for Mammy was too weak even to wash herself.

She barely attended school, afraid to leave her brothers alone with Mammy being as she was. Thankfully, she was bright, so when she did manage to go, a snatched morning here and there, she could catch up on school work.

She was looking forward to, at fourteen, leaving school and working at the sugar factory, stubbornly holding on to her dream, even though the situation at home was dire and seemed unlikely to improve.

She would walk past the docks, as near the factory as she could, as often as she could, whenever she could. She observed the women who worked there, their smart uniforms, how they tied their hair back with scarves, how they always smelled delicious, the scent of syrup and industry clinging to them, and couldn't wait to be one of them.

She wondered what it was like, being around all that sugar. Were they allowed to help themselves to it, she wanted to ask but always lost her nerve. They looked too smartly turned out. Too confident and sure of themselves. They were always in a merry group, laughing and chatting among themselves. She overheard them complaining about their shifts and how knackered they were. She watched them perk up as the conversation turned to socials and the boys they'd met and the fun they'd had.

Charity wanted, more than anything, to belong to this sodality of girls.

She was always busy but also very lonely at home.

Da grunted or shouted instead of talked. But he was also rarely with them, which was a blessing as he was unpredictable and volatile. They were never able to guess when he would blow up, what triggered his rages.

They lived in two cramped rooms downstairs and when her father was there, it was suddenly too small and claustrophobic; there was no room to breathe. No wonder her brothers started crying, somehow sensing their father's displeasure, his barely reined in rage and seething angst.

The boys' cries upset Da and he would lash out. Or else, Da would start crying himself, which would, thankfully, shock Charity's brothers into stunned silence.

Da spent his days on the street outside the public house, smoking and sharing tankards of ale with the other regulars. When he did come home after the public house had shut, and rolled into bed, more often than not, he woke up screaming in the middle of the night.

Which woke the boys, who started crying.

Their cries incited Da's nightmares and vice versa.

It was an endless cycle and with Mammy too weak to see to the kids, Charity had no choice but to do it.

She went to bed every night exhausted to her bones, glad

she'd survived the day without being subject to and protecting her brothers from her da's explosive anger.

She woke up tired, her night split open by her da's screams, the boys' sobs.

Charity loved her brothers to bits.

But... she dreaded finishing school and being stuck at home.

She barely attended school but at least she had it – something – other than home.

The few times she did go in – when she had been summoned by the headteacher, seeing as she had been racking up too many absences – she would return home to chaos.

Her brothers would be wailing, their noses running, unfed and unwashed, left to their own devices, and Mammy in bed, also crying but silently, fresh tears following the salty tracks on her face, anguished and helpless for she couldn't attend to her sons' needs.

Charity had the feeling her mother was just marking time until Charity finished school so she could take over.

And Charity resented this even as she felt sorry for her mammy, even as she cared for her.

She begrudged her mammy for being weak and ill, even though she knew it was not her fault. Even though she understood that Mammy couldn't help spending all her time in bed, whispering, or indicating with hand gestures when she needed something, not even having the energy to talk.

Charity resented Da for his moods.

She felt for the boys but was worn out from looking after them; they were always needing something and turning to Charity for it. For, although they were only little, they had learned, very early on, not to depend on either of their parents.

Charity yearned for escape from it all even as she worried

how her mammy would cope, agonised that she wouldn't, couldn't.

She dreamed of being free of all responsibility even as she fretted about the boys.

I can be an apprentice at the sugar factory and help at home, she told herself. *It will be no different from being at school.*

But even as she did so, she knew that she was fooling nobody, least of all herself.

11

CHARITY

Charity is near the docks now, out of her mind with worry.

She is walking so fast, nearly running, that she slips, stumbling over a piece of rubble on the road. Someone – the Lord – is watching out for her, for she stopped just in time. Next to her, a crater has opened up on the road, thanks to a bomb, she imagines. The scent of melted tar and earth and destruction, fiery hot.

There are bombed-out buildings, wreckage everywhere. A young boy has climbed the hillock of rubble and is placing a flag atop a jumble of bricks. He sees Charity looking and says to her, 'This was my 'ome before the Jerries bombed it.'

She feels tears prick at her eyes, even as she nods.

She passes a house, half fallen down, the other half still standing, just, but with red bricks tarnished black by smoke and its walls damaged. It leans treacherously, teetering on the verge of collapse. And yet, she sees a face pressed to the window, bloodshot eyes in a pale and stark visage, someone still living in there, despite the danger that the building might give way any time.

Smoke curls upwards into the ash and grit permeated sky, from those factories that have escaped the bombing more or less intact, and they still run despite the incessant battering they endure every night, those that are still standing.

Charity is worried out of her mind and yet still her heart bleeds for her beloved East End.

Will this war be the end of it?

For the first time, she thinks, will Fergus actually be safer at the frontline than here?

No. *No, no, no.*

She cannot bear the thought of the boy she brought up, still but a child no matter that he looks big and grown, his whole life ahead of him, fighting on the frontline, wounded by enemy bullets, dead.

No.

Smog hangs over the tired city, a translucent, gritty haze obscuring the grey sky that at night, more so recently, turns menacing, fraught with enemy threat, loud with ominous growls exploding fiery rain, precursor to devastation.

But now, it is relatively calm, unlike Charity's heart, which is beating like a trapped prisoner at the bars of her ribcage. *Please, let Fergus be all right.*

A carriage rumbles past, the clip clop of horses' hooves, the groom expertly dodging the crater on the road. Barrage balloons dot the sky over the docks.

A long line of women snakes at the butcher's clutching their ration books in one hand and baskets in the other. As she passes, she hears them grumbling among themselves that the woman being served is taking her time; there will be nothing left for the rest of them. Their bored children play hopscotch among the debris that has not yet been cleared from a previous air raid, breeze flavoured with smoke, nippy, with a sharp bite.

Over from the next street, church bells sound out the hour in sombre melody and the boy hawking newspapers beside the iron railings increases his volume to compete with the sonorous, bronze tones, waving a newspaper in front of Charity's nose, its scent of damp ink, musty sweet. 'Adolf Hitler indefinitely postpones Operation Sealion, the planned German invasion of Great Britain,' he yells almost right in Charity's ear, his hot, sour breath upon her cheek, even as he hops from foot to foot, to keep the circulation going, she assumes; his boots have holes in them and his feet must be frozen numb. He looks about eleven, the same age as Connor, and she wishes she had the coin to buy his paper. But she left home in a hurry, panic and urgency drumming a terrified beat inside her; her heart will only settle when she has gathered her wayward brother in her arms.

But even so, she is momentarily distracted by the newspaper boy's plight. He's hardly sold any news-sheets from the looks of the pile at his feet.

She feels happier when an old man digs in his pocket and says, 'Gimme it then, boy.'

The boy jauntily doffs his hat to his customer even as he hands over the paper.

The old man grins toothily at Charity, his words noisy and gurgling with the tobacco he's chewing as he says, pointing at the headline, 'We will show the Huns what's what.'

Charity nods at him as she nearly stubs her toe on a fallen tree swept aside, alongside a pile of jumbled-up bricks: their reality during these strange times. And, despite the newspapers trying to boost morale with positive news, cheery slogans, there are rumours that the air raids over London will increase.

'My cousin, who has connections in the Foreign Office, is convinced that the Germans are getting more confident, that they might start bombing London during the day as well as night!' Mrs O'Riley had relayed breathlessly last week. 'She's considering moving to the country. Dorset, she was thinking. She's invited me along. I said I'm staying right here. If I had to leave, I'd go home, to Ireland, but since that's out of bounds, I'm staying put.'

And listening to her, once again, Charity had wondered if perhaps she should think of sending the boys to the country.

As it is, Paddy and Connor are hardly getting any schooling. Most of the teachers have signed up or are doing war work. Schools are being used as rest centres. Many of the students have either moved out of the city or left to work, or to look after their siblings while their mothers work. Classes are clubbed together, older children teaching younger ones.

'Connor and I are in the same class,' Paddy announced gleefully last week, beyond pleased that he was with his older brother, finally.

A soldier, presumably just arriving home on shore leave, is trudging down the road and everyone in the queue for the greengrocer's looks at him with awe and pride.

A woman digs in her basket and pulls out a flower the sunshine yellow of glory which she sticks into his mud-caked pocket. 'God bless you, son.'

He smiles, the lines in his face, encrusted with dirt, creasing and tips his hat, which has a bullet hole through it.

Charity shivers. Thank goodness for the hat; what if the soldier had not been wearing it?

His shoes are encased in mud, as is the trunk he's carrying.

Now that she's close to the soldier, Charity can see that even his smile cannot wipe the tiredness that is etched into every grimy fold of his young face, lined beyond his years.

She quickens her step, all the more in a hurry to get to Fergus before it is too late.

Charity has been walking blindly along and now, she pauses a minute to get her bearings even as she tries and fails to settle her racing heart. *Please God, Jesus, Mary, Joseph, let me not have lost Fergus already. Give me the diplomacy to convince him rather than turn him even more against me. I know I will lose him in a couple of years, but not just yet. He's too young, still a child.*

She looks around her; in her panic, she has been racing ahead with single-minded determination without taking stock of her surroundings. Now, she realises that she is right where it happened, standing in almost the exact spot where the altercation took place that flipped the switch in her da and he was never the same again.

A sign?

12

CHARITY

It happened, they told her later, when Da, who had gone for a stroll along the docks, was walking back to the public house for his daily dose of lager and natter.

Charity had just got home; it was her last week of school, so she had thought she better attend, although she'd only stayed an hour, showed her face, made sure the headteacher spotted her, and then made her way back home again.

Mammy had been, as always when Charity was away, sitting up, resting her back against the wall, her wan face drawn with pain, too weak to tend to her wailing sons. When Charity came home, she flashed her a smile of pure gratitude and lay down.

The boys' cries had picked up in intensity and volume when Charity arrived, knowing food was imminent. Someone to listen, to care. They had been crying by rote so far, having no other way to express their angst and hoping their mother would see to them but knowing deep down that she couldn't. But now their cries had purpose.

Charity hefted Paddy on her hip, even as she heated up

gruel for the boys, talking gently to them all the while, 'Now, now, what's all this for, eh?' while inside, she was thinking, *Please let there be an opening at the sugar factory.* Just the thought was a sweet treat in her mouth, honeyed nectar.

I will walk there as soon as school finishes and gather the courage to ask.

I will deal with the fallout from not wanting to take on the family business.

For she knew that both Da and Mammy in their different ways were waiting for her to finish school. Da, so Charity could take over from him, so he could spend all day at the public house. He did so anyway. There were hardly any lodgers now and barely any money coming in. They lived off the generosity of the nuns who visited regularly, which was the only time Charity got a break.

The nuns were kind but there was only so much they could do to help.

'We are praying for all of you,' they said each time they visited. 'The Lord will provide. He will take care of you. This too shall pass, Charity, love,' they promised. 'The Lord will make sure of it.'

But why had the Lord brought this trouble upon them in the first place? wondered Charity.

She supposed she believed in God even though she wasn't completely sure if He existed at all.

But she resented Him too.

Sometimes, when Charity was being most uncharitable, in direct contrast to her name, when the boys were especially cranky and she was tired and run ragged trying to soothe them, Charity thought it would have been well and good if Mammy had stayed a nun after all. If she hadn't met Da. It would have been best all round.

Then you *wouldn't be here,* her conscience whispered.

That would be better, surely, rather than being permanently exhausted and worried and on tenterhooks, tiptoeing around Da's moods, Charity thought.

'Prayer is the answer,' the nuns promised, smiling benignly.

Fat lot of good prayers did, Charity thought as she jogged Paddy upon her hip and diluted the gruel even further to make it go round all of them.

But even if the Lord did not, at least the nuns did provide and for that, she was grateful. They came regularly every week, sometimes twice a week – 'We prayed and the Lord asked us to visit' – with baskets filled with goodies. Fresh fruit and vegetables, Irish taffy and soup. It was the only time Charity had seen her brothers smile and chuckle openly and wholeheartedly, when the nuns took them on their laps and fed them sweet chunks of apples and pears.

Hearing her brothers' laughter, seeing their joy, Charity smiled too, the muscles in her cheeks aching from the effort it took to do something so unfamiliar, so alien.

It was only then that she realised she was frowning all the time.

Only until I get my foot in the door of the sugar factory, was her refrain.

She went to bed dreaming of being one of the Tate and Lyle factory workers, woke up with the sweet taste of sugar and longing in her mouth.

* * *

Charity is tending to the boys, who have finally stopped crying and her mother is lying down now that her daughter is sorting things out and has just closed her eyes when there is a knock at the door to their living quarters.

'Yoohoo, you there, Moira?'

Charity's mammy's eyes fly open, meeting Charity's gaze in a panic.

For this is highly irregular. Mrs Kerridge has not visited since Mammy gave her the short shift after Paddy was born when Mammy wasn't coping but was too proud to admit it.

The ladies of the street, led by Mrs Kerridge, are kind, if too much into minding other people's business, and nothing gets past them.

Mrs Kerridge had dropped in just after Paddy's birth and broached the topic of Mammy's ill health.

'It's hard having bubbas one after the other. Does no favours to your body and the bubs so demanding. Believe me, I know.' Mrs Kerridge sighed deeply. 'And our men, they mean well but don't know the first thing about looking after the littluns, let alone noticing how worn out we are. In any case, they think the house and the kids are the woman's business, eh? You look all done in, Moira.' Mrs Kerridge's heart was in the right place but diplomacy was not her strong suit. 'Us ladies can take shifts and help until you're...'

Mammy took it the wrong way.

'I'm fine,' she said icily. 'Myself and my children are doing just fine. I'll see you out.'

And even though it took all she had to stand up – Charity could see how pale she got – she had walked Mrs Kerridge to the door.

Charity had felt like running after her and saying, *Please ignore Mammy. She does need help. She's just too proud to admit it. Please help. I need it. For I will be the one picking up the pieces.*

But Mammy, ill as she was, broken as she was, had stared at Charity, as if reading her mind, and shook her head, no.

'We can manage ourselves, can't we, Charity, love?' she whispered, once she heard the front door shut behind Mrs Kerridge, thrusting the baby at Charity as she lay down on her mattress, her exhausted, desperate gaze pleading with Charity to agree with her.

After that, the women of the street kept their distance, although they asked after the boys and Moira when they came upon Charity during those rare instances when she was rushing to school to keep up her attendance and avoid being pulled up by the headteacher.

'Well, we tried our best, but what can you do when someone is as stubborn as our Moira?' Charity heard the women gossip as they shelled peas of an evening, sitting on chairs in front of their polished to within an inch of their life stoops as the sun set and the ever-present smog thickened over West India Dock Road, the air scented with salt and spices and sugar and hops, raucous laughter wafting from the public house, the women tutting as the men got too loud and merry. 'She thinks we don't know what goes on.'

'Those littluns crying their heart out all day long. Breaks my heart, it does.' Mrs Ross sighed.

'And poor, sweet Charity, a child herself, run ragged doing all the work.' Mrs Devlin tutted.

'But how can we help when Moira won't take it?' Mrs Neville had the last word.

The stoop of the lodging house, in contrast, let the street down. There was a time before Da came back from war when, Mammy told Charity back before Paddy was born and she had the energy to talk, Mammy had polished it and the windows too, taking pride in making sure they shone so brightly that you could see your reflection in them.

But no longer.

Every time she saw the stoop, dirty and dust spattered, Charity vowed to clean it.

But then Paddy wailed and his cries started off the others and she forgot about the stoop and went to attend to her brothers.

Every so often, when Charity is so tired she can't keep her eyes open, pushing her aching body to do the chores that keep on building up, channelling reserves of energy she didn't even know she had, when she dreams of one hour to herself, to sleep without the boys' cries and Da's moans startling her awake, splintering her bone-weary slumber into a thousand nightmarish shards, Charity is tempted to come clean with the women of the street who look at her with kind eyes when they ask after her mother and siblings. To beg them for help, for some respite, which she knows they would gladly offer.

But then, she thinks of her mother's eyes, the entreaty in them as she said, 'We'll manage, won't we?' She was pleading with Charity to keep up the pretence.

And so, she tells the ladies of the street, 'They're fine. Doing grand.'

They nod. Not at all fooled, even for a moment. But choosing, for her sake, to believe her lie.

'And you?' they ask, eyes soft with care.

'I'm all right, thank you.'

'If you need anything at all, at any time, you know where we are,' they say, looking at her with bright, kind, understanding gazes.

Charity nods. Grateful for their reassurance.

For they mean it, she can see.

And she carries their assurance with her as she goes about her chores, the knowledge that she has the ladies of the street to fall back on just in case things get too much for her, and somehow, just the promise of it, bright as a lone star in a cloud tormented sky, gives her the strength to carry on even when every bone in her body protests and her mind is groggy from sleeplessness and exhaustion and she feels like she absolutely cannot.

The only people Mammy allowed to see her and her children were the nuns. She could not lie to them, given she had been one of them.

So when Mrs Kerridge knocks on the door and calls for Mammy, both Charity and Mammy are surprised.

Well, Mammy's surprise is, as with everything she does, more of a muted affair.

Mrs Kerridge knocks again, *rat a tat tat*, brisk and efficient. 'Moira, my dear, please let me in. It's about Paddy.'

Charity is holding baby Paddy in her arms, but nevertheless, her heart jolts with fear. Is there something she's missed? She checks the infant over, just to be sure. But the little one is fine, if cranky, so it's not him.

It must be Da then. Of course.

She sees the same alarm reflected in Mammy's eyes. And now there is nothing muted in Mammy's expression, fear and worry wrought into every premature line of her face as she sits up, with difficulty, and gestures for Charity to open the door.

Charity walks to the door carrying the fretful baby, who is about to tip into sleep, even as she follows her mother's gaze which is taking in the state of the room, mess everywhere – Charity seeing to the boys first before sorting out the chaos – in panicked alarm, swiftly replaced by tired resignation.

Connor and Fergus are sitting on the floor – they can't be trusted on the chairs; they're too wriggly and have fallen off one too many times – with plates of gruel in front of them, plus a slice of toast for Fergus.

Gruel is smeared all over Connor's face and on the floor beside him. Toast crumbs mingle with watery dregs of gruel on Fergus's plate and the floor, and his face is shiny with dripping.

Let her see, Charity reads on her mother's face. *It cannot be helped.*

Nevertheless, Charity cannot help feeling embarrassed on Mammy's behalf and her own as she lets Mrs Kerridge in, the baby hiccupping on her shoulder, Fergus and Connor crying for more food that Charity was in the process of sorting out when Mrs Kerridge knocked.

But Mrs Kerridge sweeps into the room seemingly unaffected by the mess, not appearing to notice it at all. Instead, her gaze lands on Charity and the babe in her arms, the boys who have stopped crying to stare at this strange lady in their living quarters in shock, and her mother who is sitting up but looks, Charity knows, dishevelled, pale, not the Moira that she was even just after Paddy's birth, instead a weak facsimile.

Charity registers the stunned shock that flits briefly across Mrs Kerridge's face when she sees Charity's mammy – one fleeting moment before Mrs Kerridge brings it back under control and smiles warmly at Moira.

Charity respects and is grateful to Mrs Kerridge for it.

It appears Mrs Kerridge gets the lay of the land in one glance. She understands that Charity's mammy is not up to sorting out whatever has happened with Charity's da for she nods at Mammy saying, brightly, 'All right now, our Moira?'

And then, she turns gently to Charity. 'I think you'll need to come with me, child. Hand the bubba over to your mammy now. Your da needs you.'

'What's happened?' Charity asks, her voice sharp with panic.

She steals a glance at her mother and she too is worried, tense, rocking to and fro, but that might be from the pain she is trying to contain.

The baby, picking up on his sister's distress, starts to wail louder.

His brothers join in too, each outdoing the other.

'Ach now, no point upsetting the boys further, is it? Please come with me, Charity, love,' Mrs Kerridge says, a hint of steel in her voice, even as she appears grim. Whatever it is, it must be bad.

Until now, Da has managed to contain his rages in public; he only explodes in front of his family – or at least that's what Charity has hoped. There haven't been any complaints at any rate, and in any case, he gets maudlin with drink rather than aggressive. He saves that only for his family.

That's what she's thought...

But now, ice in her veins, even as her heart pounds with fear and shame, she wonders if perhaps he's just the same with everyone but they've all been protecting her, her mother and the boys, keeping it from them out of the goodness of their hearts.

'I'll just give Connor and Fergus some more food and make up a bottle for Paddy and then I'll come,' Charity says, knowing that her mother will not be able to see to the boys and, if she left them now, they will be crying and upset until she is back. Her voice, thankfully, does not tremble and give her away.

'I'll help,' Mrs Kerridge says. 'You're looking a bit peaky now, Moira; why don't you rest?'

And it is a measure of how exhausted and in pain Charity's mother must be, or perhaps she thinks that Mrs Kerridge has seen them at their worst anyway – what's the point of hiding? – for she meekly complies.

13

CHARITY

'Your da,' Mrs Kerridge says as they walk upstairs to the reception area, which is supposed to be manned by Da, but often unattended. 'He got into a bit of a state,' Mrs Kerridge continues, pausing briefly to catch her breath.

Colour floods into Charity's cheeks, hot and bruising scarlet. 'I'm sorry.'

'Ach, child.' Mrs Kerridge is gentle. She stops at the top of the stairs, panting heavily. 'I... give me a minute. I'm not used to charging up and down stairs, you see. Not as fit as you young 'uns.'

Then, once she's got her breath back, smiling kindly at Charity: 'It's not your fault, love. It's nobody's but the blasted war's. It did for so many men.' Then, her gaze far away: 'I remember Paddy before. Such a charmer, he was. Always with a twinkle in his eyes, joking and smiling. Forever ready to help anyone in need. He was a good 'un, was Paddy O'Kelly. We were all jealous of your mammy, let me tell you. For landing such a handsome fella and kind with it.'

Charity feels tears smart in her eyes. She is glad that Mrs Kerridge has reminded her of the man her father was once.

All she feels for her father nowadays is resentment and fear, chipping away at the love she had harboured for him.

But, she realises, as her heart warms and fills, that that love is still there, although it is hidden underneath the anger, the upset, and she is grateful to Mrs Kerridge for helping her access it.

'Now, child,' Mrs Kerridge says and something in her voice pushes away the warm feeling in Charity's heart, fear once again taking hold. 'Your da... well... don't take what I'm saying the wrong way...' Mrs Kerridge stops and sighs deeply.

Whatever is to come is bad, Charity knows, for usually, Mrs Kerridge is direct but now she appears to be hesitating.

'What's he done?' she whispers.

'He lost it, child. Completely lost it. There was a fight in the street...'

'Da was involved?' Charity closes her eyes, her voice shrinking from the answer as she imagines her father's rage. Unleashing his fury on the people of the street, fists and spittle flying as he shouts obscenities, as he spirals out of the control that he only ever has a very loose handle on.

'No child, I'm not saying it right,' Mrs Kerridge says, gently.

'I'm sorry?' Charity is puzzled.

'He wasn't involved. Well, at least not at first.'

'Da was not involved?' Charity grabs at this, relief flooding through her, although she feels even more at sea. Why is Mrs Kerridge here then? Is it because... Da was hurt? Charity feels ashamed that it is only now that she is considering this; her first thought was that Da had something to do with it, not the other way round. Charity feels a pain in her heart at the thought of Da in pain and it reassures her. She does love her father. She *does*.

And now, a different kind of fear grips Charity's heart.

For Mrs Kerridge to be here, how badly is her da hurt?

'Is he...?' Her voice shrinking to a tiny, diffident whisper. 'Is he okay?'

Mrs Kerridge's eyes are soft with empathy and shiny with feeling. 'No, love, he's not.'

Charity's heart sinks and she feels the tears she's holding back bud in her eyes.

'Is he... he's not...?'

She can't say the word. *Dead.*

No. No, he wouldn't be. For Mrs Kerridge would have told her, and Mammy surely. She wouldn't keep them in suspense; she's not that sort of person. And wait, didn't Mrs Kerridge say her father lost it? Not, *he died.*

Something close to tormented relief and tentative hope clutches at Charity's heart.

She's surprised by Mrs Kerridge reaching out and enveloping her in her fleshy arms. She is surrounded by Mrs Kerridge's scent of rose talc and sweat. She is taken aback for a brief moment before she sinks into the embrace. For Charity can't recall the last time she was hugged like this, offered comfort. The only people she hugs or holds, she realises, are her brothers. And Mammy when she helps her wash and to and from the outhouse. And there, with them, she is the one who comforts.

She wants to stay in this embrace forever.

Which is why she pulls away even as her eyes sting with fresh tears.

She must not get used to this.

'I'm sorry child, for not telling it properly. Your da is far from fine, but he is not gone. Not yet.'

Mrs Kerridge's gaze is tender, her voice gentle.

Does that mean he'll be gone soon? Charity wonders. How soon? But she does not have the courage to voice the question. She'd rather not know.

There have been times, Lord knows, more often than not, when Charity has secretly wished that her father, with his simmering rages and his tortured cries, would disappear. But now, her heart sinks. She swallows and roughly swipes at her eyes with the back of her hand. *Buck up, Charity*, she chides herself.

Looking at Mrs Kerridge, she nods, acknowledging what the lady is trying to tell her.

Mrs Kerridge beams at her as if to say, *Attagirl*.

'What happened?' Charity asks when she can speak past the salt in her mouth.

Mrs Kerridge smiles kindly at her. 'As I said, there was an altercation over by the docks. Your da had gone for a walk down thereabouts and was just heading back, so they say, when it happened.'

'Ah,' Charity says, waiting for Mrs Kerridge to continue.

'There was a scene caused by a down-and-out named Davies. Looking for trouble, I imagine.' Mrs Kerridge rolls her eyes and snorts to convey just what she thinks of that. 'He intercepted Mr Cohen, who runs the textile factory on East India Dock Road. Mr Cohen was walking along, minding his own business, and this man Davies started having a go at him, saying that, "Your lot has taken all our jobs." To which Mr Cohen reasonably asked, "What do you mean, our lot?" And Davies started calling Mr Cohen and Jews like him all sorts of names. He was right in Mr

Cohen's face, even as Mr Cohen kept insisting that he had done nothing wrong. But there was no reasoning with the man, who blamed Mr Cohen and his "kind" for all his problems, yelling, "You lot have destroyed our way of life." And then...' Mrs Kerridge pauses to take a breath, digging in the pocket of her dress and extracting a voluminous, daisy-dotted handkerchief and wiping her sweaty forehead with it. 'This Davies, not content with shouting and swearing, shoved poor Mr Cohen, who lost his footing and stumbled into your da, who was walking past right at that moment... That was it for your da...' Mrs Kerridge takes another breath. 'He just...' Mrs Kerridge shakes her head, unable to describe what had happened, for once lost for words.

'I get it,' Charity says softly, mortified on her da's behalf. 'He does that at home.'

'Ah, child.' The sympathy in Mrs Kerridge's eyes is too much to bear.

Charity looks away, so Mrs Kerridge will not see the fresh tears stinging her eyes. Down at her too-tight dress, which is barely touching her knees. She has outgrown this one too, like all her other clothes, but is making do.

'He lunged at Mr Cohen and that was when he fell.'

'Oh.' It hurts to think of her father falling.

'He did his back in, quite badly, we think. A doctor has been called.'

Charity's hand creeps to her heart, which aches for her da.

'In any case, your father going berserk shocked Davies into stopping his rant...' Mrs Kerridge is saying.

'Mr Cohen, is he all right?' Charity asks when she can speak.

'Ah, child, a gem, that's what you are.' Mrs Kerridge's eyes shine with affection as she glows at Charity. 'Yes, he's fine. And what's more, Davies apologised to him after,' Mrs Kerridge clucks. 'It might have had something to do with the women of both West and East India Dock Roads turning on Davies, and his wife and his mother bending his ear too, for they were summoned by the hullabaloo like most of the East End.'

'Oh.' Charity's heart sinks even more. The whole of the East End had witnessed her father's tantrum? Her mother will be mortified. For Mammy, appearances and how they present themselves to the world matters greatly. This is why she had not let Charity ask Mrs Kerridge and the other ladies of West India Dock Road for help no matter how bad things got.

Nevertheless, Charity says, through the salt flooding her mouth, 'That's grand then, that something good came of it.'

And once again, Charity finds herself wrapped in Mrs Kerridge's warm, fusty bosom. 'You are a treasure, so you are, our Charity. Your parents are lucky to have you,' Mrs Kerridge whispers into Charity's hair.

* * *

By the time they get to where her father is, the doctor has arrived.

Charity's da is lying on his back on a makeshift pallet someone has brought out, eyes closed, seemingly unaware of the people collected around him, whispering urgently among themselves. When they see Charity and Mrs Kerridge approach, they fall silent, stepping aside to let them through.

Da's face, turned up to the smoggy and overcast sky, is scrunched in agony, Charity sees, and her heart goes out to him.

She is about to kneel down beside him but the doctor takes her aside.

'Miss O'Kelly,' he says, his eyes grave. 'Your father needs

complete bed rest. I will come and look in on him in a few days, but I doubt he will heal quickly. I understand he was already limping because of a bad hip, due to injury sustained in the war?'

Charity nods, unable to speak.

'Some of the men here will carry him to your lodgings. It's not the best idea to move him under the circumstances, but we can't very well allow him to lie here now, in the middle of the street, can we?'

Once again, she can only nod. And then, finding the words in her mouth, she manages, 'Thank you, Doctor.'

The doctor nods.

At the sound of her voice, her father opens his eyes and turns to look at her.

The lines of pain etched into his face relax as he smiles. 'My Charity,' he whispers.

And she is touched. For he has never been this gentle with her, this loving, not recently, at least.

But that might be because she is always rushing about around him, seeing to the boys and Mammy.

Her heart swells with love as she kneels down beside him, taking his callused hand in hers. It is the right thing to do for he clings to her hand as if for dear life.

'Where's your mother?' he asks.

'At home with the boys,' she says.

'Boys?' He appears confused, a deep furrow bisecting his forehead.

'Fergus, Connor and Paddy,' she says and her voice shakes like a leaf in a blustery breeze. 'Your sons.'

'My sons!' His face contorts in a scowl. 'What on bloody earth are ye talking about, Moira? Are ye out of your mind?'

A hiss of gossip swells through the gathered crowd: 'Paddy's only gone and lost his mind, he has.'

Charity turns to the doctor, who is looking at Da, a frown of concentration gracing his face.

He once again takes Charity aside. 'The confusion and loss of memory. He's exhibited it before?'

Charity nods, her cheeks on fire.

She shouldn't be ashamed, she knows. It can't be helped. It's just how her da is, at times. But does it have to be revealed in front of the whole street?

The doctor nods gravely. 'I have seen this in other men who've returned from the war. I'm sorry, my dear but your father will require constant care. And I'm afraid, from what I've seen with the other men, that it is only going to get worse.'

A baby starts wailing somewhere in the pressing mob of people...

'No,' Charity's father starts shouting. 'No. No. No. Stop. Please stop.' Slapping his ears with his palms. 'Stop.' Tears running down his eyes.

The entire street watches in horrified fascination.

Charity squats next to her father, slips an arm around his shoulders gently so as not to hurt his back further.

He turns to her, collapsing in her arms like he is the child and she the adult.

He smells pungent, of sweat and panic.

And ignoring the eyes of everyone on the street, the gossip that Charity is certain is even now making its speedy way up and down the East End, well-meaning but already, she is sure, added to and embellished, she gently soothes her father, just as she does her brothers, murmuring the same reassurances, and gradually, he settles into a trance-like quiet in her arms.

14

CHARITY

The fall, when Charity's da collapsed on the street, right where she's standing now, did for her father's back and he has been bedridden ever since.

His mental health too, just like the doctor warned, did not improve. Instead, it has progressively worsened.

For Charity, her father's breakdown marked the end of her dreams of working in the sugar factory and the beginning of her reincarnation as Charity O'Kelly, the manager of Paddy O'Kelly's Boarding and Lodging house.

And to be fair, it hasn't been a bad life.

She has her beloved brothers for company.

And the residents of West India Dock Road have been good as gold, helping her and coming to her aid every step of the way.

In those early days, as she was finding her feet running the lodging house, Mrs Kerridge, along with the other women of West India Dock Road, had taken her in hand.

If any of the lodgers gave her trouble, Mrs Kerridge was there, giving them the eye and asking them to leave immediately. 'And no, you won't get what you paid back. You should have thought of that before you treated this young girl the way you did. Shame on you.'

And off they would go, suitably shamefaced.

The lodgers soon learned that they couldn't take advantage of the young girl running the lodging house for she had the force of the entire street behind her, a formidable army of hard-faced matrons who wouldn't take any nonsense.

And of course, there was her friend Jack Devine too, once he overcame his rebel phase, who would drop by every so often just to check everything was going smoothly.

Afterwards, she wondered why she and Mammy had struggled along on their own when the street would have gladly come to their aid.

But Mammy had been too proud to ask for help.

Charity thought she understood. When Mammy had run the boarding house when Da was away, she had commanded the respect of the women of the street. But with Da the way he was, the whole street was talking about the O'Kellys, or so Mammy must have thought. And she did not want to add more grist to the gossip mill, given she couldn't even look after herself, let alone her children. As long as she did not ask the women for help, she could pretend that all was well, that she was coping fine. She had nothing but her self-respect and she was determined to hold on to it at any cost.

Charity got it, but a part of her still sometimes resented Mammy for it, especially when everyone on the street was being so helpful. Perhaps if Mammy had swallowed her pride and admitted she needed assistance, Charity could have worked at the sugar factory like she had always wanted.

But then she would firmly push those thoughts away. This was her life now. And it wasn't a bad one.

She has if not enjoyed then at least risen to the challenge of running the lodging house as well as looking after her parents and bringing up her brothers. It wouldn't have been possible without the aid and encouragement of everyone in the street and she is very grateful to them for it.

She has made good friends.

She has managed to keep the lodging house going, despite the war.

She has managed to look after her father, who has been really bad since the bombing started in earnest.

But now...

This...

She is not ready to lose her brother. The boy she has raised. Not quite yet.

Yes, she knows that if he goes to war, there's no guarantee he will become like their father.

But she thinks back to all the men who survived the first war that she knows of and they're all damaged in one way or another.

If not physically wearing their wounds, the scars of war upon their body for all to see, then in their mind.

And God help her but she is not prepared for Fergus to join their ranks.

What is the boy thinking? Didn't he come with her to visit Mrs Ross when she received the dreaded telegram?

Charity will never forget that day. Mrs Ross's grief. She had regretted bringing Fergus along, seeing his stricken face. But he had insisted upon it, which had touched her.

'Mrs Ross's Marge was only a few years older than me. I knew her from school. I will come along,' he'd said, eyes solemn and sparking with pain.

They had left Connor and Paddy at the curry house, avidly

watching Mr Brown take on Mr Stone at chess for the umpteenth time, alongside Mr Rosenbaum and Mr Lee.

Divya waved goodbye as she came out of the kitchen bearing plates of potato drops and carrot cake to sustain the boys, her face grave. She had already been to see Mrs Ross that morning.

Charity and Fergus had climbed up the stairs of the tenement block where Mrs Ross lived, that smelled of boiling cabbage and children's cloth nappies that mothers hung over the banisters and no matter how well they were washed, always carried that underlying, fetid taint of faeces.

Charity was transported as ever back to not so long ago when she would be at the wash house several times in one day, it seemed, cleaning the boys' nappies. She had heaved a sigh of sheer relief when Paddy had finally outgrown his.

Fergus, despite the sombreness of the occasion, couldn't help taking the stairs two at a time and waited at the top for Charity, peering down the dark stairwell, his hair – too long, it needed a cut; it grew rapidly, like the rest of him – falling over his face. 'Come on, hurry up, slowcoach.'

Charity knocked on the door to Mrs Ross's flat, calling for her gently.

When there was no reply, she pushed the door open.

The flat was dark, the curtains drawn.

Mrs Ross was in bed, lying fully clothed on top of the sheets, staring at the ceiling.

Her eyes wide open, tears welling from them, running down the side of her face and soaking the pillow.

One hand rested upon her heart while the other clutched a piece of paper which was crumpled in her fist.

Charity looked at her brother. His eyes bloodshot, face

pale. His body a taut spring, poised at the entrance of the door, afraid to enter, shocked by this version of Mrs Ross.

Charity tried with her gaze to impart comfort.

Then she turned to their neighbour, calling her name gently so as not to startle the woman.

Mrs Ross's face when she sat up and turned to face Charity and her brother, after having wiped her tears as best she could, was dark with pain, her eyes stark as she shivered like a tendril in a gusty storm, her face glittering with the remnants of tears.

Charity had sat down beside the woman, taken her hand, which was still clutching the telegram.

'In her last letter, she said she was missing my pork chops,' Mrs Ross said, haltingly, between sniffs.

Fergus, although appearing highly uncomfortable and like he'd rather be anywhere but here, came in and sat down beside Mrs Ross on her other side.

Charity's heart swelled with love for him. She had never been prouder of him than she was at that moment.

'I wrote back saying that when she was due home on shore leave, I'd make sure to be first in the butcher's queue. "I'll be there before the butcher opens," I promised in my letter. "Only Mrs O'Riley would have got there before me – an eager beaver, that one." I knew that would make her smile.' Mrs Ross sniffed mightily.

'She had a very good sense of humour; always up for a laugh, was Marge,' Fergus said, his voice croaky with tears.

'Yes, son, that she was.' Mrs Ross smiled wetly.

Charity's eyes pricked even as she nodded at her brother.

Mrs Ross turned to Charity, pale and ashen, despair ageing her face, contorting her familiar features in a mask of agony.

'But she's gone,' she said, and those two words were smothered in pain, choked with grief. 'She will never again eat my chops with gravy and potatoes and plenty of onions.'

She shut her eyes, the telegram scrunched in her hand fluttering to the floor.

Fergus picked it up and tried to hand it to Mrs Ross but she didn't notice.

'She's gone,' she whispered. 'She's never coming home.'

After a beat, Charity spoke into the mournful silence. 'She's a hero.'

Mrs Ross opened her eyes. 'That she is.'

'She lives on in our memories,' Fergus said.

Mrs Ross nodded, her green eyes sparkling like sodden fields, ravaged by sorrow and torment.

In contrast to his bounding up the stairs when they had arrived, when they left Mrs Ross, Fergus was subdued, dragging his feet, all the oomph gone out of him.

Charity wanted to comfort him, but what could she say? This was the reality of the times they were living in: loss and heartache. She took his hand, squeezed it and he let her, instead of pulling away, even rested his head on her shoulder – he had to bend to do it – and they shared a moment before they stepped outside, blinking and blinded by the light.

It was a grey day but even so, considerably brighter than inside the tenement block, which was dark and gloomy, permeated by the grief that had seeped through the walls of Mrs Ross's flat and into the stairwell and communal spaces.

15

CHARITY

A sudden siren, long and low and swooping, cuts through Charity's ruminations.

An air raid.

During the day? It's bad enough that the East End is being battered relentlessly every night but now they're doing it at daytime as well? It's just as Mrs O'Riley's cousin had warned.

Sure enough, the air raid warden comes up the street, crying, 'Take shelter, please.'

Her panicked thoughts run to her parents, in the basement of the lodging house.

Da will be distressed, ululating in misery.

Mrs Kerridge was in the curry house when Charity left in search of Fergus.

Charity has never really told anyone except Divya about how Da gets in an air raid, except to commiserate with Mrs Nolan when she worried about her husband, but she knows the street knows anyway.

Charity hopes, no, she *knows*, that Mrs Kerridge will sit with her parents in the lodging house basement, the air raid warden having given it the nod. Mrs Kerridge, in her firm, no-nonsense way, will deal with Da's panic attack.

Connor and Paddy will go with Divya and the other patrons of the curry house to the Anderson shelter in Divya's small patch of garden. No matter how much the matrons of West India Dock Road clean the shelters, they nevertheless get damp and dirty as water seeps into them. The boys will be cold, but at least they will be safe. If there is time, they might all trudge to the Tube station. This will please Connor and Paddy, Charity knows, alleviating their worry about their elder brother to some extent. They have heard stories of what goes on in the Underground station from the (very few) other schoolmates who, like them, have not yet been evacuated ('Mark said a rat came right up to him!' Paddy had told Charity, his eyes wide with thrilled horror), and this will be their chance to experience it.

And Fergus...

Please let Fergus be safe.

I have good friends; they will look after my younger brothers and parents. And Fergus will *be safe,* she promises herself firmly.

But it is scant comfort for she worries anyway.

The phut phut phut of Luftwaffe bombers hovering over-head intrudes into her dithering.

The enemy planes are here, about to release their deathly load.

She looks about even as a harassed-looking warden directs her: 'Go that way. Take shelter at the Tube station, which is at the junction, the next turn on your right.'

But it is too late.

She cowers under the bridge, to the dirge of sirens, the thunk crump of falling bombs.

The roar of fire and devastation. Buildings that were sound

a minute ago now teetering, then crumpling as easily as if they were made of paper. The grunt thump swoosh of destruction. The scent of burning. Vermilion flames leaping up to the death-coloured sky.

A tenement block collapses right in front of Charity, so she ducks from the rubble, fiery grit stinging her eyes. The noise, deafening, debilitating, reverberating through her very being.

Earth shattering under her feet. Tremors rocking her. Boiling debris flung at her body. Billowing rings of smoke, the orange-topped, grasping yawn of sizzling blue flames, choking everything in sight.

The heat. Oh, the ash-spiked, blistering, scorching heat.

Day turned into night by smoke. Grey ash raining doom.

The swoosh whizz bang of fire. The blinding, eye-watering, lung-choking, breath-stealing plague of smoke.

The scorching lap of heat renders her cold with terror.

Is this the end?

Fiery smoke in her throat, a salty laugh escaping in between a paroxysm of coughing.

I worried about my brother dying. Losing him before his time. But it is going to be me.

The ultimate irony.

She thinks of her brothers. Her parents. Her friends. Their faces rising before her smoke-branded, tear-swollen eyes. All the people she has loved.

Be safe, she thinks even as the world explodes before her eyes.

16

CHARITY

Charity is not aware of time passing; it could be minutes or hours in a hell of smoke and fire, crisp, scorching orange. Bright, dancing flames and blazing, crimson-topped smoke that obscures the sky, bleeding navy.

The scent of scorched flesh. The creak and groan of buildings crumbling, the screams and cries that accompany doom and destruction, agonised and panicked. Calling for help and deliverance.

If Charity wasn't trapped under rubble, she would help.

As it is, she cannot determine if she is dead.

Is this hell? Her body burning hot, flames licking close by, devouring hungrily, the world crackling and spitting, flinging grit and incandescent ash, smoke stinging her eyes, choking her throat, claiming the breath from her. The cries of children and adults, mingling with prayers.

It is what she has imagined hell to be.

But I've been good, God.

Although of course I've resented having to look after my parents and my brothers every so often. I've grumbled and complained. But mostly, I think I've been good.

She feels numb. Unable to move any part of herself. She is sobbing, she knows, only because of her chest hitching, breathlessness and fiery tears.

She is pinned down by dust and grit, hands covering her ears. Praying. For her family to be safe. *Please, Lord, look out for my parents. And, especially, my brothers. They are only young. They have so much life yet to live. Please spare them.*

She understands, even as she prays, that this must be the cry of all mothers and sisters, wives and daughters, as their children and brothers, husbands and fathers sign up for war. How will God answer all of them?

Yet even so, she prays.

Fergus, wherever he is, please spare him, Lord. And Paddy and Connor, please.

Her brothers' faces rising before her eyes, mischief and love.

Even if she is in hell, God will still listen, won't he? *Please, God.*

Ah, what's that? The urgent ringing of fire engines. There are no fire engines in hell, surely? Does that mean she is alive?

And then, there are strong arms lifting her out of the rubble, a kind voice saying, 'There there, love, you're all right.'

She opens her eyes to swirls of smog, the scent of gasoline and fire, crimson flames which are being doused by sizzling arcs of water, the sky rent with thick, black clouds of smoke.

'Am I... dead?' she whispers.

He chuckles softly. 'No, love. Although war is a special kind of hell. Now, are ye all right? Nothing broken?'

Her body hurts. But she is standing on her two feet, although she feels dizzy, disorientated.

Her eyes smart and she closes them.

'Ye all right?' the fireman asks again.

'I...' Charity swallows, trying to locate her voice in her smoke-clogged throat. It comes out hoarse. 'I am, yes.'

Let my brothers be all right. My parents. Divya, Mrs Kerridge and the others...

The fireman, strong hands smelling of fiery ash, guides her out of the debris and she allows herself to be led, blinded by the smoke.

He gently sits her down, on a section of broken wall, she thinks.

'Now, rest 'ere a while, darlin', while ye try and get yer bearings. I need to go 'elp the other poor blighters stuck in there.'

'Thank you,' she says.

'I'm just doing my job, darlin'. Ye take care now. And when ye feel up to it, make yer way to the rest centre up the road. The ambulance crew will check ye out, just to make sure yer fine, and the support staff will give ye something to eat and drink. All right?'

She sits on the wall, catching her breath, and watches the firemen putting out the fire and dragging children covered in soot out of the debris, confused, cowering, upset at finding themselves in this sweltering, breaking-apart world. They are reunited with their mothers, who burst into tears as they gather their children to their bosoms. A woman rocks on her feet beside Charity, tears spilling out of her gas mask and trembling on the folds of parchment skin on her wizened neck.

Charity wipes her own leaking eyes and stands up. She is still dizzy and waits until the light-headedness passes.

She stands for a minute or two longer, deciding where to go. She is torn. She wants to check on Paddy and Connor, on her parents. But... she's also worried for Fergus.

Now, once again, like she has several times since the war started, she wishes Jack was here. Jack, her childhood friend, who, despite his father doing well in the roofing business and moving out of the East End, is an East End lad through and through. Never forgetting his roots, always ready with a smile and a helping hand. Jack, who has been there for Charity through thick and thin. If Jack were here, he would sort things out, giving Fergus what for, but without turning Fergus against him, like Charity appears to have done. He has been a good friend to them, has Jack.

She hopes he is safe. In his letters, he is very careful to sound happy and cheerful, playing down his experiences. She prays he is all right, that the Jerries are treating him humanely in the prisoner of war camp. But... she looks at the deathly havoc wreaked by the very same Jerries and shivers, hugging herself, cold despite the heat of the fire. She does not want to think about what he might be going through. She had wished for Divya and Jack, her two best friends, to get together, but Divya's heart is promised to Raghu, the lascar who was her opponent in the curry competition conducted at West India Dock Road, oh, around sixteen months ago now but which feels like a lifetime previously. What an evening that was! A celebration, a street party, joy and festivities and lots of curry. It was going swimmingly until...

No, she won't think about that.

Divya pines for Raghu, Charity knows.

And Charity also knows, although Divya hasn't told her this, that Divya writes to him too. She found the letters when Divya, busy in the kitchen of the curry house, which was mobbed, had asked her to fetch something from her room. They were by her pillow, a thick pile, and it was the saddest sight. For Raghu, who thought he was not good enough for

Divya, had signed up for war without letting Divya know where he was, with no forwarding address or the means of contacting him.

Seeing that pile of letters beside Divya's pillow had broken Charity's heart.

Now, she shakes her head to stop her mind wandering. And arrives at a decision.

She will hope that someone in West India Dock Road – her bet is on Mrs Kerridge – has seen to her parents and that Divya has kept her brothers safe; she loves them like her own.

And she will do what she had set out to do: find Fergus.

She turns round and blinks to try and focus through the smoke and dust. She walks gingerly, trying to avoid the debris, trying not to step on splintered glass stained with blood. Bright, silver shards spattered with droplets of crimson. She shivers even though it's almost too hot to bear.

Then she starts walking towards the West India Docks, to the signing up office even as once again, she sends up a prayer for her family.

And as she stumbles through the rubble, laced with the acrid odour of burning, she hears a voice. A familiar, much-beloved voice, calling her name.

'Charity.'

Could it be? Is it?

Or is she dreaming?

Through the shifting haze of fire, which the firemen are still trying to contain with fountains of water, the navy balloons of smoke, the coarse curtain of grit and dust, she thinks she spies a familiar face.

She blinks through the smog, trying to see clearly even though it is an impossibility, the dirt and smoke stinging her eyes, inciting tears.

But yes. *Yes.*

The hazy silhouette before her takes wavering shape.

And there, a miracle. Her brother. Fergus.

Is she hallucinating?

Is her desire for him to be safe so powerful that she has conjured him up?

Please Jesus, Mary and Joseph, let this not be a mirage.

'Fergus,' she calls, though her burning, smoke-battered throat only manages a weak whisper.

And then she is running, not caring if she steps on rubble, on grit, on glass.

Please let him be real.

She runs up to him and extends a hand that trembles and shakes even as she touches his face. She has to reach up to do it. But her hand does not grasp air like she was half-expecting it to.

It really *is* Fergus.

Thank you, God.

'You are real, flesh and blood.' Her voice collapses with relief.

'Course I am, Charity.' He smiles but his voice, too, wavers and stumbles like hers is doing.

'You're all right,' she says, and it is a plea and a prayer, even as she runs a hand down his body even though he's much taller than her now, checking that all his limbs are accounted for, that her brother is in one piece. She does not know if the tears in her eyes are from smoke or relief and she doesn't care.

Her brother is here. In front of her. He is as fine as can be in the circumstances.

She opens her arms and he folds into them like he used to as a much younger child.

She holds her brother and she tastes gratitude, bright yellow, blinding white.

Thank you, Jesus, Mary and Joseph.

'Mr Singh here helped me find shelter,' Fergus is saying.

And that is when Charity sees the man he is with. Smiling at her.

Eyes the bright ebony of a dreamy midsummer's night, twinkling with stars.

17

DIVYA

October 12, 1940

Dear Jack,

How are you? Stupid question, I know.

I'm sorry. I cannot even begin to imagine what you must be experiencing. Your second letter since being taken prisoner of war, which arrived the day before yesterday, is bright and carefully light – to avoid the censor striking out anything that gives too much away and also not to worry us, I know.

But here's hoping you are as best as can be under the circumstances and that the Huns are treating you right. How is the food there? I trust they are giving you enough to eat.

Mr Brown says that he hopes they are following the Geneva Convention rules which lay out protections and standards of treatment of prisoners of war.

As I promised when you left to sign up, I will prepare all of your favourite dishes, Jack, scarcity of ingredients notwithstanding, when you get home.

Here, the days are drawing in and there is a nippy chill to the air, winter most definitely stepping on autumn's toes. I hope you are warm enough. Everyone on the street, as always, sends their best wishes and love.

We wait for your letters, all of us at the curry house. As I've said before, your letters are cause for celebration. Everyone meets here and eats the snacks I've prepared while I read out your news to all.

Mrs Kerridge gives us all patriotic speeches to try and hide her fear for her sons; her oldest came back home after Dunkirk and now he's set off again, maintaining that the country needs him. But she hasn't heard from her younger two since Dunkirk – nothing at all – and she is worried.

Mrs Ross too hasn't heard from her son.

Both Mrs Ross and Mrs Kerridge have new lines of anxiety and angst scored onto their faces. Even when they smile, the worry shines through, a part of them agonising for their loved ones.

What is this war doing to us all, eh, Jack?

'Our new prime minister, Mr Winston Churchill, urges us to be strong and brave. Well, that we are, sir, us East-enders,' Mrs Kerridge exults.

'Hear, hear,' the other women cry.

'I see our indomitable spirit reflected all over the East End as we go about our business, despite being bombed, night after night, losing our houses and our possessions and our loved ones,' Mrs Kerridge continues. 'We will not be cowed.'

Rousing cheers from everyone in the curry house.

Mr Stone and Mr Brown continue to play chess through Mrs Kerridge's pontificating. They have become a dab hand at taking their chess set with them during the air raids – when they are not busy with their civil defence duties, that is

– one of them clutching the pieces and, most importantly, the scoreboard while the other carries the set itself.

Charity's lodgers – the few who have not signed up due to medical reasons and those in reserved occupations in the railways and over at the docks – helped install an Anderson shelter, which is rather like a kennel, which the government supplied, here at the curry house. But it gets very cold and damp as water seeps in, so on wet days, and, especially now that winter is drawing in, we all trudge to the Tube station.

Yes we have endured some bombing but we are all well and quite used to it now.

For the first few months of war, life went on as before apart from the new blackout curtains and men (you) signing up and us having to take gas masks along everywhere we went. And of course we got used to barrage balloons dotting the skyline, and sandbags stacked in front of tall buildings.

But we thought, as I'm sure you did too, that the war would be over in a matter of weeks.

You and all of our brave men at the front would chase the Huns away and that would be that. Who would have thought this war would drag on and on?

And now, well, we cannot recall a time when we didn't hear the screech of the air raid sirens and the phut phut phut of German Luftwaffe bombers overhead as soon as it gets dark, even as we clutch whatever's to hand and head to the Tube station, expertly dodging the broken bricks swept aside but not yet cleared from the previous night's raid and inured to bombed-out buildings, half standing, half falling down and gaping holes where tenements used to be.

Ah, now I remembered where I was going with this.

Forgive me, Jack, I write to you and it is like I am chatting with you and I go on and on and lose my thread of thought and...

Now where was I? Ah, yes...

I am so very grateful for the curry house, which is as busy as ever. The customers pay what they can, bless them, no matter how hard the times, so it is ticking along.

Thank you, Jack for making my dream come true, and, especially for making up the shortfall when I did not have enough funds to set the place up. You were right, as always. Even, especially, during war, people need to eat and more than that, a place to gather and share their experiences while they share in the food.

I am happy when I cook something which everyone enjoys from whatever I am able to procure.

Today was one of those days when I had plenty of potato to cook with but not much else.

My small patch of back garden now houses the Anderson shelter and a veggie patch but the only crop that's thriving is potatoes.

Even Mr Lee is struggling and you know how green-fingered he is.

I made Irish potato cakes with a smattering of spice for breakfast. It was a hit not only with the Irish contingent but with everyone.

Lunch was potato curry with spiced rice. Not as much of a hit but it went down well enough. Everyone especially enjoyed the bread pudding I made for afters.

At tea time, Mrs Kerridge set me a challenge. 'I bet even you can't improve this chicory coffee we have to endure nowadays.'

I tried Jack, by brewing it with cinnamon and sweetening it.

But...

'My dear, you gave it your best.' Mrs Kerridge was expansive. 'But even a magician like you cannot improve upon sludge.'

In any case, my apple and cinnamon cake was a hit.

Dinner was lentil soup, carrot and potato hotpot and savoury potato biscuits, with parsnip pudding for afters.

Now it's dusk and I have pulled the blackout curtains shut and am writing this in the lamplight in the kitchen quickly for the air raid sirens will sound any minute, if the past few nights are anything to go by. I have one ear out for them.

Now for what I meant to tell you when I began talking about air raids. Thank you for bearing with my long asides (not that you have a choice).

When it is wet, and cold and rainy, and we don't fancy the leaking Anderson shelter, we all make our way to the nearest Tube station. And although we're cramped in there and despite the rats darting between the tracks and the mayhem being unleashed overhead, it is quite a jolly atmosphere, I must say. I imagine, but I might be wrong, that it must have been the same for you, in the barracks when you retired for the night, the heady relief of having survived another day at the war front, during extraordinary times.

Us lot, bundled together underground, are united in camaraderie, joined against a common enemy, seeding death and devastation above us.

We help the more frail among us down the steps of the station, and budge up to make space for everyone, and try and make sure our neighbours are as comfortable as can be in the circumstances. We share stories and snacks – mine go within the first few minutes, no matter how many I bring – while some of us snore loudly enough to bring down the roof (not naming names). All right then, since you twisted my arm (I learned that expression from Charity), Mr Rosenbaum and Mrs Boon are the loudest but don't tell them I told you.

Old Mr Ramsey brings his fiddle and entertains all the ladies with his music – which they love – while Mrs Murphy joins in with song, which everyone hates. Mrs Murphy never misses an opportunity to tell us that she had the sweetest of voices as a young girl. 'That must have been very long ago indeed,' Paddy exclaimed in wonder, thankfully out of her hearing; she might be old but she has all her faculties, sharp as anything.

Mrs Murphy sings in her wavering voice that stumbles upon the higher notes, and due to the close and cramped quarters, we all have no choice but to listen. Babies cry and Mr Rosenbaum and Mrs Boon protest in their sleep, their snores momentarily paused. Finally, when he can take no more, old Mr Rouse cries, 'For the love of God, woman, will you please stop. My hearing is not the best but never have I wished it to be worse than when I have to endure your singing.' But Mrs Murphy carries on screeching tunelessly regardless. Even the rats scurry away.

Mr Barney, God bless his soul, brings some ale to distribute among anyone who'd like a little pick-me-up and soon there's rousing chatter and laughter, if not drowning out then at least diluting Mrs Murphy's best efforts.

Men play cards as they take a swig or two of ale. Everyone enjoys the snacks I pass round, declaring that my *potato bhajis go so well with Mr Barney's ale, asking for the recipe for my apple and carrot fritters.*

In any case, our nights are spent in this way, broken by air raid sirens. Sometimes, the all-clear comes early and sometimes, it comes towards dawn.

Sometimes, we have sirens twice in one night, early on and then later again.

The second time, we just get in the Anderson shelter.

We are a dab hand at sleeping through noise and mayhem, through Mrs Murphy's singing and the men's raucous chatter, their jollity helped along by Mr Barney's ale. We can sleep standing up and shivering in the damp and freezing Anderson shelter, and also catch our forty winks (this phrase learned from Mrs Kerridge), sitting down, squashed by people on either side so there's no space to move.

Each morning, we give thanks that our buildings are still standing, before going across to help those whose residences have been the latest casualties of the raids.

The interrupted nights are part and parcel of our life.

The other day, Mr Crosby turned up at the Tube station for the first time in a long while.

All the men hailed him with slightly hysteric fervour tinged with relief that he was safe and well.

Mr Stone confessed later that he rather thought Mr Crosby had been one of the casualties of the bombing.

Mr Brown said that he had assumed Mr Crosby was at one of the rest centres because his lodgings had been bombed.

'I thought he had gone to the country,' Mr Barney declared.

'I was of the opinion that he had joined the Home Guard,' Mr Rosenbaum said.

'Home Guard?' Mr Barney snorted. 'He's puny as a rake and ill with it. He suffers from asthma and he also gets epileptic fits, I've heard.'

In any case, this was afterwards.

When they saw Mr Crosby in the Underground station, they welcomed him enthusiastically, making space for him, even though it was cramped, starting a new game of cards to include him, plying him with ale, and they asked him where he'd been.

Mr Crosby said that he'd been bedding down in a shelter in the wharves among the spices and canned goods, wine, brandy, rum and other spirits.

'But sheltering among spices and goods in the wharves, isn't that dangerous?' Mr Brown cried, the other men wide-eyed. 'They are what the Huns are targeting, what they're after night after night.'

Mr Crosby shrugged. 'When we go, we go,' he said.

And nobody could argue with that.

I tell you all this to give you a flavour of our war. We are doing all right, finding joy where we can, and I trust you are too.

Jack, you say you are an Eastender through and through but I bet you would not recognise the East End were you to come home. Oh, but how wonderful it would be to have you back!

Everyone on the street has missed you so.

Most children have been evacuated. So there's not much chatter of children in evidence. And with children gone and men gone, only older men, the infirm and us women, it feels odd, lacking. Of course, Paddy, Connor and Fergus have refused to leave, and Charity, while on the one hand, is grateful to have them close, on the other, worries about them no end.

Ah, here they are, the sirens.

I better go, Jack.

Take care and come home safe to us.

Much love,

Divya and all at West India Dock Road

18

DIVYA

October 13, 1940

My dearest Raghu,

    I ache.

    I miss.

    I long.

    I want.

    I need.

    I wait.

    For I will not give up hope that I will see you one day even as I fear that I may not. That you might die or I might do and that one kiss was all I was allowed of you.

    But… I will not give up hope.

    Yours,

    Divya

19

CHARITY

'I am very pleased to make your acquaintance,' Mr Singh says.

He is holding a crutch in his right hand and he switches it to his left side and it is only then that Charity, who had been mesmerised by his glowing beacons of eyes and his beaming smile, notices that he doesn't have a left hand, the sleeve of his shirt hanging limply.

Yet he manages to expertly balance his crutch on that side and extends his right hand towards her, the brightness of his smile not dimming a smidgeon.

Around them, ruins, chaos, debris. The shambles following a daytime air raid. The thrum of danger still zinging in the smoggy, smoke-stained, fiery air, even as those who've lost their homes salvage what they can from amongst the ruins before heading wearily to the rest centres and those who've been spared sigh with relief. *We have survived this. What next?*

But Charity does not see any of this. She is lost in the man's eyes, his smiling gaze. His hand which she takes, rough and weathered.

His smile, gentle. Kind.

As she takes his hand, she feels her heart settle, the worry about her brothers, Paddy and Connor, and about Mammy and Da, and how they've coped, that is centre stage now that Fergus appears unharmed, fading.

This man's smile, his firm grasp of her hand, her small palm dwarfed by his – he holds it like it is something precious – making her feel reassured. Somehow, he imparts the conviction that it will all be all right.

Her other arm is still wrapped around Fergus, loath to let go.

And for a change, the boy does not squirm out of her embrace. He seems to understand that he has given her the fright of her life.

She used to be able to kiss the top of his head not too long ago. Now he towers over her, lanky but tall, all bony limbs and awkwardness.

Now, here, in the confusion following a daytime air raid, she finds herself moved and enthralled by the pocket of calm this man somehow radiates and is surprised by the impulse to leave her hand in his a while longer.

It worries her. Charity has learned the hard way to be independent, to give the impression of competence and efficiency even when everything is falling apart around her. She has learned to smile even when she feels like crying, to go on when she feels like giving up. She cannot start changing now, just because she was terrified by her brother running away to sign up and is vulnerable after having been caught in an air raid. She is made of stronger stuff. She extracts her hand and he drops it immediately, moving his crutch back under his right arm deftly.

She feels bereft even though she was the one who had pulled her hand away first.

She clears her throat, which is parched and feels burnt. Her voice, when she finds it, tastes of smoke and is croaky with it. 'It is I who am very pleased to make your acquaintance, sir. Thank you for helping Fergus to a shelter. I was worried about him.'

Mr Singh twinkles at Fergus.

He really has the most gorgeous eyes, Charity thinks, long-lashed and beautiful, like a lake at midnight holding the reflection of the star-spangled sky within its undulating depths.

'He realised he must have worried you.'

'He did,' she says, pulling her brother closer.

'I have only just been demobilised. I was in search of a lodging house my friend recommended when I bumped into Fergus here. He was at the signing up office, trying to convince the officers he was of age. I took him aside and told him a bit of what he could expect when he signed up, eh, Fergus?'

Fergus nods, looking sheepish.

'I have recently been invalided out of the army. I took a bullet to my thigh and one in my left arm. The arm couldn't be saved, as you can see.' He shrugs in a matter-of-fact way, flapping his armless sleeve. 'But thankfully, my leg could, although I will need a crutch for the rest of my life.'

'I'm sorry,' Charity says.

'I'm fine,' he says. 'It could have been a lot worse.' And now, his eyes shadow, throbbing with pain briefly and she understands from their stark depths that he has been briefly transported to the battlefield, and is haunted by those comrades he has lost, and the horrors he has surely seen and endured.

Then, his expression clears.

'You understand now, don't you, young sir, that the age limit is there for a reason?' Mr Singh speaks easily, treating Fergus with respect.

Like Jack would, Charity thinks. And like Jack, there is nothing patronising about the way this man talks to Fergus; instead, he is gentle, matter of fact, chatting as if to a friend.

'You might be physically strong but you need to be a little more mature too, to deal with some of the things you might see and endure.' And now his eyes cloud over again and he rubs his right hand over them. 'I'm several years older than you and I don't think I was ready. In fact, I will be having nightmares about what I saw and went through for the rest of my life.'

Charity does not look at Fergus, but she sees her brother nod and knows that he is, like her, thinking of their da.

Charity has said the exact same things to Fergus countless times but she sees clearly now that what he has been lacking is a male role model to look up to. Jack used to fill that role easily but Jack is not here.

And serendipitously, just when she needed someone to, this man has stepped in.

Thank you, God.

Now, once again, Mr Singh's gaze clears as he looks at Charity. 'In any case, as we were talking, the air raid siren sounded and we went into the shelter the warden pointed us to. And we continued chatting in there.' He turns to Fergus, 'And you've decided that you will sign up in a couple of years, when you are of age, right, sir?'

Fergus nods.

Now, Mr Singh addresses Charity. 'He was a bit disappointed as he hopes, like the rest of us, that the war will be over by then. But the country needs its men, not only at the war front but also here, at home. While I was being demobilised, they said that the Home Guard is always in need of volunteers. It is doing nearly the same thing as we did in the battlefield, but at home, protecting the country in the event of a German invasion. I am going to join as soon as I have a place to stay and I said that perhaps he could consider it, too, if his guardian was agreeable.' Twinkling at her. 'We did not realise that his guardian was so close by, just paces away.'

She loves the way he speaks, enunciating each syllable. His accent is more pronounced than Divya's, lending his words a melodic slant. Charity thinks she could listen to his rich voice, like sipping hot cocoa, forever.

What is happening to her?

She is light-headed from having rushed out of Divya's curry house agonising about Fergus, and then being caught out during the air raid, seeing it happen in front of her eyes, being felled by rubble, thinking she was dead and worrying about her family…

Speaking of which…

'Mr Singh, it is wonderful to make your acquaintance and yes, I will discuss with Fergus about him joining the Home Guard. But right now, I need to check that my other brothers and parents are all right.' Charity says, even as she feels bereft about having to part ways with this man.

What is going on? Why is she feeling like this? It is most uncharacteristic of her.

'Please drop by to the Paddy O'Kelly Boarding and Lodging House on West India Dock Road. I would like to thank you properly for helping Fergus and I am sure he would like to see you too.'

And I would too, she thinks, surprising herself yet again.

She looks up at her brother, who nods and smiles at Mr Singh. 'I really would,' he says.

Mr Singh's face is aglow, the smile he is sporting seemingly lighting up his whole body. 'I say, this is such a coincidence.

You are Miss O'Kelly who runs the Paddy O'Kelly Boarding and Lodging House?'

'Yes, I'm sorry, I should have said,' Charity says, taken in by his smile, which seems to tingle through her body, and flustered that she did not think to introduce herself. The smoke from the air raid must have messed her mind up, rendering it foggy.

And then, as what he said sinks in...

'A coincidence?' she asks, looking at him.

He is still beaming, a starburst beacon of a grin. 'Do you believe in miracles, Miss O'Kelly?'

'She does.' Fergus speaks for her, for Charity seems to have misplaced her voice.

'The Paddy O'Kelly Boarding and Lodging House is the very place my friend recommended,' Mr Singh says.

Just like Divya, Charity thinks. The nuns recommended the lodging house to her and she bumped into Jack along the way.

Divya found her community and her vocation on West India Dock Road. 'It was a miracle – meant to be,' she says often.

Now another miracle has guided this man there too and also engineered it so that he rescued her errant brother along the way. Is this man meant for West India Dock Road too?

The thought incites a flutter in her heart. What on earth is happening to her?

She says, 'Your friend recommended our lodging house? Who is it? One of the sailors who stayed with us before signing up? Mr Juma, perhaps?'

'No, it was my mate in the barracks. He went on about the curry house on West India Dock Road, declaring that Miss Ram made the best curry in the country. I said I had yet to eat vegetable curry that could top the one my ma used to make. And he said that if I ever went on shore leave, I must stay at your lodging house opposite Miss Ram's curry house and try her curry and then write to tell him whether or not it topped my ma's. He sounded very sure indeed that it would. He talked so much about Miss Ram and the curry house that I feel like I know them very well. He is a good man and became a very good friend, and I miss him sorely, but as to his claim that Miss Ram will beat my ma's curry, I don't think so.'

While this man has been talking, Charity has been thinking of her best friend, and the pile of unposted letters beside her pillow, which she is sure is growing daily. Charity's hand goes to her heart, which is beating very loudly, swelling with hope on her friend's behalf. 'What is his name, this mate of yours?'

'Ah yes, you must know him, Miss O'Kelly, since he recommended your lodging house. His name is Raghu Kumar.'

PART II

20

CHARITY

West India Dock Road is a bit more battered and worse for wear, the air swirling with dust and debris, thick with smoke and rent with ash and the hot scorch of fire.

There are gaps where buildings have been bombed, like teeth missing in a crowded mouth, all the more obvious in their absence, but no more than before.

Everything is as it was when Charity left it.

The lodging house is still standing, as is the curry house.

Charity lets out the breath she had been holding.

Charity, Fergus and Mr Singh had walked back companionably together, Charity not letting go of Fergus's hand and her brother, uncharacteristically, allowing her to hold it, knowing that she needed to. Mr Singh was gentle, unobtrusive company, and they walked mostly in sombre silence, as fire engines and the Air Raid Precaution heavy rescue vans keened around them. Firemen tried to put out the fires still blazing while the ARP squad clad in overalls and steel helmets and what looked like capes and clutching respirators and torches made their way into the smouldering ruins to ensure that they were safe to dig around in before the search for survivors began in earnest.

'One of my mates in the barracks had been in the ARP heavy rescue squad during the first war.' Mr Singh's voice took on a wistful strain. 'He would entertain us – well, bore us more like – after a long day at the battlefield, with tales of what he did in the first war. No matter how much we told him that we had had enough of experiencing war, we did not want more stories of it in our downtime, he would go on. And on.' A smile in Mr Singh's voice, which was sad. 'When the first war began, he was like you, Fergus, keen to sign up but not old enough to, so he volunteered with the ARP instead. All these jobs are just as important, I think. Here too you are risking your life to save others, putting yourself in jeopardy for the greater good.' Mr Singh's eyes clouded over. 'And my mate, he was a good man. One of the best.'

'Was?' Charity asked gently.

'The same day I got injured, he... he died. I found out, when I came to in hospital and asked after my fellows. He was to the left of me. I lost my arm. He lost his life.' Mr Singh's voice was a hollow reed of pain.

'I'm sorry,' Charity and Fergus said at the same time.

'It's his wife and children that I feel for.' Mr Singh sighed. 'I... It should have been me. I am an orphan. I lost my parents a couple of years ago. I don't have any dependents. But he is gone and I am still here. I might have lost my arm and injured my leg, but I'm one of the lucky ones.'

He sounded very melancholy, and Charity was going to distract him with a question but Fergus, her sensitive, understanding brother, got there first, sparking a burst of sisterly pride within her.

'What's happening over there?' Fergus asked, pointing to a

ruin where the headlights from the ARP vans and the torches set upon a wall of bricks illuminated the area the ARP heavy rescue squad were working on. Although it was daytime, visibility was compromised because of the smoke and dust and dirt strewn air.

'They are shoring up the damaged walls and floors with timber to prevent further collapses,' Mr Singh said. Then, 'You know, no matter how tired and worn out we were after a harrowing day in the battlefield, there would be at least a couple of us, more actually, most nights, who couldn't sleep. Nightmares, you see. That was when old Russ – we called him old because he was older than the rest of us – would regale us with stories of his time with the ARP in the first war. And then there was Raghu, who would drive us mad with hunger as he described in detail the dishes Miss Ram would cook in her curry house. Whether she beats my ma's cooking or not, and I hugely doubt it, whatever Raghu says, I cannot wait to taste her food.'

'It is a treat, I can tell you,' Fergus said with great feeling.

And now, the shadows crowding Mr Singh's eyes were chased away by his sunbeam of a smile. 'I'll take your word for it.'

* * *

Everyone at the curry house cheers as Fergus enters.

Connor and Paddy, who Charity had seen through the window, her heart settling at noting that they appeared safe and whole, launch themselves at their brother, little hurricanes, nearly knocking him off his feet and Mr Singh beside him off balance.

'Gently, boys,' Charity chastises, even as Mr Singh steadies himself, his eyes twinkling at Connor and Paddy.

'You haven't signed up, have you, Fergus?' Paddy asks, his gaze wide and worried.

'No, squirt,' Fergus says. 'I'm going to join the Home Guard instead, with Mr Singh here.'

Paddy regards the newcomer curiously. 'You fought in the war, Mr Singh?' he asks.

'I did, young man,' Mr Singh says.

The whole curry house now bursts into applause.

'You are a hero, sir,' Mr Brown cries.

'Hear, hear,' everyone agrees.

Mr Singh colours, his smile abashed. 'I was just doing my duty,' he says softly.

Charity has been looking around the curry house. Mrs Kerridge isn't there.

As if reading her mind, 'Mrs Kerridge is with your parents,' Divya says to Charity even as she comes up to Fergus and pats his back. She can't reach up to tousle his hair like she used to just a few months ago.

'I'll go and relieve her now,' Charity says to Divya. 'Thank you for taking care of the boys.'

'You don't have to thank me.' Divya smiles. 'It's always a pleasure. They kept everyone taking shelter entertained and Paddy helped hand out my onion bhajis.'

'I did too,' Paddy says, nodding gravely. And then, scrunching his nose in disgust, 'Although Mrs Smith's daughters took two each even though they were allowed only one.'

'Here,' Divya says, handing over two steaming bowls to Charity. 'Porridge for your parents.'

Charity smiles gratefully at Divya. 'You think of everything. I don't know what I'd do without you.'

Then, turning to Mr Singh, who has been watching their exchange, a smile gracing his face, 'Mr Singh, this is the famous Miss Ram.'

'Famous.' Divya laughs. 'Hardly.'

'You are,' Mr Stone calls. 'You make the best curry in all of London.'

'You come highly recommended, Miss Ram,' Mr Singh says.

'I will leave you two to get acquainted.' Charity says. 'I need to check on my parents. Once you've tasted Miss Ram's food, Mr Singh, come across to the lodging house; it's right opposite as you can see, and I would be happy to show you to a room.'

Mr Singh nods, his smile and the warmth in his eyes causing Charity's heart to flutter strangely again. She turns away before the blush that is creeping up her throat turns her face bright red. 'Fergus, Connor, Paddy, I'm going to check on Mammy and Da.'

Before she shuts the door of the curry house, she winks at Divya. 'Mr Singh has something to tell you that you're really going to like.'

And with that, ignoring the question in Divya's eyes, but feeling very pleased for her friend, her heart lighter now she knows all her brothers are safe, Charity runs across the street to the lodging house, making her way to the basement.

21

CHARITY

Da is in a bad way but Mrs Kerridge is managing him in her usual efficient, no-nonsense manner.

'Now, now, Paddy, you're all right, aren't you? I'm here. And your Moira is over there saying the rosary, asking God to look out for us. So what's there to get in a tizz about, eh? And look,' she says, as Charity comes in the door, smiling fondly at her, 'here's your girl. Here's Charity.'

'Thank you, Mrs Kerridge,' Charity says.

'Ach, it was nothing, gel. Any time you need me, you know where I am.' She stands up, knees creaking. 'Fergus all right then?' she asks softly.

'Yes, he's with his brothers at the curry house.'

'That's good.' Mrs Kerridge smiles. Then, to her parents, 'Right I'm off, Moira, Paddy. Take care now.'

Mammy opens her eyes, her hands stilling upon the rosary beads she is never without, and smiles wanly at Mrs Kerridge.

Da continues to lament, rocking back and forth.

'I'll let myself out, gel; you see to him,' Mrs Kerridge says and then the door closes behind her and Charity can hear her heavy tread labouring up the stairs.

She sets the bowls of porridge down and goes to her da, gathers him in her arms.

He is but skin and bone no matter how much she, thanks to Divya, makes sure he and Mammy have nourishing food three times a day and healthy snacks in between.

He rocks in her arms, sobbing. 'I left them there. I should 'ave helped. Done something. I should 'ave. I... I left them.'

'It's all right, Da. Shush. It's all right.'

'It's not. How could I 'ave left them...'

'Da, it's all right. Here. Eat something.' She picks up one of the bowls, tries offering him some porridge.

'I don't deserve it.' He bats the bowl away.

It would have tipped, but Charity manages to catch it just in time. 'You do, Da. You do,' she reassures.

'I don't. I saved my skin and left them to die.'

'They would have died anyway, Da,' Charity says gently.

'They would?' Her father looks at her with wide eyes, a plea in them for deliverance from his all-consuming guilt, looking for all the world like his youngest son, who bears his name, when he wants Charity to reassure him that everything will be all right.

'They would. And if you had stayed to help, you would have died too.' She has reiterated these same words a thousand times.

They go through this back and forth every single time there is an air raid, or when her father wakes up gasping from a nightmare.

Sure enough, her father whispers, like she knew he was going to, 'Perhaps I would have.'

'And then you wouldn't have had Fergus and Connor and

Paddy. Thanks to you coming back from the war, there are three wonderful young people in this world, Da.'

Her father looks at her with incomprehension in his milky eyes. 'Moira?'

'I'm Charity, Da. Mammy is over there, see?'

And through it all, her mother prays, her mouth working silently, fingers clasping her rosary and moving down the beads.

'Charity,' Da's eyes clear and he beams. 'My babby.'

'Yes, that's me.'

'You're all grown up.'

'I am, Da. I surely am. Now then, how about some porridge, eh?'

And finally, her father takes the bowl from her and starts eating.

And Charity turns her attention to her mother.

22

CHARITY

When she has tended to her parents and washed the bowls and she comes back upstairs, Mr Singh is waiting in the hallway.

He beams when he sees her, his starburst smile making her heart flip.

'Ah, I'm sorry, I hope you've not been waiting long,' she says.

'I could wait forever, Miss O'Kelly, just to see you smile,' he says.

She blushes and tries to hide it by ducking her head to search for her ledger.

He notices anyway. 'I'm sorry, that was very forward of me.' Laughter pleating his voice so it sounds like wind chimes ringing in honeyed celebration in a sunshine-gilded summer breeze.

'You don't sound very sorry,' she says archly.

He laughs properly now and it is festive joy, sparklers exploding silver stars into a russet-wine sunset.

She can't help but join in.

Afterwards, 'So, what did you think of Miss Ram's food then? Was Raghu right?' she asks.

'Hmmmm...' he says, rubbing his chin, which, she sees, is dusted with dark stubble. 'It was a close call. What Miss Ram does with the scarce ingredients she has available is nothing short of magic.'

'See, what did I tell you?' she says, triumphant.

'But... whether it's better than my ma's... well...'

'It is. Go on, admit it.'

'I was hungry. I haven't eaten Indian food since I left India. So of course Miss Ram's food was absolutely delicious. But... I need to taste it when I am not so famished...'

'You are making excuses,' she teases.

'I'm being honest...'

Their banter is interrupted by her brothers tumbling through the door.

'Mr Singh.' Paddy beams. 'You're staying with us! What a great honour, sir.'

Charity's littlest brother executes a very smart salute and Charity's heart swells with pride.

'Thank you, Mr O'Kelly,' Mr Singh says and Paddy looks fit to burst with joy at being addressed thus.

'Oh, you can call me Paddy,' he says expansively.

'As you wish, young sir.' Mr Singh nods and Paddy appears even more overjoyed if that is possible. 'I rather think it is *my* honour to be staying here at this lodging house which comes very highly recommended and with such wonderful young men such as you and your brothers.'

And at that, Paddy beams even wider, his whole body glowing, it seems.

'I will show you to your room, sir,' he says gravely and to Charity, 'Where are you putting him, Charity?'

'The room on this floor, Paddy,' Charity says, pleased that it is empty, knowing that Mr Singh would find it a job to handle the stairs.

She is glad now that she changed the sheets, aired it and made it ready for occupation, praying that someone would come for it, just the previous day.

Mr Singh turns to her. 'Thank you, Miss O'Kelly. I intend on staying for a few weeks until I find my feet.'

Behind him, her brothers cheer, and he smiles, as does Charity.

'You have firm fans in my brothers, sir.'

'I'm not sure if I deserve it but I'm glad of it.' Mr Singh smiles at Fergus, Connor and Paddy. And, to Charity: 'Given that I intend to stay here for a time, I'd rather you called me by my first name. I'm Veer.'

She nods, even as she feels her face once again flood with colour. 'And I'm Charity,' she says.

'Charity. That's a beautiful name. Suits you, I think,' he says.

I love how you say it, in your beautiful voice with its musical accent and the smile threaded through it, she thinks but is too shy to say out loud.

'The Ursuline nuns named her,' Paddy tells Mr Singh. Veer.

'And I like your name,' she says. 'What does Veer mean?'

'It means brave.'

'Well that definitely suits you,' Paddy says firmly and Charity smiles, saying, 'I have to agree.'

'Me too,' Fergus says and Connor nods assent.

'Thank you, O'Kellys,' Veer says and then, to Charity, 'Now... um... Charity,' he says, leaning against the alcove and taking out his wallet. 'Would you prefer it if I paid you by the week?'

'Yes, please,' she says. 'Soldier's rates for you. Fifty per cent off.'

Even as she says it, she hears Mrs Kerridge's voice in her head: 'You are running a business, not a charity. Just because you're named so, does not mean you have to live up to it.' But she just can't help herself.

'Thank you kindly, Charity.'

Again, she thinks of how much she loves the way her name sounds when he says it. Like a gift.

'Now that's settled,' says Paddy officiously, 'I will show you to your room.'

'Lead the way, sir,' Veer says, nodding and smiling at Charity as he turns to follow Paddy, Connor and Fergus falling into step beside him.

She stands there, a hand upon her heart, which is fluttering with that strange thrill he occasions, smiling widely at nothing in particular.

23

DIVYA

October 25, 1940

Dear Jack,

It was, as always, so wonderful to receive your letter, which arrived the day before yesterday.

I read it out to everyone and we were all reassured that you are fine, doing well, eating well. That the Huns are treating you all right.

Mr Brown in particular is pleased that the Huns, for all their barbarity, are still following the Geneva convention rules.

He informed us that it is because the Huns know that when we win the war and they have to release the prisoners, they will be answerable to us. Then he added, 'In any case, I'm glad Mr Devine is all right. He's a good man, he is.'

We are thrilled that you have made friends with men from all over the world. It's nice to hear about the Australian *medic and the Geordie spitfire pilot who arrived at the POW camp around the same time as you. When I read out the bit about the Irishman, Kilroy who is on the cooking rota with you this week, it roused a cheer from the Irish contingent here. That bit where you said that you wished you'd learned some recipes from me, for it would have made you very popular with the other POWs, made me smile.*

'I imagine he's already popular enough. That lad can charm the socks off even wizened old ladies like me,' Mrs Murphy cried and we all smiled.

Thank you for your message to Fergus, advising him to wait until he is old enough to sign up.

Ah, Fergus. He got into a bit of a pickle, that lad.

Yes, it's exactly what you think; he was impatient and decided to run away and sign up.

In any case, Charity went to find him and bring him back before it was too late – the recruiting officers want able-bodied men and don't really pay too much attention to age – they take what the boys say at face value.

Mrs Kerridge told me, out of Charity, Connor and Paddy's hearing, of her friend Pam's son, a lad of just fifteen like Fergus, who signed up and is now missing in action. Her eyes were sparkling as she said it, no doubt thinking of her two younger sons whom she has not heard from and who might be suffering the same fate.

So, Charity left Paddy and Connor in my care and went to the recruitment office after Fergus. And guess what? That was the moment the Jerries, not content with their nightly assault upon the East End, decided to bomb us during the day!

As soon as we heard the air raid sirens, I bundled Paddy

and Connor with me to the Underground. Mrs Kerridge volunteered to sit in the lodging house basement with Charity's Mammy and Da.

We were all right, Jack, all of us.

Yes, Fergus too.

There was this kind man, an Indian man, actually, Mr Veer Singh, who has been invalided out of the army. He talked Fergus out of signing up.

Charity says that Mr Singh told Fergus the exact same things she had been telling him, over and over, that he would do more for the country by helping at the Home Front, but that while he ignored her, he listened to this man who had been at the frontline.

'I don't mind,' Charity said, and she was smiling, her face lighter than it has been in recent weeks. 'At least he's got rid of that idea of joining up before his time now.' Her face clouded over slightly. 'He says he will sign up for the Home Guard and that is dangerous too, of course.'

'Charity...' I began.

'Yes, I know that everywhere is dangerous now. I know, Divya.'

I gave her a hug. She smelled of exhaustion. 'I am glad he's home and safe for now,' she said against my shoulder.

I read out your message to Fergus and he looked sheepish (another new word learned courtesy of Paddy's dictionary, now mine – so I should stop calling it Paddy's, I suppose), colour flooding his cheeks.

'Yes, I understand. Please thank Mr Devine from me when you next write to him. And tell him to take care,' he said.

So there. I've written his message here word for word.

We are all fine, as best as can be in the circumstances.
Everyone sends their love.
As do I.
Take care, Jack and come home safe,
We are waiting.
Divya and all at West India Dock Road

24

DIVYA

October 25, 1940

My dear Raghu,

   After all those months of writing into the ether – yes, I have written letter after letter to you; I will show you when you are here and now I have hope that you will be here – finally, this letter will actually be making its way to you.

   And what's more, I have actual news of you, that you are all right. I can't tell you how wonderful that is after months of hoping and praying for your safety and yet not knowing where you were, how you were. I now know that you are not taken prisoner or wounded – you are still fighting for God and country – and for this, I am grateful.

   Raghu, I obtained your address from Mr Veer Singh. It appears you were full of praise about me and the curry house and insisted he visit once war was over. But, he was able to do so much earlier than that, given he was invalided out of the war – he's all right, please don't worry; he's lost his arm but he said it could have been a lot worse.

I fed him a hearty meal: chapatis, pilau rice, potato curry, carrot halva, rice kheer. He said the pilau rice and potato curry reminded him of his mother's cooking. I also made dhal, which he loved, but I told him that yours was better.

When Charity introduced me to Mr Singh and he said that he knew of your whereabouts, I couldn't believe it.

After months of fantasising about a way of contacting you, not knowing if you were alive, but hoping, and believing fiercely that you were, suddenly, here was someone saying that they had shared barracks with you.

I must admit that I did worry if, feverish with longing, I had conjured this man who said he knew you, dreamed him up, that he wasn't actually there, that it was all a fantasy.

I wondered if when I blinked, he would disappear and this reprieve that fate, destiny, fortune had granted me would be gone.

Raghu, I am writing this and I will post it knowing it will make its way to you.

I hope that you will read it. I think you will. If you talked about me and the curry house in the barracks, then I think – I believe – that you have missed me.

In these long months of writing to you but not being able to send any of my letters, I had sometimes (all right, I'll admit it, often) wondered if what I felt for you was one-sided, despite you confessing that you loved me that one magical night. I had agonised whether my feelings for you were not reciprocated, even as I watched my pile of letters to you grow and grow.

But now, after having met Mr Singh, I'm hopeful again, the doubts about whether you care for me are gone and I know that you do. Just as I know you will read this letter.

But whether you will write back – that I'm not certain.

You might stubbornly still hold on to your conviction that you're not worthy of me.

But whether I get a reply or not, rest assured, I will keep on writing until I can convince you that I love you and you alone and that as far as I'm concerned, you are the only man for me.

You know, I quite like the medium of letters. Here, I can put down all my thoughts: things I would be too shy to say face to face. And during these last few months of writing to you with no hope of reply, I have become very open with you. You might be shocked by my honesty, my frankness.

But people are dying around us. Nothing is certain, except what I feel for you and I will put it in writing for I may not get another chance given the precariousness of our existence these days.

Mr Singh told me that one evening after a particularly brutal day at the battlefield, you were all taking turns to talk about what you would miss the most if you were to die the next day.

Mr Singh said that while everyone else mentioned their mother, their wife, their children, you said you'd miss my curry.

This is why I'm hopeful.

Mr Stone and Mr Brown note that I haven't stopped smiling since I met Mr Singh.

'He bring good news,' Mr Lee said, beaming. 'You happy like I no see since war begin.'

This is true. I'm happy. You see, Mr Singh said you told all your mates in the barracks to visit my curry house when possible, taste my food, for there wasn't anything like it.

You might have been drumming up business for me.

Or maybe you missed me.

Or you wanted them to visit and bring news of you.

Or perhaps all three.

I don't care what it is. I am writing to you and finally, I know this letter will make its way to you.

I won't waste any more words; I will get straight to the point.

And it is this. I have railed against you. I have been angry with you. But most of all, through it all, I have never stopped loving you, no matter what you said in your letter which I have read so many times that I know it by heart. Which I treasure not for what it says – I don't agree with your conviction that you are not right for me and that I should move on, wipe you from my life – but because it is the only tangible thing I have of you.

Raghu, I love you. Only you. Always you.

I don't want anyone else. I will not move on.

So when you next apply for shore leave, come home to me. Please.

I have lived and relived our one kiss. I would like more such memories to tide me through the long days and weeks and months of parting. The world is at war. People are dying every day. Nothing is certain.

So please come to me. Let's have whatever time we can together.

Yours,

Divya

25

CHARITY

Veer soon settles into the wartime rhythms of West India Dock Road, and it is as if he has always been there, staying at the lodging house, taking his meals at Divya's curry house opposite.

He and Fergus sign up for the Home Guard, and Veer promises Charity solemnly that he will keep an eye on her brother for her.

Fergus apprentices at the shipbuilders' during the day and attends to his Home Guard duties after.

'They have given me a uniform,' he said, when he returned after having joined the Home Guard, pleased to bits. 'And we are being trained.'

'In what?' Charity asked.

'That's top secret,' he said, preening, chest puffed out and in that moment, he resembled his youngest brother so much, it took her breath away. He was, essentially, a child playing at being an adult. And she sent yet another prayer up to the heavens to keep her brothers safe, even though she knew that God must be inundated with prayers from mothers and sisters, wives and daughters. And although Charity knew that nothing was beyond Him, it was still not feasible that he could save all of them, now could he? *But please spare Fergus, Connor and Paddy, God. Please.*

Her brothers look up to Veer.

He is gentle with them, patient, kind.

He has fitted into their lives seamlessly and Charity must admit, she enjoys having him around, hearing him laugh and joke with her brothers, his smiling face – and he is always smiling, even when there is scant to smile about – a gift, causing that strange, thrilling flutter in her heart every time she sees him.

26

DIVYA

November 14, 1940

Dear Jack,

    As always, such a joy to receive your letter yesterday.

    Reading between the lines – it appears German censors are even more stringent than ours, for nearly everything you write is crossed out – we understand that you and your fellow POWs are finding it frustrating to spend your days in captivity when you are wanting to fight, to protect your country.

    But, crossings out or not, we are so grateful for any communication from you.

    Mrs Kerridge has still not heard from her two younger sons. And Mrs Ross, who lost her daughter in the first few months of war, also hasn't heard from her son.

    We are all very worried for her as she is not herself at all.

    She is fragile physically and emotionally. When her husband was a casualty of the first war, her children kept her going. Now, with her daughter dead and with no

*communication from her son, she appears to have lost the
will to go on.*

*She eats very little and then only when one of us
coaxes her.*

*'I tell her she must keep herself together for when her
Tom comes home.' Mrs Kerridge sighs. 'I tell her she
mustn't ever give up hope. I haven't,' Mrs Kerridge says
fiercely. 'I never will. But I suspect she has, the poor dear.'*

*Mrs Ross sits for hours staring into the distance; she is
so weak now that she needs help climbing the stairs to her
flat.*

*Mrs Boon, who lives in the same tenement block as Mrs
Ross, told us yesterday that worryingly, Mrs Ross doesn't
bother responding to the air raid siren any more. She said
that she was heading to the Underground station the day
before yesterday when she noticed that Mrs Ross wasn't
there. Mrs Boon ran back inside and up the stairs. It took
her an absolute age, she said, what with people pushing
past on their way down. She reached Mrs Ross's flat only to
find her friend lying in bed on top of the sheets, fully
clothed, contemplating the ceiling as if it held all the
answers while the sirens screamed blue murder around her
and the last of the stragglers thundered down the stairs.
Mrs Boon said she only managed to convince Mrs Ross to
join her at the shelter after she was tough with her, admon-
ishing her that she was no use to her son dead. Mrs Boon's
eyes were stark with sadness on her friend's behalf as she
told us this. 'Took us an absolute age to get to the station;
we made it just as the Jerries started dropping their bombs
over Stepney way. Thank you for saving space for us.' She
smiled at Mrs Kerridge, who nodded. In any case, Mrs
Boon said that from now on, she would knock on Mrs*

Ross's door when the siren sounded and make sure to chivvy her along.

Mrs Kerridge cried that what she found most concerning was that Mrs Ross seemed to have lost her faith. It kept her going after she lost her Henry, Mrs Kerridge said. But now... she no longer attended church, which was worrying as she would be at mass religiously every day, and it was partly because of her and the few other regulars that Father O'Donnell was conducting services even though the church had been bombed. She was not even reading her Bible, which she'd once claimed was her comfort. Mrs Kerridge had tried handing it to her, but she just sighed and tenderly patted the book as if a child, but she did not open it, did not read the pages, worn from use. It was a worry for sure, Mrs Kerridge tutted.

'She gifted me a Bible after I lost my Joe and my boys in the first war,' Mrs Devlin said, her gaze soft with reminiscence. 'She claimed it held all the answers. At the time, broken as I was in heart and spirit, I wondered, how could it be? I even challenged her, asked her if it would bring my husband and boys back. But Fanny just smiled gently and placed the Bible in my hands. "Try it," she said. "It will help, I promise."' Mrs Devlin sniffed. 'And do you know, it took a while, but it did help. She will be all right, will Fanny. She just needs time. And meanwhile, she has all of us.'

'That she does,' everyone agreed fiercely.

Sorry, Jack, once again, instead of giving you good news, I've brought in the war. But you did say that you'd like me to be honest and provide a more rounded picture of what's going on over here. So here it is, warts and all. Hope you're not sorry you asked.

The women of West India Dock Road have also been

worrying about Mrs Murphy, who is getting very absent-minded.

'She forgets things often; her mind is not like it used to be. She's taken to talking about her beloved Barry as if he has just popped to the shops when he has been dead nigh on forty years.' Mrs Neville fretted yesterday over tea and eggless fruit cake. (Eggs are hard to come by.)

'On Sunday, I found her wandering on the street looking more than a little lost,' Mrs O'Riley said. 'I asked her if she was on her way to church. "Oh, that's where I was going." She smiled. "Do you know, my dear, I quite forgot where I was meant to be." We walked to church together and I made sure I walked her back after the service.' Mrs O'Riley sighed deeply.

The ladies have created a rota to drop in on Mrs Murphy in such a way so as to not make her aware that they are keeping tabs on her. One of us will also accompany her to the Underground station during an air raid.

Do you recall when I first came to the East End, you said to me, 'We look out for each other here; us Eastenders are family.'

I have never forgotten that and it is at times like these, with war and devastation everywhere you look that family is all the more important. And I am so very grateful that I have found my kin here on West India Dock Road.

In other news, Mr Veer Singh, who talked Fergus out of lying about his age and signing up, is now a regular fixture on West India Dock Road. He is staying at Charity's and takes his meals here. He even played chess against both Mr Stone and Mr Brown – and lost.

'You are now our friend for life,' they said to him, slapping his back expansively.

'Would he have been your enemy for life if he had won?'
Paddy, always literal, asked and everyone laughed, although
Paddy appeared puzzled, maintaining that he hadn't been
joking.

The worry lines furrowing Charity's forehead have eased
a little and she is smiling more.

It's funny, the things you become accustomed to, take
for granted, when the world is at war. We have become
used to the dearth of food, rationing, blackouts, carrying our
gas masks around.

But yesterday, as I was closing up, the night was calm,
for a change, and the air, while usually thick with debris and
ash and grit from the relentless bombing, was blessedly
clear, tasting of frost. Except for the blackout, everything
absolutely dark, you couldn't have said we were at war. All
that would change in an hour, or less, when the air raid
sirens would shatter the glorious peace. But I stood there
and breathed in the air, savoured the taste of it, untainted
with smoke and fire and devastation, and whispered a
prayer of thanks for moments such as these, all the more
precious for being so rare.

That's it for now, Jack. Take care.

Our love and very best wishes,

Divya and all of us here on West India Dock Road

27

CHARITY

Charity staggers into the lodging house from the wash house with two baskets of laundry, trying to hold the door open with her hip.

She manages, just about, but it means that she cannot see where she is going, and she walks right into someone.

'Sorry,' she says.

'Here let me help,' she hears.

She is relieved of one of the baskets of laundry and she can see again.

She looks up into twinkling eyes that she could get lost in.

'I was just off to my training at the Home Guard when I walked into a mountain of laundry.' Veer grins.

'Please go; I can manage now. Thank you,' she says.

'You do so much, single-handedly,' he says.

'I'm used to it.' She shrugs, feeling, as is always the case when he's around, a blush creep up her throat. He must think she's permanently red-faced.

'And you have been doing it since...?' He is genuinely interested, his gaze sincere.

'I've been running the lodging house since I was fourteen,' she says.

He nods. His eyes are admiring as well as empathetic. 'You are quite something, Charity.'

His words warm her heart, even as her body is taken captive by that strange thrill he excites.

Fergus comes clattering down the stairs.

'I will join you once I'm done at work,' he says to Veer.

'Right you are.' Veer nods at Fergus. Then, smiling at Charity, 'I'm off now. Good day, Charity.'

'Good day,' Charity says, the warmth of his smile once again causing her heart to swell.

* * *

That evening, at the curry house, Divya says, 'You keep looking out of the window.'

Charity looks down at her plate, at the curried carrot and potato turnovers that she enjoys, trying to stop the flush taking over her face.

'Are you waiting for someone?' her friend asks, eyes twinkling.

'No, I'm not,' Charity says, shoving a forkful of turnover into her mouth, tasting nothing. But her burning cheeks give a lie to her words.

And then, Veer arrives with Fergus, greeting the regulars before making his way to where Charity is sitting, smiling widely at her, causing her whole body to tingle.

'Ah.' Divya smiles.

Fergus goes to join his brothers, who are watching Mr Stone and Mr Brown's game, and Veer sits himself down next to Charity.

Mrs Kerridge, who is with the other ladies of West India Dock Road by the window, raises an eyebrow at Charity, as if to say, *You are getting very friendly with your lodger, aren't you?*

The other ladies too are looking at Charity, their gazes variously worried, thoughtful, curious, speculative.

There might be a war on but that doesn't stop the matrons of West India Dock Road minding everyone's business.

It's wonderful that they care and when someone needs help, they will step in, even if they are going through hell themselves, but now, Charity feels very exposed.

She does not want to analyse why she feels this way even though she is doing nothing wrong.

In any case, once Veer arrives, Charity recovers the appetite she seemed to have misplaced and turns her attention to her food.

Later, after he has eaten his fill, sitting companionably next to Charity, Veer says to Divya, 'Thank you, Miss Ram. Your food was outstanding as always. Raghu was absolutely right and I'll be ever grateful to him for recommending both your curry house and the wonderful lodging house where I'm staying.' Twinkling warmly at Charity, he adds, 'I have an amazing landlady.'

Charity once again feels her face burn.

'Ah, she is brilliant, isn't she?' Divya says, draping an arm around Charity. She smells of spices and love and Charity leans into her friend's hug as she wrestles her emotions under control.

'Go on, admit it,' Charity says to Veer. 'Divya's food is better than your ma's, isn't it?'

'Ah, Charity, that's unfair,' Divya says. 'You cannot ask him that.'

'She can ask me anything she likes.' Veer smiles at Charity

and once again, pinned by his gaze, her body betrays her. 'Whether I will answer it is another matter.' He laughs. Then, 'I will take your leave now, ladies,' he says, nodding at them in turn. And he's gone, calling goodbye to the other regulars.

Once the door closes behind him, Divya turns to Charity. 'Is there something you're not telling me?'

'Nothing at all,' Charity says, toying with the cutlery on her empty plate.

'I've seen the way your eyes follow him. You watched him just now until he disappeared into the lodging house,' Divya says gently.

'I don't have time for romance.' Charity voices out loud what she's been telling herself ever since Veer's gaze started playing havoc with her heart. 'There's work, my parents and brothers to look out for, and we are at war.'

'All the more reason for there to be romance,' Divya says earnestly. 'Tomorrow is not certain. Grab today with both hands, I say.'

'Are you doing that?' Charity asks.

'Yes. I have written to Raghu. Oh, I cannot tell you how thrilled I was to actually be able to post this letter, thanks to your Veer.'

'He's not *my* Veer,' Charity protests, blushing again.

'Isn't he?' Divya asks archly. Then, her gaze wistful, 'Raghu will receive my letter but whether he will write back, I don't know.'

'Ah, Divya.' Charity hugs her friend.

'I hope he does. I hope he is not stubborn like you.'

'I'm not stubborn.'

'If you say so, Miss Charity O'Kelly.' Divya surveys Charity, hands on hips, and she smiles.

28

DIVYA

December 5, 1940

Dear Jack,

How are you doing? Hope you are well.

We are well here. Coping as best we can.

Your message to Mrs Ross really touched her. She said it meant the world when you asked her not to give up hope, that the authorities, because of the craziness of war, cannot notify everyone, and that letters go missing with alarming frequency. Your assurance that Tom will turn up, that not having heard from him is good news of a sort has perked her up. She said that hearing from someone who's been there has made a difference.

So now she's looking altogether more hopeful. And she's started attending mass and reading her Bible again. So, thank you, Jack.

You reiterated in your letter that you didn't mind me telling you about the harsher aspects of wartime life over here. Well, the grim reality is that there are air raids even during the day now. But we are well, so far. We truly are.

Mrs Porter, who runs the mobile canteen service, told us about Nurse Chambers over at the hospital, who, when she heard the street where she had left her child with her mother had been bombed, sprinted home through the scorching wreckage, the bruising ash.

Firemen and air raid wardens called to her to take shelter as bombs were still falling. But she was a panicked mother and she shut her ears to the caution of the fireman, tears leaking down cheeks assaulted by fiery confetti, as she ran through the blistering earth, to her street which was lit by the blaze, death machines hovering above, persistently dropping their deadly cargo.

Her baby was spared. But when she came back to the hospital, her best friend was one of the many casualties being wheeled in.

Mrs Porter told us that Nurse Chambers managed to keep a brave face in front of her friend, holding her hand while she took her last breaths, promising to break the news gently to her children, who had been evacuated, but when she came to Mrs Porter's mobile canteen after her shift, she broke down.

'There have been casualties during my watch, despite all the care I have taken. And when I have lost a patient, I've mourned them and prayed for their souls, for they were someone's child, someone's sibling, someone's spouse, someone's parent, someone's friend. But this time, it was my own friend and I could not pray,' she wept, Mrs Porter said. 'At the start of each shift, I usually cross my fingers and send a prayer heavenward but today, I didn't even do that. I appear to have lost my faith, perhaps that is why...'

Mrs Porter, who's said more than once that her job is as much to administer comfort, a listening ear and a gentle pat on the back as it is to dispense tea and toast, sat with Nurse Chambers and gently reminded her that what had occurred had nothing to do with faith and everything to do with Hitler. She coaxed her to drink her tea and once she had recovered somewhat, she sent her home to her mother and her child, even as Nurse Chambers cried, guilt and sorrow writ large upon her face, 'Margot's children will not have their mother returning to them.'

'This is what the war is doing to us,' Mrs Porter said, sighing as she recounted the tale, her eyes bright with pain. 'We feel guilty when we and our loved ones are spared while also knowing that we might be spared today but...'

She did not complete her sentence but we all knew what she meant, nodding along, the sheen of tears in everyone's eyes as we thought of our beloved lost and our beloved who are still with us but whose fate is not certain; for that matter, neither is ours.

I don't have to tell you this. You know better than most that we live in uncertain times.

Even the Tube stations are not safe.

Over in Balham, a bomb fell on an intersection of Tube tunnels and the pipes burst, killing the people sheltering inside, the station master among them.

Just yesterday, Mr Brown told us of a bus packed with people falling into a crater that had suddenly and without warning opened up on the road due to the bombing.

And that's not all.

I don't think I've told you this but much like everyone gathers in the curry house to hear your news in your letters, they also come here to listen to the news bulletin on Mr

Stone's wireless. It gives us a feeling of solidarity and even when there's bad news, we feel better able to face it.

It is, I will hazard a guess, like how you must feel being a prisoner of war: having others there from all over the world sharing the same fate as you. Together, it might feel less daunting, facing whatever each day has in store. It is definitely like that for us. Somehow, sitting in the curry house bunched around Mr Stone's wireless, with the blackout curtains drawn, we feel better able to stomach the doom and gloom (even though the presenters try their best to project a positive front), as we are together.

Sometimes, programmes go off air, and the eerie fading of the radio is an early sign of an impending attack. Then, even before the siren sounds, we all get ready to trudge to the shelters and sure enough, just as we are leaving the curry house, it starts up.

We were listening to the news bulletin the other day when we heard a loud crash.

We all rushed to the windows to peer outside, thinking a bomb had fallen near us, without prior warning, it was that loud.

But no...

'It's on the wireless,' Mrs Kerridge whispered. 'It must have fallen on the broadcasting house.'

The East End is being battered ruthlessly, but having said that, nothing and nowhere is sacred.

But this is the best part: the news presenter, Mr Bruce Belfrage, merely paused before carrying on in his usual impassive baritone.

And you know what? The war might be ruthless and might be taking it out of all of us, but it also brings out our best selves. It has made us resilient and resourceful, and we *all try our best to keep calm and carry on, regardless. Hitler might be hell bent upon destroying our homes and our loved ones and cutting our lives short but he will not crush our spirit. I feel so proud to be part of the East End, part of this wonderful community here on West India Dock Road.*

So there, even though this letter has been mostly grim, I have managed to end it on a positive note.

We will not be beaten and we will meet soon and celebrate victory together.

Here's to that, Jack.

Love from Divya and all of us on West India Dock Road

29

CHARITY

Another air raid. Another broken night, punctuated by the drone of enemy planes and the boom thump doom of bombs falling.

Charity is in the basement with her parents. Her brothers have taken to going with Veer to the Tube station alongside Divya and others from the street.

Da is more agitated than usual. Mammy prays silently, clutching her rosary beads, eyes closed.

The all-clear arrives with the dawn, and with it, the news that Mrs Porter, who runs the mobile canteen bringing refreshment to the aid workers and victims in bombed-out areas, has herself been bombed.

When, after settling her parents, Charity, her brothers, Veer and the other lodgers go to the curry house for breakfast, Mrs Kerridge says, breathless with upset, that Mrs Porter has been taken to the Poplar hospital on East India Dock Road. 'A few of us are going to see her,' Mrs Kerridge tells Charity. 'Will you come along?'

* * *

Half the hospital is bombed and yet it is operating at full speed, packed with all manner of patients, bloodied and battered, with more being brought in every minute. A nurse is directing patients where to go.

'We are equipped for wartime care; our operating theatres are in the basement. We bury radium used in medical treatments to protect against radioactivity in the event of a direct hit,' a nurse tells Charity and the other ladies from West India Dock Road as she accompanies them to the ward where Mrs Porter is. 'On hearing an air raid warning, anti-splinter blinds are drawn across the windows, babies are moved to a "gas refuge room" and mothers are given gas masks along with a cup of tea,' she says cheerfully. 'Now, here we are. I'll see to my patients while you cheer up Mrs Porter.'

Mrs Porter is looking the worse for wear, her face and body bruised and yet she summons up a smile when she sees the contingent from West India Dock Road.

'Been in the wars, 'ave you, our Ethel?' Mrs Neville cackles.

'Just about,' Mrs Porter says. 'Got off lightly, didn't I?'

Beside and around her, nurses tend to the ill and the wounded, in their brisk, no-nonsense manner.

They spend an hour with Mrs Porter, who says she will be back to running her mobile canteen as soon as she's pronounced fit.

* * *

When Charity returns from the hospital, she goes to check on her parents, reminded afresh of how fragile life is.

She pauses at the door to the basement, hearing voices from inside.

Not the boys. They visit each morning and last thing before bed.

It is not her father grumbling to himself, shouting in agitation. It is not her mother praying.

She hears laughter. A voice she has grown to care for.

Then... a miracle.

She hears her da laughing. A deep-throated chuckle. Something Charity has not heard in what feels like forever. Definitely not since the war began.

'You're a good man, you are,' Da is saying.

'I'm in good company, sir.'

And Da laughs again. Hearty. Wholesome. Magical.

She touches her cheek and her palm comes away wet.

A hand upon her heart, she goes back upstairs.

After a bit, he comes by, whistling merrily.

'Ah, Veer,' she says. 'I haven't seen you about this morning. Where were you?'

'Oh, just in my room,' he says easily.

She nods, liking him all the more for not making a big deal that he has been to see her parents, keeping them company in her absence.

After that, she catches him often, visiting with her parents, having long chats with her father.

It eases her burden, for one of her constant worries is that her parents are lonely and that she is never able to spare enough time to spend with them, just a few rushed minutes while she brings them their meals. And it warms her heart, hearing her father laugh, thanks to Veer, affording a brief glimpse into the Paddy O'Kelly who was, back in the day, the life and soul of the street.

30

CHARITY

Charity and Veer become close. He helps her with her chores whenever he gets a chance, not taking no for an answer.

'Please,' he says, 'let me make myself useful.'

And he does. It is a blessing.

As they work together, she asks him about his life before he ended up here in England.

'I grew up very poor in a small village near Amritsar, in the Panjab,' he says, matter-of-factly. 'My ma was a maid servant. My father, a farmer, who spent everything he earned on drink. My ma wanted a better life for me. I was good at my studies, you see. The priests at the missionary school in my village put me up for a scholarship and I won it. I earned a university place here in England. But it did not cover my accommodation.'

'Ah,' Charity says.

'My ma urged me to go. She was convinced I would find a job which would pay for the accommodation and sundries. She was so proud. "You've done the hard bit, winning the scholarship," she said, eyes shining. "They've invited you to

England. Finding a job and a place to stay once there will be easy compared to what you've already achieved.'" He takes a breath. Then, 'She died,' his voice stumbles, 'a week after I came here.'

'I'm sorry,' she says. She wants to touch him, offer comfort. But she worries it will be too forward of her.

He nods, composes himself.

'My father died soon after. I did not have the means to go back for either of their cremations. The villagers set fire to their funeral pyres, although it is, by rights, a son's job.' His voice hollow with pain.

Charity aches for him. His hand is right next to hers and she gently places her palm upon his. Her heart jumps at the connection; her body thrills. He grips her hand as if it is his lifeline.

'In a way, it is good they went when they did,' he says softly. 'For soon after, the war started and they... Ma would have worried something terrible.' He pauses, then, 'And even before the war, I... I was not happy and Ma would have divined it, even if I wrote cheerful and upbeat letters. She had a way of knowing exactly what was going on with me, whether I shared it with her or not.' He looks at her hand, small and pale, ensconced within his brown, rugged palm.

'This, Charity. You offering comfort by touching me, allowing me to call you by your first name, it is a privilege I do not take lightly.'

She looks at him. His eyes are stark, deep wells of pain.

'You see... the racism...' he says softly. 'After a while, it chips away at you, the constant treatment as inferior because of the colour of your skin. It undermines who you are. You begin to lose your self-worth; you stop seeing yourself as someone worthy and start seeing yourself through their eyes.' His pain, palpable, bleeding into his voice as he recounts his experiences as a brown man in a white country. 'Since the accommodation was not included in the scholarship, I had to find a place to stay and a job to pay for it, you see. It was not as easy as my ma had hoped. In fact, it was much harder than winning the scholarship. The only job available for the "likes of me" was cleaning loos and the only place to stay, well...' Another pause. A breath, then, 'All I could find was a leaky hole of a basement, with an ever-growing family of mice as houseguests, the landlady charging me a premium even as she kept her coloured lodger a secret. The basement had its own entrance and she made sure to tell me that the room was available only if I kept away from the other tenants. She also insisted that I must never use the main entrance, nor cook foreign food, nor entertain anyone in my room.' He takes a deep, tortured breath. 'What she was not saying but was implying with every word and pointed look, was: "Don't be seen or heard. Don't put my other tenants off." What she did say was, "This is a respectable boarding house and I'd like it to remain that way. I'm only renting to the likes of you out of the goodness of my heart, for you look quite desperate." Which, to be fair, I was. In any case, as soon as the war started, she made noises about wanting to convert the basement into a shelter, only keeping me on when I agreed to even more of an increase in rent.'

'I'm sorry,' Charity says. It is all she has.

'It's not your fault. You have been nothing but kind.' He smiles but there is such hurt in his eyes. She wishes she could make it disappear.

'I don't know who was more relieved when I signed up: myself or my landlady,' he says. 'I thought things would be different in the army.' He sighs. 'But people are people. Their attitudes don't change just because we are at war.' Such resignation in his voice, underscored by hurt. 'Brown sparrows are accepted everywhere but brown people are not. Why this discrimination based on colour? Just because our skin is a shade darker, we are not filthy, we are not dumb.'

Her eyes sting, her heart spasming with pain on his behalf. He has suffered more than he is telling her. She wonders how much abuse he endured in the army, if the worst injuries he received were not physical but emotional, the most painful wounds not inflicted by the enemy but from the blackballing and racial abuse of his own side.

After a bit, 'Your university place?' she asks.

'Ah, I might go back to it after the war. I was doing it more to realise my mother's dreams for me than for myself, I think. I miss her terribly, but in many ways, I am glad she is gone. She died happy, crowing to all and sundry that her son was in England on a scholarship, doing something with his life, unlike his drunkard father. As I said, she would have worried herself silly when I signed up. And she would have been devastated when this happened...' He nods at his missing arm. 'When Raghu told me about your place, he insisted that you didn't make judgements based on colour and I did not believe it, not after what I had experienced.' He looks at their entwined hands and smiles at her and it is genuine, his eyes shining. 'Now I do.'

And she smiles too.

'Now tell me what you'd like help with, Charity,' he says. 'Even one-handed, I am a dab hand at cleaning loos.'

31

CHARITY

Charity is sitting at the table in the kitchen of the lodging house, attempting to wrestle the accounts into adding up to a favourable amount, when Divya comes running in, waving a letter.

She kneels in front of Charity, breathless, her eyes shining stars. 'I've heard from Raghu.'

'Ah, Divya!' Charity gathers her in a hug.

'He's wounded. He is here, in England, at a convalescent home in Guildford, Surrey, which Mr Stone says is not too far away.'

'No, it isn't,' Charity says, feeling warmed by Divya's barely contained joy and excitement.

'Charity, I am thinking of shutting the curry house for Christmas and going to see him.' Divya breathes. 'He says he will go back to the frontline once he's better as they need people. I would like to see him before then.'

Divya's eyes are alight with hope and plea, as if willing Charity to tell her it is a good idea.

Charity thinks of her own feelings lately, her heart suddenly swelling whenever a certain person is near.

'Go,' she says.

'I'm not married.'

'It doesn't matter. Life is short. Precarious. You love him. You must be with him.'

Divya beams, her eyes shining, throwing her arms around Charity, whispering in her ear, 'Thank you, Charity. You are a good friend.'

'If I had said it wasn't a good idea, would you have listened to me?' Charity asks, eyebrows raised.

'Most likely not,' Divya says and they both laugh.

* * *

Afterwards, Veer says to Charity, 'I was just coming to see you and I confess, I overheard you give sound advice to Miss Ram.'

'You think it was good advice?' she asks. His opinion matters to her; she does not want to admit just how very much, even, especially to herself.

'I do,' he twinkles at her.

'She is closing the curry house at Christmas. The whole street will likely be in uproar.' Charity sighs. 'But we can all manage without her for a few days. The poor dear deserves a holiday.'

'You're a good friend to her, Miss Charity O'Kelly.' Veer beams at her.

'She is to me too,' Charity says, even as her heart warms at his compliment and she feels colour once again ambush her cheeks.

32

DIVYA

December 10, 1940

Dearest Raghu,

I cannot tell you what a wonderful miracle it was, what joy to receive a letter from you at long last!

When Mrs Jennings, the postmistress, walked into the curry house this morning, we all looked at her worriedly, for from her face, we can usually tell if it is bad news.

But thankfully, she was smiling.

She handed out letters to some of the regulars and then… one for me.

I thought it was from Jack Devine. He writes to all the street through me.

But to my absolute delight, I saw that it was from you!

It has been weeks since I posted my letter to you, and a part of me was resigned to not hearing back. Although of course, I hoped otherwise.

And you did write and I now have another souvenir from

you to carry around next to my heart until it is in danger of falling apart!

Oh, Raghu, now I can confess that I worried, oh how I worried, that you were no longer of this world, but lying lifeless in a foreign battlefield in the weeks since Mr Singh had been invalided out of the army.

Even though I maintained that since I loved you, I would know if you were dead, I still could not help agonising anyway.

So to get a letter from you! I cannot tell you how much it means.

Although of course, this letter too engendered mixed feelings in me, like your last. Happiness that you are alive and worry upon reading that you are injured and recuperating in a convalescent home in Guildford.

How bad was your injury? You don't say. Instead, you fill your letter with details of the postal system, that the reason it took so long for you to reply to my letter is because my letter took a while to reach you, having travelled all the way to France and back again, after being forwarded on to the convalescent home from the barracks! I am worried that your injury must have been bad if they brought you back from France and if you have to recuperate now.

'My dear Divya,' your letter said.

My dear. The words, and my name in your handwriting, were like a warm hug, easing, briefly, the melancholy of missing.

'Thank you for your letter.'

So formal, Raghu. And that same formal tone continued throughout the letter.

I must confess that once the initial joy had passed, I was furious with you.

You were injured, brought to a hospital here, in England, then moved into a convalescent home. (I didn't know how far away it was, so I asked Mr Stone. I just dropped it into conversation, said, 'I heard there's a convalescent home in Surrey where injured soldiers recover.' 'Yes, Chalmer Grange in Guildford. It is not too far from here,' he said. 'Only thirty-five miles or so.')

You are so close and yet you did not write to let me know that you had been injured. If not for Mr Singh sharing your address, and my writing to you, I wouldn't have known. So close and yet... you might as well have been across the world.

You don't even tell me how long you have been in the country.

I am upset, for you, and with you. You could have convalesced here!

But I know your arguments: the same old ones. You don't want to cause trouble. You are not worthy of me. I don't care. We are at war. I want you and that's that.

And in any case, you are now a celebrated soldier, injured in the line of duty. You will be feted, not looked down on for being a lascar. You have shed blood for England and once you are well enough, you tell me you will be going back again to fight on behalf of all of us.

I was proud of you before but now I am more so.

I don't know how many times and in how many different ways to tell you this: you are the only one for me.

I have been dreaming about you even more than usual recently. Waking up with my heart pounding in my chest, convinced something is not right. Perhaps some part of me knew you were injured. Perhaps it was a premonition.

I was brought up to be a good girl, a dutiful girl. Cover

your face in front of men. Absolutely no consorting with, talking to, touching them. Your reputation is precious. If you lose your reputation you will bring shame not only to your parents but to your entire village.

But my village kicked me out, saying I was bad luck when my parents died, just when I needed them most.

And we may not be married, but you are my family.

I have thought long and hard since your letter arrived – actually, that is a lie. I did not have to think at all; I knew the moment Mr Stone said that Chalmer Grange is near to here, what I must do. But... I have had battles with my conscience which berates me in the voice of the elders from my childhood village since I made my decision.

In any case, I am not listening to my conscience.

I have spoken with Charity, and she is all for it, but I would even have disregarded my best friend's opinion, if it had gone against what I have made up my mind to do.

Which is to come and see you. Visit you before you go to war again.

I have to, especially since you are so close by. I feel that it is destiny urging us together. Fate conspiring that we meet. Something stronger than mere human whim.

Otherwise, how do you explain Mr Singh coming here to West India Dock Road and giving me your address to write to? And you writing back to tell me you are nearby?

Christmas is coming. A time for family. And as I said, you are my family. And so, I am coming to visit.

I will not be able to live with myself otherwise.

What if I die next week?

Or... I shudder to think this... what if you do?

I want more than that one kiss.

I am prepared to ruin my reputation, even if just in my head.

Life is precious, incredibly fragile, our time on earth too limited to squander on propriety.

I must see you.

I will not post this letter, although you have given me the address for Chalmer Grange.

I will bring it with me, along with all the other letters I have written to you.

I will surprise you.

I don't want you to say no.

I don't want you to do what you did before, when the war first started, posting that one letter, which was all the communication I had from you until now, on your way to the train headed for France so that when I did come in search of you, you had already left.

Raghu, I never thought I would be this forward or this stubborn.

What if you don't want to see me?

What if you have already left?

What if you are worse off than you are making out?

But… loving you has made me strong.

I stood up for you back before the war, even when nearly everyone on West India Dock Road was against you, convinced that you had started the fire at the public house.

I never thought I would one day run my own curry house and in England too but I am doing so even during the war.

And now, for the first time since it opened, I am planning to shut the curry house for a couple of days over Christmas so I can visit with you.

I am nervous.

I haven't travelled in this country, beyond the East End,

since I arrived here to West India Dock Road and found my place.

I haven't gone anywhere since the country has been at war.

But I will come to you.

Just the thought makes my heart sing even as I worry and as I fear.

I have an image of you, imprinted upon my heart.

But I want a fresh one.

I want more memories with you to cherish when you are away at war again.

Your love gives me wings, makes me do things I would never even have considered before.

Perhaps I am foolish.

My conscience says so.

My parents would not approve and I have never gone against them, even just in my mind.

But I must do this.

I will bring this letter and all the others: a testament of my love for you.

Please be there, Raghu. Please let us have this time together, stolen from war, from pain and injury, treasured moments, together.

I love you.

Yours,

Divya

33

DIVYA

December 12, 1940

Dear Jack,

Just a quick one to wish you as good a Christmas as is possible over there, from all of us here at West India Dock Road.

Do write to us about how it went.

Hopefully, the Huns make a concession for Christmas and allow celebrations, such as they are.

Here we will be celebrating the festive season during wartime. Again.

Traditional carol singing has been cancelled due to the bombing and blackout, but that does not stop the residents of West India Dock Road bursting into festive song while at the curry house, out and about in the street as they attend to their chores, and even in the Tube station with enemy planes hovering above.

There's something so celebratory about carols, isn't there? Bombs might be raining overhead but when the street's voices are joined in song, it breeds a merry jollity which assures us, even though we might know otherwise, that Christmas is coming and all will be well.

Well, except when Mrs Murphy sings…

Those nearest to her flinch and try to move a little away from her, a losing battle as the Tube station is always packed. But that doesn't deter her one bit.

'I wish it would,' grumbles Mr Brown, who claims he used to lead the choir in his hometown in Accra, The Gold Coast, back in the day. He does have a very pleasing baritone.

'What about over here?' I asked.

'Ah, it might be a place of worship, God's house as they say, but they don't want a coloured man in their midst stealing their thunder, my love.' He sighed.

So Christmas is coming but given the war, festive lights are not to be found anywhere in the streets.

But having said that, extra rations are available which everyone is very grateful for.

Mrs Boon announced happily that the tea ration was doubled and the sugar allowance increased.

Mr Barney complained that Mrs Barney was in a mood, for wine and spirits were aplenty but there was no brandy to be had for love or money.

'And the prices being what they are, and going up daily, we cannot afford turkey or goose this year.' Mrs O'Riley sighed.

'Well there are always substitutes, dear,' Mrs Porter said gently. 'We all must keep calm and cheerful, don't you know.'

'I am following the recipes provided by the Ministry of Food.' Mrs Nolan smiled, although it didn't quite reach her *eyes, given her worry about her husband who, although home in one piece, is struggling to deal with the trauma he endured and steadily getting worse instead of better, much like Charity's da.*

In fact, this is true of everyone on the street, and the country, I suspect. We are determinedly cheerful but our smiles lack sparkle much like the streets bereft of Christmas lights. For almost everyone is spending Christmas apart from their loved ones. The mothers with their children evacuated, wives and daughters and mothers and sisters with their loved ones spending Christmas in the battlefields or sacrificed to war, like Mrs Ross (who still hasn't heard from her son).

Mrs Kerridge's smiles too do not reach her eyes; she still hasn't heard from her two younger sons either. And her eldest, who came home from Dunkirk and, once recovered, went back to the battlefield, cannot get shore leave for Christmas.

The children of the street, who have not evacuated, have been hard at work making Christmas decorations from old card, newspapers and scraps as there is a paper shortage. We save any paper we have and give it to the children to use. They are so good, turning the scraps into something so festive and beautiful; war shortages have made artists of all of us. The colourful decorations remind me of the curry competition and also the grand opening of the curry house, when you were here, celebrating with us, and the children made bunting and hung it up and down the street.

Happy times.

We will have happy times again, when we win this war and are reunited, hopefully very soon. In the meantime, we will try and find happiness where we can. Bombing may not stop at Christmas but the shelters and the Tube stations are decorated to the hilt, again with handmade ornaments and baubles, everyone pitching in, a mishmash of styles, but somehow it works, reminding us of this special time of year.

Green-fingered Mr Lee even managed to get a sapling and decorate it, one for the Tube station and one for the Anderson shelter, serving as a Christmas tree. He hung little bottles filled with his baijiu liquor well out of reach of little fingers and also baubles and trinkets that he has fashioned at the lower levels for the children to play with and admire.

Mr Lee has also proved adept at crafting toys from scrap materials. He has enlisted the help of the O'Kelly boys with Mr Singh joining in and they are making toys and gifts for all the children in the street and beyond! Intricate dollhouses complete with furniture, beautiful dolls fashioned from wood and card, trolley buses and train sets and miniature farm implements. You name it, Mr Lee makes it.

'Mr Lee is a genius,' the women of the street proclaim in wonder and gratitude. 'He is saving Christmas for our children.'

Word has spread the way it does around here and women have taken to queuing at Mr Lee's shop with requests. Mothers whose children have been evacuated have posted the toys to their loved ones. They thanked Mr Lee with tears in their eyes, touched. 'You are a magician.'

'It nothing,' Mr Lee said, busily fiddling with something on the counter to hide the blush that made his face glow rosily.

The women of West India Dock Road have been busy knitting, unravelling old jumpers to make scarves, gloves and hats to give as presents and post to loved ones.

Mr Stone and Mr Brown declared that they were getting

war bonds to give as gifts as they will help with the war effort.

Both men told me, separately and in secret, that what would make Christmas special for them would be to beat the other at chess once and for all.

'Ha, no it would have the opposite effect and far from crowing, you'd be miserable. You'd immediately challenge Mr Stone to another game, wanting him to beat you just so he could still prove a worthy opponent.' Fergus, who'd overheard Mr Brown's comment, laughed.

Everyone is looking forward to the King's speech, which will be broadcast on Christmas Day, even as we hope he will be able to overcome his stammer for the duration of it. I hope you get to listen to it where you are. If not, do let me know and I will write you a gist. (Another word I have learned from the dictionary. I love it: 'gist'. Small, perfect, just exactly right.)

I am posting this letter nice and early (in keeping with the Ministry of Information's edict to send any messages and mail sooner rather than later to avoid disappointment), along with a care package which includes something from every family on West India Dock Road, to say how much you mean to us and to wish you a merry Christmas.

I am keeping everything crossed that it reaches you before the big day. Wishing you a good one, Jack, despite the circumstances.

Much love from Divya and all of us here on West India Dock Road

34

DIVYA

December 20, 1940

Dearest Raghu,

I am coming to see you.

I have made my decision. So just don't you say a word. In any case, you can't for, like with my previous letter, I'm not posting this one but bringing it to you.

I can't help writing to you. I've got into the habit and it is like having a conversation with you, however one-sided. It eases the missing somewhat.

I have researched how to get to you, with helpful pointers from Mr Singh, and I know the journey by heart. Now all that remains is to undertake it.

I just cannot bear the thought of you spending Christmas all alone in a convalescent home. I know you don't celebrate the festival and neither do I but when everyone is together, although of course this year, most have someone missing, I cannot bear the thought of us spending it apart, especially given you are so nearby.

Last Christmas, we were apart and who knows what will happen next Christmas? I want at least one Christmas with you.

Yes, Raghu, I am becoming very English, perhaps, but Christmas is a time for family and you are mine. When you are so close, it would be remiss of me not to at least try and see you. And Charity thinks it's a good idea.

Ah, Charity. My friend is glowing, Raghu; the worry that had etched premature lines onto her face and weighed her shoulders down has eased lately. I suspect it has much to do with a certain lodger. Yes, it is your friend from the barracks, Mr Veer Singh! I smell romance in the air, honey sweet and invigorating. For Charity and also for me. For I can't keep the bounce from my step; everyone has noticed and remarked on it.

'Glad to abandon us to our own devices are you, Miss Ram?' Mrs Kerridge was moved to ask sternly. 'I've noticed you haven't stopped smiling since you decided to shut the curry house for Christmas and you're walking as if the ground is a cushion filled with air.'

'Floating is the word you're looking for, I think,' Mr Brown teased, winking at me, heartily chuckling in his booming baritone when I blushed.

I cannot keep my happiness at seeing you at bay. I am so excited and at the same time, very nervous. I understand the expression now: 'butterflies in my stomach'. That's exactly how I feel. I cannot sleep, counting down the hours until I can see you.

You will still be there, I hope. I pray.

Surely they won't send you out over Christmas?

Don't go anywhere just for a few more days, please, until I get there.

Needless to say, my regulars at the curry house were at a loss when I announced that I would be closing the place over Christmas.

'How will we manage without your wonderful dishes to supplement our bland, rationed meals?' they cried.

'And where will we come to play chess?' Mr Stone and Mr Brown asked, looking a tad lost.

'You are welcome to spend the day in here as always, but do remember to draw the blackout curtains when you leave, please,' I said.

'It won't be the same without you, my dear, supplying meals and snacks, Indian-style spiced tea for me and regular tea for Mr Brown throughout the day.' Mr Stone sighed. 'But you very much deserve a holiday. You haven't shut once since the curry house's grand opening. You have a nice time now with your acquaintance in Surrey.'

I have told them that I am meeting a friend of mine, a fellow ayah from the ship to England who has written to tell me she is in Surrey and invited me to stay with her. In addition to everything else, I appear to have also become a very adept liar.

However, Mrs Neville, shrewd old bird that she is – much as she complains of short-sightedness and 'the old memory which is not quite what it was' – looked me up and down and said, 'Don't get up to mischief, mind.'

I turned away to hide my blush but not evidently soon enough for she sucked her teeth and tutted, while shaking her head.

What did I tell you? Nothing gets past her.

'We will all miss you very much.' Mrs Devlin said kindly, the other women cooing their assent.

Mrs Kerridge, as usual, had the last word, 'Make sure to

come back, won't you. West India Dock Road won't be the same without you.'

Again, everyone in the curry house agreed enthusiastically.

I must admit, I was overwhelmed by Mrs Kerridge's words, the affection in her voice, all my regulars nodding along.

I have so much to be grateful for, Raghu. I came to this street destitute, looking for a room for the night, but I have found my community and my place here. I belong, which is all I ever wanted after I was chased out of my childhood village in India because of my supposed bad luck.

I know you worry that my association with you threatens this but I disagree. Given they accept me, they will accept you, for you are my soulmate, my family.

Only Charity and Mr Veer Singh know the truth: that I am in fact coming to see you. Charity told me that Mr Singh overheard our conversation, when I asked for her advice on what she would do if she were in my situation.

'He is the soul of discretion and has promised me it will not go any further,' she said, knotting her apron worriedly.

I noted how anxious she was on his behalf.

'I know that I can trust him, Charity,' I said gently. 'Because you do.'

She beamed then, her anxious expression ironed out, and I was glad for it. She looks so much younger when she smiles.

Mr Singh joined us just then, and I told him we were talking about my trip to see you.

'I was at Chalmer Grange before I was demobilised.' He smiled. 'What a shame Raghu and I missed each other.' Then, grinning widely, 'He will be so happy to see you, Miss

Ram. Honestly, he would talk about you at every opportunity; he missed you very much, I think.'

My heart swelled. I know you care for me, but your letter was friendly yet formal, not giving a clue as to your feelings for me. I know it is because you don't want to encourage me, for you think you're not good enough. So it was nice having what I know in my heart confirmed by Mr Singh.

And then, his expression clouding, he added, 'The nurses are kind but they are not used to us, you see. It can be very lonely and isolating, recuperating in a country where hardly anyone else is like you, especially when you are wounded and vulnerable. Raghu will benefit from seeing a friendly face, someone who cares.'

That made me all the more determined, even if I am nervous and keep having arguments with my conscience haranguing me in my parents' voices. And also there's a small voice at the back of my head which chirps up every so often to ask whether you really want to see me. Perhaps you've moved on since your declaration of love, and now only think of me as a friend. Perhaps, far from being pleased, you will be irritated, annoyed, even scandalised when I turn up. What if I am making a mistake?

But Mr Singh's reassurance fortified my resolve. He was very helpful, giving me precise directions on how to get to Chalmer Grange. 'As hospitals go, it is a very nice place,' he said. 'I think you will like it. Please give Raghu my best. Hopefully, we will meet again when he gets back from war.'

So there it is, Mr Singh's message for you, in his own words.

With this war, that's the best we can hope for: that one day, we will be reunited.

Which is why I'm coming to see you even knowing there is a possibility that you might not wish to see me.

I don't want to regret giving up on this opportunity later. And I want to hand over this letter and the others I have written in person.

I write the words down, 'in person', and I cannot begin to imagine our reunion, even as I am thrilled and nervous and excited, my heart beating in anticipation and trepidation.

Yours always,

Divya

35

CHARITY

Veer comes upon Charity doing the accounts, her face scrunched up in a frown even as she chews the end of her pencil, a bad habit she's acquired while trying to make the sums look better than they are.

'What's the matter, Charity?' he asks. 'I've never seen that expression on your face before.'

Charity sighs deeply even as she smiles at him. 'Ah, these accounts!' she grumbles. 'This is the part of running the lodging house that I least look forward to.'

'May I?' he asks, indicating the chair beside her. 'Please shoo me away if I'm being a nuisance.'

'No,' she says, shutting her ledger gratefully. 'I'm glad of the distraction, to be honest. The numbers were starting to swim before my eyes.'

And I'm always happy to spend time with you. You make my heart sing.

He lowers his crutch and sits himself down next to her. 'Was running this lodging house what you always wanted to do? Was it, as they say, in your blood?'

From a hidden recess of her heart, she unpacks her child-hood dream, long since put away but never forgotten – she still fantasises about it, every now and then – to share with this man who has his intense, soulful, deeply interested gaze trained upon her in that way that makes her whole being thrill to him.

'Ah no,' she says. 'I wanted to be a sugar girl.' Her voice wistful, even as she looks past him, towards the docks where the factories still stubbornly operate despite enduring the daily bombardment of enemy fire.

'A sugar girl?'

His voice and the smile gracing it drag her attention back to him.

'That is what they're calling themselves, I've heard, now that there are only women running the factory,' she says.

'You wanted to work at the sugar factory?' he asks.

And she shares out loud what she hasn't told anyone else before now, nursing the secret desire in her heart, trying and failing to let go of the fantasy once her life took a different turn. 'For as long as I can remember, yes, that's what I wanted. I had this romantic notion of it. The scent of syrup clinging to my clothes, my hands sticky with it.'

'Your eyes sparkle when you speak of it,' he says.

'Ah well, in a different life, perhaps. Not this one,' she says.

The warmth in his eyes, his expression...

She feels hot all over, her body wanting to move closer to him.

And so she babbles on, in order to distract herself from what he is making her feel. 'In any case, when I talk to the sugar girls, they sound tired, fed up, saying it's not all it's cracked up to be. They are envious of my life here. Proprietress of my own lodging house. No one to answer to.' She shrugs.

'It's all well and good, I suppose, until I have to do the accounts, that is.' She laughs, somewhat unsteadily, trying to ignore the fluster he is causing in her entire being.

'Ah, Charity,' he says and the way he says her name makes her heart flip. 'You are doing a great job.' His gaze never leaving hers, the intensity of it, that expression that makes her want to lean into him, lose herself in him... 'I wish you could see what I see.'

'What do you see?' A whisper is all she can manage.

'A girl who is so caring, so kind, so selfless...'

'I'm not—' she begins, thinking of how, at times, she has resented the burden she carries.

'Please let me finish,' he says softly. 'A girl who gave up her dream to run the lodging house. Who if people can't pay her for their room, takes anything or nothing as she is too kind-hearted, which is why she dreads doing the accounts.'

How does he know this? she wonders.

As if reading her mind, he says, 'When I was in the curry house the other day, we were talking about artefacts and I said your lodging house could easily double up as a museum given there were so many knick-knacks from all corners of the world. "Oh, those are from sailors who've stayed there and have gifted relics in lieu of payment," Mrs Kerridge tutted. And then, lowering her voice and waiting until Miss Ram was in the kitchen, out of earshot, she added, sighing deeply, "Charity even pays for their meals in here out of her own pocket. At this rate, and I've warned her often enough, those pockets will be empty sooner rather than later."'

'Oh.' Charity blushes. 'I thought nobody knew about that.'

'You think anything gets past the matrons here at West India Dock Road?' Veer smiles. Then, tenderly, 'She also told me that you've single-handedly brought up your brothers, even when just a child yourself, while also looking after your parents.'

'I...' She thinks of how, quite often, she is fed up and does what she has to with bad grace. 'I had no choice. It's not the same as—'

He does not let her finish. 'Ah, Charity,' he says, his voice oh-so very tender. 'You are amazing, believe me.'

And she sees that in his eyes, she is.

36

CHARITY

Charity, her brothers, Veer and the other lodgers, and the residents of West India Dock Road, those not away at war, spend Christmas day at the curry house, although without Divya there, bustling about bringing food and drink with a wide smile, it feels rather odd.

But the curry house is the only place big enough to host all of them, a patched-up family of sorts given their loved ones are at war or missing in action or, like Jack, German prisoners of war.

Everyone brings food, whatever they can cobble together given the rationing.

By the time they arrive, Mr Lee has decorated the curry house the best he can and it is looking very festive indeed.

There is a small, make-do Christmas tree in the corner festooned with Mr Lee's beautiful, handmade baubles. There are intricately patterned paper doilies (fashioned from old newspapers given the paucity of paper), painted pine cones and colourful bottles of *baijiu* at every table. The ceiling is strung with newspaper chains, sprigs of holly and other garden greenery dangling from them.

It is beautiful and festive and Mrs Neville gives Mr Lee a hug.

'You've outdone yourself,' she cackles.

Paddy looks alarmed and jogs Charity's arm. 'She's recruiting Mr Lee for her witchy army.'

Charity laughs but Paddy looks even more worried. Hands on hips, he hisses, 'I'm not joking. This is very worrying. Why does nobody ever take me seriously?' He shakes his head in exasperation, sounding quite fed up, and Charity bites her lower lip to try and hide her smile.

She pulls him close and deposits a kiss on his forehead; he still lets her do so which is a privilege she does not take for granted, given how Connor and Fergus are now shying away from her hugs. She is overcome with affection for her earnest youngest brother, even as she hopes he will like his present, a model Spitfire fashioned by Mr Lee from scrap metal which Fergus had scrounged from the shipyard. Connor is getting one too, while for Fergus and Veer, she has knitted scarves and hats and gloves from scraps of wool she has been saving.

By the time everyone arrives with food and drink, there is quite a spread, even though most of it is made using substitute or mock ingredients, the ladies of West India Dock Road carefully following recipes as laid out by the Ministry of Food and the programme, *The Kitchen Front*, broadcast by the BBC on the wireless each morning.

Mrs Kerridge has brought along an impressive-looking Christmas cake which all the ladies coo over and which Connor and Paddy eye longingly.

'Iced with mock marzipan, hides a lot of sins.' Mrs Kerridge sighs. 'It will not be as sweet as you're used to, boys,' she says, ruffling Connor's hair.

Paddy deftly steps out of her reach even as he says, 'I'm sure it will be delicious, Mrs Kerridge.'

She beams and Charity is once again overcome with love and pride for her brother.

'Mock marzipan? What's that when it's at home?' Mrs Neville asks.

'You don't want to know,' Mrs Kerridge says.

Mrs Boon has fetched candied carrots and carrot fudge. 'It's not strictly fudge as there's no sugar in it, but I do hope the sweetness of the carrot makes up for the lack.'

There's roast pork cooked by Mrs Neville and Mrs Devlin, all the ladies having pooled rations so that it's big enough to go round, and also rabbit, courtesy of Mr and Mrs Barney.

'I laid traps and caught the blighters myself,' Mr Barney booms.

Charity has brought carrot soup for starters, Veer having helped peel and chop the carrots.

The others have brought along roast potatoes, mash, Irish boxty and a variety of vegetables.

The BBC Home Service, which has been playing in the background, is turned off briefly while Mrs O'Riley leads them in prayer, all those present sniffing away a few tears even as they call upon the Lord to look out for loved ones away fighting the war or lost or missing or in prison.

'And now, let's eat! Merry Christmas, all!' Mrs Kerridge declares even before Mrs O'Riley has drawn a breath after saying, 'Amen.'

They eat while listening to the *Christmas Under Fire* broadcast which includes the King's speech.

The speech is rousing and they all clap and cheer when it is done.

'He came through, he did, our King. Did not stutter one bit, did he?' Mrs Kerridge beams.

The food, despite all the substitutions, is delicious and there isn't a morsel left when they are done.

Charity's soup comes up trumps.

'What's this hint of spice in the soup, my dear? It's delicious,' Mr Stone enthuses.

'Ah, a girl can't give away all her secrets, Mr Stone,' Charity says archly, even as she mouths a thank you to Veer, who, after tasting the soup, suggested that she add a tablespoon each of ground cumin and cinnamon, from Divya's stash, to lift the flavour.

Mrs Kerridge's cake is highly praised and Mrs Boon's carrot fudge and candied carrots are relished by all.

'You cannot tell that there's no sugar in this fudge. Melt in the mouth, it is,' Mrs Neville praises, helping herself to more, and Mrs Boon glows with pride.

'It's not the same without Miss Kumar, is it?' Mr Stone says and they all nod agreement.

Afterwards, as *Music for Christmas* plays on the wireless, they exchange presents.

Charity's youngest brothers are very happy with their Spitfire models and give her a hug and when she tells them that Mr Lee made them, they shake his hand while solemnly thanking him and he turns red to the tips of his ears with pleasure.

Veer is touched with his hat and scarf and so is Fergus.

The boys and Veer have clubbed together to gift Charity a beautiful, rose-scented bar of soap and she is very pleased.

Her eyes meet Veer's and he smiles at her and she smiles

back, feeling her heart swell as it always does when this man is around.

Fergus is dozing, Connor and Paddy running about the room with their airplanes.

Mr Stone and Mr Brown have got out the chessboard, Mr Lee and Mr Rosenbaum watching intently. Mr Barney is on his third mug of ale, his wife scowling at him.

The other residents of West India Dock Road, stomachs sated, presents exchanged, are smiling and chatting away.

Charity thinks of Divya and hopes she is having a glorious time with her love. She closes her eyes, allowing the gentle murmur of conversation to wash over her. Soon, she will go across the road to the basement of the lodging house to check on her parents; she has been once already with food for them and she will do so again in a few minutes, but for now, she will savour this moment, beauty and joy and togetherness in the midst of war.

37

DIVYA

December 27, 1940

My dearest Raghu,

I cannot believe that it's been only a day since I saw you, that yesterday, we were saying goodbye, not wanting to let each other go. It feels like forever ago.

I miss you with my everything already.

I wish it was yesterday again; I would hold you to me and not let go.

What a beautiful, charmed Christmas that was! I'm so very glad I came to spend it with you.

And you whispered to me that you were too. Overjoyed. Grateful. Touched. Overwhelmed.

Oh, how you enjoyed the pilau rice and the potato curry, the potato pakoras and the carrot halva that I brought for you, even though they weren't my best, given what little there is to cook with. But you ate every last crumb with relish, your face beaming, exulting about how much you had missed my food. It was incredibly gratifying and my heart felt full just looking at you. I could never get enough of looking at you, being with you. I had to remind myself that it wasn't a dream, that we were together at long last.

And while you were happy with my food, you were beyond thrilled by the huge stack of letters I handed over, cataloguing my feelings for every day we had been apart. You have saved them for reading when away in the battle-field, when the hours drag, you said, and missing me gets too much.

While I hoped when I set off that you would be happy to see me, I hadn't dared wish for more. But your reaction has been so wonderful, beyond my wildest dreams.

You said you would save my letters to read later but nevertheless, you couldn't help reading a couple immedi-ately, stroking them tenderly as if it was my face you were touching, exactly the way I do with your missives. You handled them like precious treasure, and I was so very touched. You said you loved how I put all my feelings down, everything I was thinking.

I looked at your shining face, your eyes soft with love and I had to resist the urge to pinch myself, to check that this was really happening, that this wasn't all a fantastic dream.

You made me promise to continue to write that way, without editing or censoring. 'Write anything and everything that occurs to you, please,' you said.

So that is what I will attempt to do here.

And we had so much to talk about, such a lot to catch up on, that I didn't get around to answering your questions about my journey to Chalmer Grange and my impressions of the place.

I will record it here as much for you as for myself, for, in the process, I will be reliving our meeting again, which I have been doing a thousand times in my mind since we parted. But writing it all down will make it more vivid, I feel. And also, it will be there in black and white, in case I forget something a few weeks down the line, although I don't think I will forget a single moment of our enchanted time together.

In any case, here they are, my thoughts as I set out to meet you and the moment of our meeting and everything that happened afterwards.

If I have missed something out, let me know in your reply, will you?

For I want every moment of it preserved for it was sheer magic.

On the train, on my way to see you, I saw soldiers on shore leave for Christmas, their faces etched with tiredness, their eyes hollow with everything they had experienced, and I prayed, please let Raghu be all right. I was imagining the worst, even though you had said in your letter that you were recuperating well enough to return to the war front in the next few days. And that thought spawned another prayer: please let him not have left already.

From the train station, I took a bus to Chalmer Grange. In my head, I thanked Mr Singh, who had not only described the journey to me in great detail but also told me where to queue for tickets and how much they would cost, so I was well prepared.

The bus took us through narrow country roads, twisting like a ribbon in a capricious breeze. Hedges crowded the lanes, kissing the sides of the trolley bus. Children skipped alongside and waved to us. We passed a scattering of dwellings beside a church, spire piercing the wide awning of sky, a butcher's, a greengrocer's and a public house abutting a village green. So different from the city, which was crowded, noisome, bombed, bedraggled. Barely standing.

And suddenly, it was dark, like a candle abruptly snuffed out. Night came early out here in the country, it seemed. The interior lamps of the bus were fitted with cowls so it was as if we were moving in a dark, shadowy world, the only people left. The headlamps of the bus, masked to account for blackout, allowed only a thin crack of light through, barely illuminating the winding road, slick with rain, silvery droplets dancing like starburst dreams.

When the bus dropped me off at Chalmer Grange, the grounds going on for miles, it seemed, the house itself a sprawling manor serving as a hospital during wartime, I must admit, I was a bit cowed. All my bravado on setting off on this journey deserting me, leaving only nerves, fluttering in my stomach and doubts multiplying in my head.

Why had I been possessed of this madness to come here? What if you weren't there, if you had left for war already? What if you were and didn't want to see me?

I took a deep breath, told myself, sternly, You are here now. You might as well go through with it.

As I approached the manor, I saw soldiers resting in beds under awnings in the vast grounds of the house, nurses tending to them. Some, those well on the road to recovery, sat at tables playing cards. Like mine, their eyes too must have adjusted to the darkness, pulsing with shadows, for they seemed adept at squinting at the cards. I tried, in the dusky gloom, searching their gaunt faces for the familiar face of my beloved. But you weren't here. Did this mean you had already left?

No. I wouldn't think that way.

*In the gloaming, the lawns glowed a secretive shadow
tinted navy emerald. The air that brushed my face was nippy
with frost, not gritty with debris and fiery with smoke like in
the East End. Here, arrowwood and winter honeysuckle and
witch hazel perfumed the air, a cornucopia of scents
accented by the convalescing soldiers' raucous laughter.*

*I concentrated on all this to stop the thudding of my
heart, which was remonstrating, very loudly, What are you
doing? What on earth are you doing?*

*The inside of the manor was as high ceilinged and
magnificent as on the outside, but it smelled, for all that, like
hospitals everywhere, of antiseptic and ammonia and
illness. Soldiers hopped about on crutches, others were
wheeled by nurses, some heavily bandaged, several missing
limbs, haunted gazes. There was a Christmas tree in the
corner of the room, draped with handmade baubles,
wooden and paper ornaments. I privately thought Mr Lee's
tree, festooned with the decorations made by the children
of West India Dock Road and Mr Lee's baubles much better
but of course, I fear I might have been biased.*

*I was standing at the door, hesitant, gripped by a sense
of unreality, when a nurse approached me, smiling briskly
and asked if I was looking for someone.*

'Er… Mr Raghu Kumar,' I said.

*She smiled, looking me up and down. 'Let me guess,
you are Miss Ram?'*

*I was taken aback. I hadn't told anyone I was coming,
least of all yourself, Raghu. 'How did you know?'*

*'We were all hoping you'd come. He talks about you
enough,' she said.*

*I felt warmed, my worry that you might not want to see
me easing.*

'I... is... is he... still here?' I stumbled over my words, anticipation and excitement causing me to stutter.

'Yes, you caught him, just. He's due to rejoin his battalion after Christmas.'

Thank you God, I prayed.

And that was when I felt eyes on me.

I turned.

And found myself looking at a face, so very familiar and beloved, that visited my dreams, was with me in my every waking moment.

You blinked. Once, then again, your mouth open but no words leaving it.

You... you were you. And yet...

And yet...

A skeletal, extremely gaunt version of you.

When I had seen you just before you were imprisoned, our last meeting before this one, when we had declared our love for each other, I had thought you gaunt then.

But that was nothing compared to now. You were thinly stretched skin over a collection of bones. The scars on your face standing to attention. A constellation of lines etched upon it. Your eyes hollow and haunted with the spectres of all you had seen and endured.

But... it was you.

I smiled but you only blinked, unable to believe, I imagine, that I was really here.

You came up to me, then.

You walked with a slight limp, I noticed.

You stood in front of me, extended a hand, wanting to touch me but afraid to, as if, if you did so, I would disappear.

'Am I dreaming?' you mouthed, your voice a whisper of awe. 'Or is it really you, Divya?'

My name, uttered by you, prayer and adoration and poetry.

That jolted me from my inaction, for I had been rooted to the spot, shocked by your appearance, my body going rigid, even as my heart simultaneously danced and bled, sheer, uncontrolled joy and desperate anguish at seeing you like this, hurting for you, worrying about you, even as I breathlessly, hungrily took you in, unable to quite believe that it was actually happening, what I had dreamed of and imagined for so long.

I reached out and took your hand.

When we touched, an electric thrill jolted through me, that you felt too, I could see, in the tears shining in your eyes even as your hand closed around mine. And I finally felt that flailing, rootless part of me find anchor, all my doubts and torment, the tortured back and forth with my conscience, falling away.

This was love, I thought then. How could you deny it, Raghu, this thrilling connection between us? The love that I had cried into my pillow every night that we'd been apart, the love that visited, vivid and vibrant, in tantalising, glorious dreams that rendered every day colourless with your absence.

That meeting after our time apart, on Christmas Eve: I will relive it always.

It took place in the crowded foyer, but we weren't aware of anyone else. Not the soldiers milling about, nor the nurses looking on. It was just the two of us in our cocoon. Reunited at long last. Unheedful of the tears that were overflowing our eyes as we breathed the other in, learning each *other by heart once again, our faces alight with love and gratitude for this moment, this gift of togetherness, our hands joined.*

'Divya,' you said, your voice, your body aglow with hope and love.

I had thought I'd never hear you saying my name again, except in my dreams, even as I'd hoped otherwise.

You were wan, washed out, a shadow version of the vivid man I'd known.

But… your eyes, that soft, gold gaze, tender as you took me in…

I revelled in the miracle of it.

'You travelled here to see me,' you whispered, awe and wonder, looking at me as if I was a vision your imagination had summoned, that would disappear any minute. 'You are real, aren't you, Divya? I… I haven't conjured you up?'

'Would you?' I asked, breath catching in my throat. 'Conjure me up?'

'I have. Millions of times since our parting…'

The pain… Oh, the torment on your face as we both recalled our last, fraught meeting, bookended by danger, when we had confessed our love for each other.

'Come,' you said then, gently tugging at my hand.

And then you led me out of the manor, across the grounds, past the soldiers convalescing under awnings, under the dark-navy canopy of sky pierced with twinkling diamonds of stars.

You took me to a cabin, nestling in a copse of trees, to the left of the main house. The small cabin that had been given to the only Indian convalescing on the premises.

You shut the door on the shadows flirting with night.

And then you gathered both of my hands in yours,

looking at me, your eyes soft and shining with emotion, devouring me with your gaze.

I was suddenly shy, feeling a blush creeping up my neck, heating my cheeks.

You angled your right hand, the other clasping both of mine; it hovered tantalisingly close to my face and I could see it trembling.

When you cupped my cheek, I closed my eyes, leaned into you and you dropped my hands and put your arm around me, gathering me close. I breathed deeply of your scent: spice and sweetness, familiar, beloved.

And all shyness disappeared.

That charmed night, the laughter outside died as the soldiers retired to bed.

The darkness, utter and still, would be broken, very soon, by hovering enemy planes, buzzing and droning overhead, heralding bombs, war intruding, relentless, even in Surrey, never mind that it was Christmas Eve.

Houses would crumble and lives would be destroyed by the orange-winged, smoke-topped, violent ire of the enemy, paying no heed to the fact that the next day was Christmas, usually a time of feasting with family, of celebration.

Or perhaps, the Jerries would show some mercy, because it was Christmas? Perhaps West India Dock Road would not, like it had these past few weeks, be noisy with air raids, the residents' dreams blazing, choked with smoke, confettied with ash, clamorous with sirens. Perhaps the residents would get to sleep in their own beds, instead of trudging to the Underground station, the icy, Christmas Eve night smoking hot and bright yellow as around them, the city burned.

Inside the cabin, you and I kissed, Raghu. And it felt so very right, so absolutely perfect.

It was everything I had ached for and imagined in my dreams. Only better, my imagination unable to conjure this perfection, which could only be experienced to be realised. This coming together of hearts and souls. This utter communion.

We undressed each other gently, tenderly. Your touch on my skin igniting goosebumps of desire.

You kissed every bit of my body.

Your own was a map of wounds, riddled with scars. I kissed every one, as you recounted the story of each.

The ones you got from the sailor who had a vendetta against you.

The ones you acquired in prison.

The ones you earned in war.

'And now you have made them your own, baptised them with your love. Now, that is what I will remember. Your kisses claiming them,' you whispered.

You told me you had been unconscious, delirious from your wounds, tucked away in a secluded corner of the hospital basement, away from the other men by virtue of being the only 'coolie'. You told me you had almost lost your leg to infection, hence the limp, and your stomach wound became infected too.

It had been touch and go for a while, your infections flaring, and a couple of times, the doctors had given up hope.

'Oh, Raghu, you could have died,' I lamented.

You kissed my tears, and then you kissed me, the taste of salt and love.

'I recovered. I'm here, see? With you.' You smiled, love

shining out of your chocolate gold eyes, making me wish we could stay in this moment forever.

'I dreamed I had an angel tending to me, like the night of the curry competition,' you said.

'I wish I had been there,' I said.

'I heard your voice in my fevered dreams,' you said.

'You did?'

'I did. I… I had no reason to live, you see, before.'

'Don't ever say that,' I cried.

'But when I heard your voice, I did.' Your eyes shining, so full of love. 'I've missed you, Divya. Ached for you. Dreamed of you.'

I could not look away from the magnetic force field of your gaze.

I had imagined you saying these words countless times.

And now, you were.

'And here you are,' you said.

'Here I am.'

And then, there were no words, only loving.

Outside, war was raging, or perhaps, hopefully, it had been suspended just for Christmas.

Inside that cabin, you and I were joined in a love as beautiful as it was desperate, as wanton as it was poetic, as right as it was wrong.

We spent Christmas Day in your cabin. We loved and we talked and we loved again.

For me, although the world was at war, even with the sorrow of our imminent parting hovering at the edges of my loved-up contentment, it was the best Christmas Day ever.

We lost track of time, we forgot everything except each other. We did not even experience hunger pangs until a soldier banged on the door and yelled, 'Kumar, they're serving Christmas dinner. Believe me, you don't want to miss it.'

We joined the soldiers walking, limping, being wheeled towards the dining hall. Everyone sporting huge grins.

The dining hall was decorated with paper chains and sprigs of holly.

The food was delicious. Despite the rationing and the scarcity, the cooks at the convalescent centre had gone all out. There was no turkey but there was roast chicken – mere slivers to make it go round – but with plenty of roast potatoes to bulk it up. Vegetables were sparse but everything was served with liberal lashings of gravy.

For afters, there was Christmas pudding with breadcrumbs and grated carrots in place of dried fruit which was hard to come by.

Later, there was carol singing, the hall rocking with voices raised in song, out of tune but jolly all the same.

Then we listened to the King's speech and there were cheers and a few discreet tears from those missing loved ones, when the King said, 'War brings, among other sorrows, the sadness of separation,' quickly wiped away and replaced by brave smiles.

I squeezed your hand under the table, feeling so lucky and blessed to be spending this special day with you. You looked at me, your eyes shining, your face glowing, and I knew you felt the same.

And there was even a pantomime! Soldiers with legs and arms in plaster, hobbling about in dresses and hamming it up for the audience.

So much laughter. Such joy.

It was a thoroughly magical day. A day of happiness and

fun snatched from the grim reality of wartime and all the more beautiful for it.

Afterwards, we went back to your cabin.

I wished we could lay there, entwined, loved up, in our bubble forever.

I wouldn't have minded if we had died at that moment.

We were happy.

We had each other.

We would be together forever in the afterlife.

I did not think once of the curry house, how it was faring, whether it was still standing.

I did not think of anything but you.

I breathed you in.

I loved you.

And it was enough.

I felt complete again.

I did not listen to the voice of my conscience and my dead parents' disapproval, their shouts of, 'What are you doing? Have you gone mad? You are a single girl. You are not married. You shouldn't be doing this. Stop. Now.'

Instead, I kissed you.

Learned every inch of you by heart.

That night, we loved each other enough to sustain us during the barren weeks and months when we would be apart.

Your touch. What wouldn't I give to experience it again! Come back to me my love, safe and whole.

I wanted that visit to last forever, but dawn inevitably arrived, flinging back the shrouded curtains of night, throwing light upon the darkest corners, hidden recesses, secret desires, heralding another day in this war, of rations and scrounging, making do and carrying on, suffering and death, telegrams and reunions, bombing and fighting, and our enchanted, magical time together came to an end.

This is what I will always remember, what will stay with me in the days and months to follow. Your voice, thick and husky with love, pouring sonnets of longing and adoration into my ears, our lips tasting of each other, our hearts heavy and suffused with impending loss as outside, the misty caress of dawn was kissing the edges of darkness, night dancing away on stealthy tiptoes, the grounds thick with frost, blades of grass misty with dew.

'I love you,' you whispered as the veil of night gently lifted, shadows tenderly chased away by the pre-dawn milky light, your tears mingling with mine. 'I always will.'

And this is how I remember you, your song of love steeping my heart in your chocolate voice, your face orna-mented with tears, your eyes hungry as they recorded my every feature, 'to remember you by when we are apart.'

'I love you,' I whispered, leaning in for one last kiss, tasting your sorrow, longing and ache.

And then, my eyes blinded by tears, I slipped on my clothes, every one smelling of you.

'I love you,' I whispered as I left you, your eyes following me, my last glimpse of you, silhouetted against your cabin in the grounds of the manor, blurred by the tears I was with-holding and yet, stamped upon my heart.

My love, you have promised to write to me.

You have promised also to, as far as it is possible, come home safe to me.

I will hold you to your promises.

I love you. Now and always. You are the only one for me.

My beloved, be safe. Be well. Come back to me.
Yours,
Divya

38

CHARITY

The longer the war goes on, the more agitated Charity's da becomes.

Charity doesn't want to admit it, but he is getting very difficult for her to handle. All her tried and tested techniques do not seem to be working any more.

She is glad the boys have taken to going with Veer to the Underground station along with Divya, Mrs Kerridge and the other residents of West India Dock Road.

Her brothers would be upset to see their father in such a bad way. Charity finds herself in tears the entire time as she tries and fails to console her father. He doesn't know what he's doing, she knows and yet still it hurts when he clasps her arms so hard they bruise, his nails digging into her skin, drawing blood, leaving crescent-shaped welts, shaking her so hard, she thinks her head will fall right off her neck.

One day, when Veer is helping her clean the lodging house before his shift, the sleeve of her dress rides up and he sees the bruises.

'Charity, what happened?' he asks, voice worried, eyes wide with upset.

'Ah, it's nothing.' She tries to wave his question away.

'It's your da, isn't it?' he says softly.

'He doesn't mean it.'

'I know,' he says and she sees that he does. 'But nevertheless, from tonight, can I please come and wait out the air raid in the basement with you, so I can help you with him?'

'I...'

'Please, Charity, allow me.'

She can only nod, the concern on his face causing a lump to form in her throat.

'Wait here,' he says.

He leaves the room, returning with her first aid kit.

'I'm sorry if this hurts,' he says, as very gently, he tends to her bruises. His touch is so tender that, although *he* winces when he dabs at the welts, she doesn't.

Tears prick her eyes but they are not because of pain but the opposite. She is used to caring for everyone. It is novel to have someone care for her.

Afterwards, 'May I?' he asks and when she nods, he puts his arm around her.

She rests her head against his chest and listens to his heart beat and she feels her heart beat in tandem even as her whole body relaxes into his.

This feels right. It feels like it is meant to be. She wants to stay here, anchored against his chest, forever. She wants more than this.

She pulls away.

'Thank you,' she says.

'Don't thank me,' he says, his eyes aglow with... is that what she thinks it is? 'I care for you, Charity,' he says. 'I'd like to take care of you. Will you let me?'

He feels the same way she does. *I care for you too, Veer.*

But then she thinks of her responsibilities. Her brothers. Her parents. The lodging house.

She wants nothing more than to go back into his embrace where she had finally felt her heart, always anxious, thinking of everything and everyone she is accountable for, settle. Felt thrilled and at the same time comforted.

He misunderstands her hesitation. 'I know you can do better,' he says. 'A man who is whole, who has all of his limbs accounted for. A man who is white...'

'It's not that,' she says fiercely. 'I don't care about any of that.'

'But *I* do. I hate that I'm not the best...'

'Don't say that,' she says. 'To me, you are perfect.'

He smiles and it is sunshine after a snowstorm. It is happiness and caring. It is everything.

'I love you, Charity. Dare I believe that you feel the same?'

He loves me.

'I love you too,' she whispers.

And now he holds out his arm and she goes into his embrace.

He kisses her and it is beautiful. It is perfect. It is the taste of sugar and nectar, the explosive celebration of dreams she hadn't dared envision come true.

PART III

PART III

39

DIVYA

January 19, 1941

Dear Jack,

Oh, but it was wonderful to receive your letter yesterday and to hear all of your news.

We are all so thrilled that the care package arrived safely. We are also pleased that you shared the jams and chutneys with everyone and that the scarf knitted by Mrs Neville, the hat knitted by Mrs Kerridge, the jumper knitted by Mrs Boon and the socks knitted by Mrs Devlin are all very useful in helping keep the cold at bay.

When I read your letter out, especially the bit where you said you were touched and moved to tears that despite rationing and the challenges everyone faces, they still put aside something to send to you, there were tears here too, plenty of sniffing and clearing of throats and blowing of noses. Thank you for such a lovely message.

And I am so happy you loved my cardamom biscuits and spicy snack mixture, that it was wonderful, magical, to *taste my food again. I've said this before and I'll say it again: come home as soon as you are able; I'll have all your favourites waiting.*

So good to know that you did celebrate Christmas after all, that the Huns did make an event of the day.

We are all very grateful that the Red Cross had sent parcels and you were able to have a Christmas meal.

'Wish we could 'ave seen the play they all put up that 'e tells us about,' *Mr Stone cried, echoing all of our sentiments.*

Sounds like you had a good Christmas, captivity notwithstanding. It appears you too, like the rest of us, found joy where you could.

London had a reprieve from the bombing on Christmas Day and Boxing Day.

Did you know, the royal family had to spend the holiday in secret in case they were attacked while King George was giving his Christmas broadcast? The royal Christmas card reflected what we've all had to endure this year, royalty and commoner notwithstanding. It was a picture of the King and Queen in the grounds of the bombed Buckingham Palace. Yes, even Buckingham Palace was not safe from the bombing. As for the King's speech, it was rousing and energising, promising us that we would win the war, thanking us and especially everyone on the frontlines for all you are doing for God and country. 'The future will be hard, but our feet are planted on the path of victory, and with the help of God, we shall make our way to justice and to peace,' *King George declared and it gave us all hope, it did.*

Mr Lee's handmade presents were a huge success. Mothers everywhere came to thank him for making their children's Christmases so very special.

Needless to say, he blushed and waved their thanks away. 'It nothing,' he said. 'I do my bit.'

He blushed even more when old Mrs Neville gathered him in a hug. 'You're a good man, Chen,' she said. 'You'll make someone a good husband.'

'Ah,' he said and will you believe it, he actually dug a handkerchief from his pocket and mopped his eyes for Mrs Neville had reduced him to tears! 'How you say... That ship sail long time back.'

'Never say never.' Mrs Neville winked and Mr Lee turned redder than Mr Barney when drunk on Mr Lee's potent baijiu liquor.

'I rather think Mrs Neville has set her sights on you,' Mr Brown teased, causing Mr Lee to blush even more, if that was possible.

Paddy looked horrified.

As soon as Mrs Neville left, he took Mr Lee aside, his voice earnest, eyes out on stalks, as he said, 'Mr Lee, I have to warn you, Mrs Neville is a witch. Don't let her cast her spell on you.'

'I be careful,' Mr Lee said, nodding gravely, and Paddy's expression relaxed, his shoulders slumping in relief.

So that's the news from here, Jack.

Here's hoping 1941 is the year we win the war and we are reunited at long last.

Take care and we live in the hope that we will see you soon.

Much love,

Divya and all on West India Dock Road

40

DIVYA

February 15, 1941

My dearest Raghu,

It is a few weeks into a brand-new year and yet still, I haven't heard from you.

After we parted at Chalmer Grange, once you went off to war and rejoined your battalion, you wrote to me, like you promised.

But since then, I've heard nothing.

I hope it is just the post taking its time to reach me.

I pray that I am worrying for nothing and that I will receive two or three of your letters all at once.

Every minute of every day, I recollect and relive our short, sweet, perfect time together. Lately, I have been having nightmares in which something bad has happened to you. I wake with my heart drumming foreboding and fear in my chest, my cheeks and pillow wet with tears and my throat hoarse as if I have been screaming for you in my sleep. There is a constant, hollow ache in my heart, a thrumming anxiety, a dull dread. And a debilitating feeling of emptiness. Lack.

Needless to say, I am worried but I dare not think the worst.

I am not posting this letter. I have written another, cheery missive which will be making its way to you. But I wanted an outlet for my worries and the only way I know how is by writing to you.

You're all right, aren't you, my love?

I hope. I pray. I wish that you are. And yet, my heart does not thud with the same conviction that it did before. And that scares me.

Come back to me, my love, won't you, please?

I love you,

Yours always,

Divya

41

CHARITY

The ladies of West India Dock Road pay Charity a visit.

'We've noticed you're getting awfully close with your lodger.' Mrs Kerridge is the spokesperson, as per usual, the others nodding along, wearing identical expressions of grave concern.

Charity has told no one, not even Divya, of Veer and her mutual declaration of love. She is keeping it to herself for now, revelling in the beautiful, sweet wonder of it. They share hugs and kisses when they can, snatched moments of furtive intimacy. A part of her is afraid that if she tells anyone, even her best friend, she will somehow jinx it and something will go wrong.

But she should have known that the matrons would somehow sniff it out. Nothing is secret on West India Dock Road for very long.

Nevertheless, 'Mr Singh is a friend,' she says.

'More than a friend,' Mrs Kerridge says. A bald statement of fact.

Charity says nothing, neither contradicting nor agreeing with her.

Mrs Kerridge waits for a couple of beats and when Charity is still not forthcoming, she says, mouth set in a grim line, 'We heard from your brothers that Mr Singh is spending the nights during the air raid in the basement with you and your parents.'

'There's nothing untoward going on. He's helping me with Da, that is all.' She aims for matter of fact, but nevertheless, a shrill note of defensiveness creeps into her voice.

Yes, there has been nothing untoward but it has been wonderful to have him beside her helping with Da during the long hours of night, broken and bookended by air raids. For Charity, the nights no longer drag, for in between caring for her parents, she and Veer chat about everything and nothing, loving each other with their eyes, their expressions, holding hands when they can.

'It won't do, Charity, love,' Mrs Kerridge says gently. 'You are young and he is right there, while all our young men are away at war. We understand. But...' And now, Mrs Kerridge is firm, 'Since your parents are indisposed, it is our duty to tell you that this pairing is unnatural. It won't work. If you persist in this madness, you will be mocked, shunned and worse. And think of your brothers...'

'Mr Singh is just like the rest of us, if anything, more kind and—'

'Perhaps. But that doesn't mean you can change society, expect years of prejudice to just disappear...'

Charity thinks then of Veer telling her about the racism he has endured. How, when he had been brought into hospital, wounded, the matron had sighed. 'Now where shall we put this coolie, then? As if I didn't have enough problems to deal with.'

'I was a problem, not a person, although my blood was the

same colour as that of my fellow white soldiers,' he had said, his voice haemorrhaging.

She could only guess at how it felt to be ostracised, to be at the receiving end of this casual, ingrained prejudice. Such a brave man, who had signed up, fought for, and nearly lost his life for this country, to be treated in this way.

Charity thinks back to before the war, when the pub had burned down, and everyone pointed fingers at Raghu, despite Divya's insistence that he was innocent. Charity too had been guilty of not quite believing Divya, of siding with the residents of West India Dock Road, quick to blame the man who was different, not one of them.

She has never considered herself as someone who judges people by their skin colour, but perhaps, at some level, she too is just as guilty. For she has never thought about it too deeply, if at all; *she* has never experienced racism. Before she met Divya and Veer, she never had to put herself in their shoes, what they might feel when treated differently everywhere, their skin branding them as 'other'.

'There might be a war on but it doesn't change people's attitudes, their blinkered prejudices one bit,' Mrs Kerridge is saying.

Exactly what Veer had said, his gaze melancholy, adding, 'In their own way, the so-called enlightened English are just as bigoted as the Germans. They might be waging war against the Germans but they too are guilty of the same narrow-mindedness.'

Charity may have been party to racism by not speaking up against it before, but no longer.

'Mr Singh is a good man,' she says firmly. 'That's what matters.'

Mrs Kerridge's face is suddenly sharp, all angles. 'My dear, he might be a good man but he is Indian.' Then more gently, cupping Charity's face, although Charity is tempted to pull away. 'He is not one of us. You don't know anything about him.'

'I know enough. That he's kind. A good man,' she repeats. Then, 'God made everyone, of all colours.'

'Yes, but he didn't mean for them to mix.'

'How do you know?' Charity asks.

Mrs Kerridge, instead of replying, parries with a question of her own: 'What do you know of his past? What he might have done? What made him run away to join the army?'

'If he ran away from anything, it was the racism he suffered in this country when he came here to study. He thought things would be better in the army, but sadly, they weren't,' she says, her voice rising indignantly.

In contrast, Mrs Kerridge is calm. 'All you know is what he's told you.'

'Are you implying he's a liar, just because he's brown?'

'My dear, we care for you. Our ways are different to theirs. How do you know that what he's told you is the truth?'

She thinks of the shadows crowding Veer's eyes, choking the light from them when he talked of his mother, his father, his life before he came to England.

'Do you miss India?' she had asked.

'Yes,' he had replied. 'I miss it like I miss my limb: a dull, throbbing ache, constant, always there. Sometimes, a smell, a taste, Miss Ram's food will intensify the longing as well as temporarily easing it. I would like to go back, one day, perhaps.' Those dark shadows shuttering his eyes again. Then, smiling softly at her, a sad ghost of a smile. 'Perhaps we could go together.'

She had thought of her own responsibilities, her parents,

her brothers, the lodging house and matched his sad smile with one of her own. 'Perhaps.'

Both knowing it would never happen but dreaming anyway.

He had taken her hand in his, squeezed it. 'One day, we will.' His voice wistful with longing.

And Charity had imagined travelling with him on a great big ship bound for India. Tasted the spicy adventure of it briefly on her tongue, and then briskly shrugged it away. It was one of those dreams that wouldn't become a reality in her lifetime.

Now, to Mrs Kerridge and the other ladies who have taken it upon themselves to impart advice, she says, 'He is good to my parents. My brothers love him. There is a war on. We don't know what might happen tomorrow. Why not be with who we want to without thought to colour and difference?'

The other ladies gasp in shock for Charity has all but admitted that she cares for Veer.

Only Mrs Kerridge is unfazed. She says kindly, 'Charity, love, war does not give pause to prejudice. It seems to feed it. As people get more desperate, they seem to want to feel superior to, have power over, someone to feel better about their own dismal situation. And those that don't match their ideal of what is right, who don't fit the norm, are the casualties.' She pauses to take a breath, then, 'Take one of my good friends from Green Street, Mercy. She's black, has lived in this country for years. When the war started, she wanted to do her bit. But when she responded to calls for citizens to help with the war effort, one look at her and she was turned away. Subjected to suspicion and mistrust: "What does the likes of you want at a munitions factory?"'

'I would have thought war would be colourblind,' Charity persists stubbornly even though Veer has told her different.

'Ah, love, *nothing* is.'

This distrust because of race makes her furious. Before Veer and Divya, she was guilty of not noticing it. But now she does and it galls her. People deciding somebody is better than someone else because of the colour of their skin. Just because people are dark-skinned, they are not given a chance.

'Charity, love, we care for you,' Mrs Kerridge says gently. 'You've had a hard enough life. We don't want you to suffer further. And if you persist in this infatuation—'

'It is not just an infatuation,' Charity cuts in.

The other ladies gasp again, louder, but Mrs Kerridge continues, as if she has not been interrupted, 'You will be subjected to mistrust and scorn. You will be treated like them and perhaps worse for putting your lot in with them.'

'*They* are not different. They are people just like us.' Now Charity cannot help the angry rise of her voice. She has had enough, all her reserves of patience exhausted. 'You all enjoy Divya's food. You said she is one of us.'

'And she is, but not everyone feels the same way, which is what we've been trying to tell you,' Mrs Kerridge says firmly, the others nodding along. 'Charity, if you persist with this, nothing good will come of it. And you deserve good after all you've been through. You must be with your own kind.'

Charity opens her mouth but Mrs Kerridge is not finished.

'These attachments won't work in the long run. Believe me. He too will resent you after a bit.'

'He wo—'

'And what if you have children? Do you want to subject them to abuse, discrimination? Have you thought of that? It will be too late to backtrack.'

And this stops Charity short, gives her pause.

Mrs Kerridge, sensing that her words have at last struck home, adds, 'Give some thought to what we've said, before you do anything rash.'

And Charity does. Despite herself, she does.

For the matrons' caution festers in her brain. The women of West India Dock Road helped her at her lowest, when she was a young girl out of her depth taking over the management of the lodging house while also bringing up her brothers and looking after her parents.

There is no doubt that they care for her. They have all been there for her, in their different ways.

Mrs Kerridge has been like a mother to Charity, protective and no-nonsense, giving advice when she needed it and also, like with Veer, when she hadn't asked for it.

Charity cannot wipe Mrs Kerridge's parting shot from her mind. 'And what if you have children? Do you want to subject them to abuse, discrimination?'

How would she feel if her children were reviled? Shunned? Treated differently because of the colour of their skin?

No.

No, no, no.

She shouldn't care about what people think, but she is realising that she *does*.

42

DIVYA

February 24, 1941

My dearest Raghu,

I cannot believe it. I do not want to.

But in my heart of hearts, I do.

I have felt down recently. Out of sorts.

I have missed you more than ever, but the ache of missing, it has been different, despairing, hopeless.

I knew. I have known for a while now.

I worried when I did not hear from you. The post is temperamental in wartime, I told myself. Letters don't come for weeks and then several turn up at once, I reasoned. And yet, I understood that at some level, I was lying to myself, refusing to entertain the nagging feeling gnawing away at me that something was very wrong.

And then... after weeks of nothing but worry, it arrived. Intimation of the kind I did not want but somehow knew I would receive even as the postmistress, Mrs Jennings dropped in at the curry house looking grim.

They found my letters to you and that's how they knew my address. That is why the telegram came to me.

All of my letters were next to your heart, they said.

Under your uniform.

Splattered with your blood.

Oh, Raghu.

You are not coming back.

I don't know how else to process this so I am writing to you.

Once again, letters that I will not send.

Before, I had the hope that I would give them to you.

Now I do not even have that.

I ache.

I mourn.

I miss.

I yearn for you.

This letter is getting splattered with my tears.

And yet still I write for I have got used to writing to you, my love, pouring my heart out, and I do not know what else to do.

You are with our beloved lost now. My ma and baba. Your ma.

You are watching over me, I hope.

Now I understand why I had this compulsion to come and see you when you wrote to say you were in Surrey. My heart urging me to visit even though I worried that you may not want to see me. I was scared of making the journey, of shutting the curry house. But I felt I had to see you.

Perhaps even then a part of me knew we would not get another chance.

I am glad we had that magical, stolen time together.

It is not enough.

But it is all I have and the memories of it will need to sustain me.

Goodbye, my love.

Rest now.

I am glad I had the privilege of loving you, even if our time together was too brief.

You were kind. Gentle. A great cook.

Your smile lit up my heart.

You touched me. You completed me.

I love you, now and always,

Yours,

Divya

43

CHARITY

Charity and Veer are in the basement with Charity's mammy and da, waiting out the air raid.

Da has been refusing food recently and Charity is worried. Her father is but skin and bones and remorse and pain, grieving his fellow soldiers from the first war even more than usual.

She is glad Veer is beside her, helping with Da during the long nights punctured by sirens. Veer is so calm and steady. His voice and his gentleness appear to, if not soothe her father, then at least ease, to some extent, his anxiety, stopping him from lashing out.

When Charity is with Veer, all the doubts occasioned after being given a talking to by Mrs Kerridge and the other ladies of West India Dock Road disappear and she feels only love, all-encompassing and glorious.

She hasn't confessed to Divya either her feelings for Veer or her worries about whether she should pursue the relationship. Her heart wants to but her mind, in the voices of Mrs Kerridge and the other ladies of West India Dock Road, advises caution.

For her friend is going through a terrible crisis of her own, having lost Raghu, the love of her life, to war.

Charity had held Divya as she sobbed in her arms.

'When I went to see him...' Divya had choked out in between sniffs, '...it seemed foolhardy although it felt right. But now,' she said, her face swollen and grief-stricken, splashed with sorrow, 'I am so glad we had that time together.'

The residents of West India Dock Road know Raghu is dead; the regulars were in the curry house when Mrs Jennings delivered the telegram.

They know that Raghu was a good friend of Divya's, that they were close. But they do not know that it was him Divya went to see at Christmas.

Charity, Veer, Mr Stone, Mr Brown, Mr Lee, Mrs Kerridge and the others urged Divya to shut the curry house for as long as it took for her to come to terms with the shock. But Divya insists on going on as usual, claiming she needs the distraction of work, that cooking the dishes she and Raghu prepared together helps her, as it is a sort of communion with him.

Charity wishes she could do more for her friend, who is looking wan and wrung out. She is sad about Raghu's untimely death herself and cannot begin to imagine what Divya must be going through. She'd liked Raghu. He had made Divya so very happy.

'I am here for you. You can talk to me at any time,' she has reiterated to Divya often.

Veer too is very cut up about Raghu's death. 'Another one of us gone,' he'd said and his eyes were wounds, his voice was hollow with pain.

Charity had held him, tears stinging her eyes, both of them grieving for the man they had known, separately, briefly but in that short time, grown to like him very much.

And this is why Charity feels she should throw all caution and doubts to the wind with regard to Veer. Life is uncertain, especially now. Nobody knows what's in store, what's coming next. And Veer makes Charity feel good. Protected. Safe. Beloved.

There is a whistling sound overhead and an almighty crash, a banging thud. The whole house jolts. The basement shudders as if a giant is shaking it in a rage. Da and Mammy's beds tremble and judder as if the giant's hand is pushing them this way and that at whim.

Veer, who was beside Charity's Da, nearly falls onto the bed, managing to steady himself by holding on to the bed frame.

Charity, who had been sitting by Mammy's bed, is scooted across the room, even as she feels the tremors rock her. She stands with difficulty, the ground unsteady beneath her feet, trying to get purchase.

Leaning on his crutch, Veer extends his hand to her. She grabs it as if it is her lifeline. *He* is her lifeline, for he squeezes her hand, offering comfort.

Their eyes meet as the building shakes, as beside Veer, her father cries, 'This is it. The reckoning. I deserve it. I left them. Now my judgement is coming.'

Almighty groaning, thuds and bangs, crashing and splintering above, causing them to flinch, to cower.

An expression of alarm, mirroring what Charity is feeling, crosses Veer's face for a brief instant before he replaces it with a serene steadiness.

But Charity saw it. She knows what's happening even before plaster dust rains on them from above. They have been bombed.

Her da cries out and Veer offers comfort, dropping Charity's hand, which leaves her feeling bereft, unanchored.

'We will be okay,' he says. 'We will be all right.'

How can he keep his voice even when the world is crumbling around them? Isn't his mouth gritty with dust?

Cracks appear in the ceiling and they are ambushed by a swirling snowstorm of ash-licked debris. The room feels too hot suddenly, rife with smoke, stinging their eyes, blinding them. It feels like the end of the world.

We are going to die, Charity thinks, catching Veer's eye.

He shakes his head, *No, we are not,* imparting calm.

She is so very grateful for him, here with her, Mammy and Da.

The scent of fire, the charred taste of it in her mouth.

If anything happens to us, at least the boys are spared, she thinks. Divya, Mrs Kerridge and everyone in the street will look after them, look out for them. I am so glad that they are with the others in the Tube station and not here.

'We will be fine,' Veer says to her father, but he is looking at Charity through the curtain of ash and grit, his conviction bolstering her.

Mammy is huddled under the sheets, her hands tapping her rosary beads, her Bible open beside her. She is praying: 'God is our refuge and strength, a very present help in trouble.'

She looks up at Charity and then, as if knowing Charity is petrified, she pats the space beside her and Charity climbs in next to her, breathing in her mother's scent of illness and musk.

And there, ambushed by plaster dust, singed by smoke, touched by fire, as the lodging house burns overhead, Charity holds her mother and listens to her tremulous voice quoting from her Bible: 'Cast your burden on the Lord, and he will sustain you,' through the pervading miasma of ruin, even as Veer maintains, firmly, 'We will be all right.'

* * *

Charity does not know how much time has passed, only that it is still going on, the endless crashing, banging, splintering, thuds overhead. The crackle and whoosh of fire. The taste of ash-slicked smoke, scorching their bodies. The smell of burning and devastation. They are blinded and blanketed by a storm of grit.

She and her mother pray while lying side by side.

The cracks in the ceiling are widening. Surely it's just a matter of time before it collapses on them?

I am ready, she thinks. I will die with Mammy and Da and my love. My brothers will be all right. They will cope.

She pushes her desire to see her beloved brothers' faces one last time, to kiss them, to hold them, firmly away. They are old enough now to cope.

But Paddy... her youngest brother. Who thinks prayer is insurance against anything bad happening to you. His earnestness, his sincerity. His innocence...

And Connor, who doesn't talk much but whose smile lights up his whole being. Who is so wise and loving and kind.

And Fergus, fiercely moral, always wanting to do the right thing, so very idealistic.

They will be *fine*, she tells herself.

'Charity,' Veer says, and there's something in his voice, in the way he says her name, that makes her heart thrum with concern.

Until now, he's been steady, balanced, apparently unfazed by what's happening. His voice imparting comfort to her as much as her da. But... is that a skein of anxiety threading through his voice? Has Veer given up hope too?

'Your da,' Veer says, 'he needs you.'

And that is when Charity realises that her father has stopped crying. There's silence in the room, broken only by the juddering thuds from above.

And her father's laboured pants.

Her father is gasping for breath.

She scoots off her mother's bed and wades through the fog of plaster dust to her father's side.

Veer hobbles over to Mammy's side and pulls her bed next to Da's.

Then, he kneels beside Charity, and she is grateful for his reassuring presence.

She takes her father's hand in hers. It is gnarled, a tissue of fragile skin stretched thinly over brittle bones. 'Da,' she says, 'Da, we will be all right.'

She doesn't know this. The ceiling might cave in on them at any moment.

'Can't you see?' he says, in between laboured breaths, his teeth chattering. But... his voice is calmer than she has ever heard it. 'This is the end,' he says in between gasps. 'Finally, this is the end.' He sounds relieved.

'Da, hang on, we are going to be fine. We are still alive. The all-clear will sound in a minute and then the firemen will rescue us.' *Please let this be true.*

'It's too late,' her da pants. 'Far too late.' A pause while he scrambles for breath. 'Tell my Moira I love her.'

'Mammy is right here.'

Mammy says, in her thin, shaky voice, 'I'm here, Paddy, love.'

'I love you, Moira. You are the love of my life,' Da says.

'And you are mine,' Mammy says, tears speckling her face even as her hands steadily tap at her rosary beads.

'And my children. My Charity and my boys. I love you but I don't deserve you. I deserve nothing. I let my friends die. I abandoned them.'

'Da, please, don't give up. We will be rescued soon. Hang in there,' Charity sobs.

'Holy Mary, Mother of God, pray for us sinners, now and at the hour of our death. Amen,' her mother chants.

'You are a good 'un, my Charity,' Da says, smiling right at her.

His gaze is finally clear after years of being clouded with remorse and agonised regret.

And then he closes his eyes.

44

DIVYA

March 15, 1941

Dear Jack,

I am so sorry to be the bearer of sad news.

Charity's lodging house was bombed. Charity, her mammy and the boys are fine, I hasten to add. The boys were with all of us in the Tube station. Mr Veer Singh, one of Charity's lodgers, was in the basement helping Charity with her da and mammy.

The house collapsed, but the firemen were able to rescue Charity, Mr Singh and Charity's mammy. They were shaken and bruised and suffering from smoke inhalation but otherwise unharmed.

But the trauma was too much for Charity's da. Paddy O'Kelly died, Jack. I'm so sorry to have to tell you this in letter form. I wish it was otherwise. We all wish, now more than anything, that you were here.

Please don't worry. I know it is easy to say this and that you will worry. We deliberated whether to tell you, but in the *end, we all decided that it would be worse to keep it from you.*

Charity has told me to assure you that she, her mammy and the boys are all right, given the circumstances. Coping. She is organising the funeral, with the help of the Ursuline nuns.

She, her mammy and the boys are staying with Mrs Kerridge at the moment. Her lodgers have moved to other boarding houses around the docks.

This is a short one just to update you on what's happened.

Please, please try not to worry.

I will write a longer letter with more news soon.

In the meantime, keep safe, keep well.

We will see you soon, we hope.

Much love,

Divya and all at West India Dock Road

45

DIVYA

March 15, 1941

My darling Raghu,

You are gone.

And yet I haven't got out of the habit of writing to you.

Charity's da died. Is he where you are? I imagine you reunited with your ma, meeting my ma and my baba and also Charity's da. All of our loved ones, uniting in the afterlife to look out for us, with our earthly foibles and burdens, our aches and our worries.

I miss you, Raghu. My heart is hollow with loss. The pain of losing you is constant, throbbing with every beat of my heart.

Imagining you just behind the incorporeal curtain that separates us mortals from those passed on, watching over me, is the only way I can go on. I look for signs from you everywhere: a white feather, a tiny shoot, a burst of hopeful green pushing through the cracks in the icy pavement, a ray of sun angling through the glower of clouds and gilding my face like a divine blessing.

Raghu, I cannot tell you how scary it was, for all of us from the street bar Charity, her parents and Mr Singh, huddling together underground, hearing the drone of enemy planes and then the thump, whizz, crump of bombs dropping very close by.

We exchanged worried looks while making sure the children among us remained unaware. But the older ones divined what was happening soon enough, their expressions bleak, while the young ones picked up on our anxiety and started to wail and could not be consoled.

We waited on tenterhooks for the all-clear and charged out of the station, although once we were in the open, and were ambushed by smoke, scorched by the distinct brand of fire, heard its gleeful crackle, too close, our steps faltered.

And when we had blinked away our stinging tears occasioned by smoke and apprehension, to be greeted by the devastation of bricks and destroyed belongings where Charity's lodging house used to be! I cannot tell you the shock, the upset, the sheer, uncomprehending terror.

The boys burst into tears. Paddy loudly. Connor and Fergus silently, silver tracks running down their cheeks.

Mrs Kerridge took charge, telling them not to worry, that their sister and parents were just fine, although I could see the hand she put around Paddy shook as if beset by tremors and the brisk smile she was affecting wavered at the corners, while her face was stark, her eyes agonised.

Mrs O'Riley started praying while the rest of us were rooted to the spot, our expressions washed out with fear.

I am sure the same chant was going through everyone's

heads, as it was in mine: please, please, please let Charity, her parents and Mr Singh be all right.

That abode that had sheltered me when I first came to West India Dock Road, like it had countless other displaced souls, where I found friendship in Charity, who welcomed me with a warm smile and open arms from that first moment I set foot in her lodging house, seeing past my colour to who I was within, and where, through cooking, I found my vocation, was no more.

Please Christian God, Hindu gods and goddesses, I prayed. I have lost the love of my life. Not my best friend too.

But looking at the smouldering devastation of bricks and belongings, singed by smoke, branded by fire, even as, alongside Mrs Kerridge and the other matrons, I comforted the boys and told them their sister and parents would be fine, I wondered how anyone could have survived this.

Yet, please gods, I prayed. As if the gods, Christian, Hindu, Jewish, who were already inundated by hundreds of thousands of prayers from tormented souls from all over the world would listen to mine. There were people who had lost everyone dear to them. Just because one of your beloveds was dead didn't mean you would be spared another. Look at poor Mrs Devlin, who lost her husband and her boys all to the first war.

Paddy was inconsolable and I concentrated on trying to soothe his hiccupping sobs.

'The ARP squad have given the all-clear. The firemen are going in,' *Mrs Boon said, her voice stumbling and stuttering with the fear we were all barely holding in.*

Please gods.

Some of the women joined Mrs O'Riley in prayer.

Their quiet and purposeful voices punctuated by Paddy's sobs were the only sound as we waited, hopeful and terrified, both at once.

And then Charity emerged, blinking, covered head to toe in plaster dust, coughing like nobody's business. But there was never a more beautiful sight.

The boys ran to her and threw their arms around her, all of them sobbing.

Then the firemen carried Charity's Mammy out, followed by Veer, who, accompanied by a fireman, hobbled out, balancing heavily on his crutch.

And then they brought Charity's da.

And there was not a dry eye on the street.

Raghu, I am crying too much to write any more. This paper is turning very soggy.

More soon, my love.

I will believe that you are watching over me, over all of us, alongside Ma, Baba, your ma and Charity's da.

That thought gives me comfort.

All my love, always,

Divya

46

CHARITY

All through her da's funeral, Charity is gripped by a feeling of unreality.

She watches her brothers heft the coffin which contains her father and she feels removed from herself, as if she is floating far above and watching the proceedings, like the lone bird hovering against a sky the vivid blue of fantasies, a dark shadow marring its sapphire perfection.

Her brothers, oh-so handsome in their suits, their too-long hair tackled into submission, neatly combed and slicked back, no doubt thanks to Mrs Kerridge. They look so very young, that vulnerable arch of their necks, their faces set in grim determination, Paddy's lower lip wobbling as he tries not to cry, Mr Barney helping him hoist the coffin.

The lodging house, her parents' legacy, gone. A smoking pile of ash and ruin.

Her da, the gregarious Paddy, life and soul of any gathering before he went to fight in the Great War, gone.

His eyes, clear and untroubled in that last moment before he shut them forever, the love in them, the pride. She wishes her brothers had seen it, although she does not wish for them what she, Veer and her parents endured during those fraught hours when she was convinced that the ceiling would give way and crush them all.

The relief when the firefighters came for them, mingling with sorrow that it was too late for Da.

Veer turning to her, saying, 'Charity, you go first.' Taking her hand, helping her over the debris and into the firefighters' arms.

A shaft of pain pincers her heart, which aches for him.

No. Fiercely, she pushes thoughts of him away. She cannot. Not now when she has so much to deal with.

The Ursuline nuns sing farewell to Paddy in the bombed-out church with the sky for ceiling, blue and cloudless, plastering the holes, contrasting with the broken, soot-stained bricks, golden arcs of occasional sun angling down like bounteous blessings, prayers drifting right to heaven without the hindrance of roof tiles.

Birds startle as the nuns burst into song, wide-arced shadows silhouetted against the gilded firmament, wings flapping frantically as they take flight, as below them, the congregation – the church is packed, the entirety of the East End turning up to bid Paddy goodbye – kneel, rustle and creak and sigh, on scarred pews. All these people, on intimate terms with suffering, reeling from loss, many who have lived through one war and are enduring a second. Praying in a bombed-out church, praying even when they know the next moment is not certain; nothing is.

Charity sits numb, her brothers weeping beside her, Mrs Kerridge on her other side. Mammy was too weak and ill to be moved, even though Mr Barney offered to carry her to church. She assured Charity that she didn't mind, that she had prayed with the nuns when they visited her before the funeral, for her beloved Paddy's soul and she would continue to pray in her room in the basement of Mrs Kerridge's house while they were at church.

Now, Charity's mind shuts down, unable to process this loss, still so woundingly fresh. She swallows down the pain, does not allow the tears pricking her eyes like barbs to fall.

A shaft of sunlight angles through the sky-ceiling and falls upon the congregation, haloing them in golden light just as the nuns' choir crescendos to Hallelujah.

And suddenly, as Father O'Donnell asks them to join him in confessing their sins, she spies Veer across the pew, and her heart flips over with that familiar swell of joy, thrill and love. He is staying at a lodging house in Bermondsey. She misses him with an all-consuming ache. But it is what she deserves.

She feels (irrationally, perhaps, but she can't help thinking so anyway) that if she had not been distracted by her love for Veer, if she had focused on her da, then perhaps he would be alive.

Veer tries to catch her eye but beside Charity, Mrs Kerridge slips her hand in hers, steadying her.

She cannot think of him now. She has to be there for her mother, her brothers, who are all floundering and grieving in their different ways and need her, like Mrs Kerridge has advised. She has responsibilities. She has no time for the frivolities of love.

She pretends not to see him, staring straight ahead, not allowing her gaze to swivel in his direction, like it wants to.

And yet, even as she bids goodbye to her father, she is aware of Veer. Her heart throbbing with yearning, wanting him.

* * *

After the funeral, she sees him coming towards her and her heart jumps, anticipation and happiness and love.

But Mrs Kerridge beckons to her. She needs Charity for something.

When, after a bit, Charity looks again in the direction she had seen Veer approach, he is not there.

She searches the congregation, looking over and behind the heads of all the various people wanting to speak with her, offer their respects and share their memories of Paddy.

But there is no sign of Veer. It is as if he was not there at all.

47

DIVYA

March 18, 1941

My darling Raghu,

I went to visit Mrs Ross, who still hasn't heard from her son. She is living in a world of her own, increasingly oblivious to this one, even more so recently. I took her some apple fritters, which she used to love back when she knew the whereabouts of both of her children. Now her daughter is a casualty of war and her son is missing.

I didn't tell Mrs Ross about you but somehow, she knew.

'You've lost someone,' she said softly.

I could only nod, tears budding in my eyes.

'It doesn't get easier, the ache of missing, yearning for them. We carry them with us always, our beloved lost,' she said. Then, 'It's amazing what the soul can bear. I unpack one memory of my Marge and my Tom and my Henry every day and relive it. It gets me through the long, endless hours.'

'Thank you,' I said.

She squeezed my hand, and we both shed a few tears for our beloved lost.

Do you know my favourite fantasy? That you are not gone.

That day, when we parted, I will miss you so very much, I thought, trying to stop the hot tears tormenting my eyes from escaping down my cheeks.

'Promise me you will come back to me,' I said.

You wrapped your hand around mine. That thrill, electric, trembling through me. And I thought of the previous night, our breaths mingling, hot and sweet, the poetry of our entwined limbs.

Your thumb stroked my wrist. I shivered as layers of feeling consumed me, as you conveyed everything you wanted to say but could not through touch.

You said, 'I… I didn't mind dying before when I thought you were lost to me. But now I…'

I trembled as your fingers etched tender messages upon my palm.

'Promise me,' I said again.

Your hand caressing mine, your eyes upon mine.

'Yes,' you promised. 'I will.'

You couldn't keep that promise. I don't hold it against you.

Yours, always,

Divya

48

CHARITY

Mrs Kerridge is away doing her shift for the Women's Voluntary Service and Charity's brothers are at the curry house. Charity, having made sure her mammy is comfortable in Mrs Kerridge's basement and will be all right for an hour or so, is just about to leave to join her brothers when there is a knock at the door.

She opens it to find Veer standing there, his hand raised to knock again.

She takes him in, her heart blooming with that familiar jolt of joy and love.

He looks thinner, haggard, as worn out and run-down, as ravaged as she feels.

'Charity,' he says and her name in his mouth is a poem of love and longing.

She wants to go into his arms. She crosses her own to not give in to the impulse.

'May I come in?' he asks, knowing, like she does, that the eyes of the street are on them, that even now, the news is making its way on wings of gossip all the way to the docks and beyond. That Mrs Kerridge will be hearing of it in the next few minutes, if she hasn't already.

Take me in your arms. I want to stay in them forever.

She stands aside, still keeping her arms tightly crossed.

As he brushes past her, his proximity raising goosebumps of yearning, she breathes in his scent: lime and the outdoors and something sweet, uniquely him. She wants to be wrapped in that scent. She wants him so much. She can't have him.

Mrs Kerridge had sat her down, after Da died. 'Your mammy is more fragile than ever. Your brothers are very distressed. They need you. You must concentrate on them for now, child, without distractions.' Then, clearing her throat and looking sternly at Charity, 'You do not have time for love, especially with a coloured man, not now.'

Charity, wrenched apart by grief and guilt, nodded. In any case, it was easy to agree with Mrs Kerridge when Veer was not around.

But now that he is here, within touching distance, all her resolutions and good intentions disappear in the face of the magnetic pull she feels towards him.

Oh, how she loves him.

But he... he is not...

She, her brothers and her mother are homeless, reliant on the kindness of Mrs Kerridge. She has to find a way to support her brothers and mother. She doesn't have time for love.

'I have been coming every day since...' Veer pauses, takes a breath, 'since we were bombed and Mrs Kerridge has been turning me away.' Then, his gaze upon hers, he extends his hand.

She wants to take it.

But she doesn't.

His hand drops to his side. 'I love you, Charity,' he says. 'And I thought you loved me too.'

I do. So very much.

Somehow, she finds her voice, which comes out a hoarse croak. 'I... I have my brothers and Mammy to think of.'

'I can help with your mammy and your brothers. I can help get the lodging house back to what it was. Lean on me, Charity. I love you.'

She is sorely tempted.

I love you too. It would be such a relief to take you up on your offer. I want that more than anything.

But, at the back of her mind, Mrs Kerridge's words, echoed by the street: 'He is different. Not one of us. It will not work.'

'I just...' Charity says. 'I need some space.'

'Is it because of my colour?' His voice is so sad. Defeated.

Mrs Kerridge's voice in her head again: 'You might think you love him, but what are you prepared to risk to have him? Your life has been hard enough. And with the lodging house bombed, it just got harder. If he is in your life, it will *never* be easy. Not for you and especially not for any children you have with him.'

'This is time for my family,' she tells him.

'I thought you were different,' he says and his voice, his eyes are bright with despair. 'But you... you are just like all of them.'

And with that, he turns and wrenches open the door.

Wait, she wants to cry. Her heart howling for him. *Wait. I love you.*

But she does not say a word.

She watches him limp away and then she shuts the door on him, leans against it and sobs.

49

DIVYA

March 20, 1941

My dearest Raghu,

Charity's da funeral was heartbreaking.

If there's one thing I have learned during these inter-minably long and endless months of war, it is this: war does not respect grief. It does not discriminate. It does not give pause.

Charity is broken in more ways than one.

She is grieving for her father and missing Mr Singh.

Yes, your friend. Yes, she cares for him.

I knew she had feelings for Mr Singh, and he for her. It was obvious when you saw them together; they only had eyes for each other.

The news was up and down the street in minutes, that Mr Singh had declared his feelings for Charity; what was he thinking? He, a brown man wanting to be with a white woman? He was made welcome on the street, yes, but there were certain rules you didn't break, certain lines you didn't cross. Didn't he know that?

Charity, rightly, the street agreed, sent him packing.

I can see she's devastated, undone by missing and yearning; it takes one to know one. But of course, everyone in the street has put it down to her mourning for her father and the loss of her home and business.

Mr Singh professed his feelings for her at the wrong time, the silly sod.

Just when she was overcome by grief for her da and at a loss after her livelihood was destroyed.

So she said no.

He of course thought it was because of his colouring.

Perhaps there was an element of it. Charity doesn't see colour. But I know she worries about what people will think. And the opinion of the residents of West India Dock Road matters to her as they were there for her when she took over the running of the lodging house although but a child herself. It doesn't help that she and Mr Singh were separated after Charity's lodging house was bombed; Mr Singh is stopping at a boarding house in Bermondsey and Charity, her mammy and her brothers are staying with Mrs Kerridge.

I would have happily had them stay with me, and I did offer. 'I'll sleep in the kitchen. You, your mammy and the boys can have the upstairs to yourselves,' I said.

'Ah, Divya, you're a gem,' Charity said, tears in her eyes. 'But Mrs Kerridge happens to have a basement where she's installed a bed for Mammy, and which will work in the event of an air raid.' She paused, took a breath, eyes shining. 'It will be traumatic after what happened…'

'Yes,' I said.

'But it's best in the circumstances. The boys can go with

Mrs Kerridge and all of you to the Tube station and I'll stay with Mammy.'

'I can come and be in the basement with you and your mammy,' I offered.

She hugged me, eyes wet. 'I know, but me and Mammy will be fine. Please look after the boys for me.'

'You know I will.'

'I know,' she whispered into my neck.

And so, Charity is lodging with Mrs Kerridge, who is not one to mince words, and the first to offer advice and opinions, whether wanted, asked for, or otherwise.

You see, Charity's mammy was very proud and refused to admit that she needed help after Paddy was born. She did not want to lose face with the women of the street.

And Charity, although only a child, absorbed that. She too does not want to lose face.

The women of West India Dock Road, especially Mrs Kerridge, have done a lot for her over the years. And so their opinion, even if she knows it is prejudiced, matters to her.

Yet still she loves Mr Singh and she is hurting.

I want to shake her, want to say, 'Forget everyone else's opinions. Listen to your heart. You love him, I can see. So go to him, Charity. Don't lose him. He's alive. Isn't that something?'

I have tried hinting at it but she's not in the right frame of mind to listen.

In any case, she's getting more advice than she knows what to do with from Mrs Kerridge and the other ladies of West India Dock Road, which is not helping, and which confuses and upsets her all the more.

I will be there for her and offer my thoughts when she

asks for them. But she has to come to this realisation about Mr Singh in her own way. In her own time.

I need to give her time.

Charity's da's funeral was a sombre affair. But in a strange way, also comforting.

In the churchyard, the yew trees that had miraculously survived the bombing, although some had shrapnel embedded in them, which young Paddy, ever observant, had pointed out to all of us, sighed over the newly dug grave as snatches of hymns drifted on the mournful wind, chilled by, tasting of death.

But inside the church, it was different.

The nuns' voices raised in song echoed solemnly in the hushed confines, rainbow patterns of light filtering through splintered glass, painting the ceiling (most of it bombed out, the sky angling through the gaps) and the myriad statues, in a golden glow. My feet rested on bricks beneath which lay centuries-old dead. It was strangely soothing, all our sorrows put in perspective in this hallowed space of death and afterlife, heaven and hell, devils and angels, saviours and demons.

Since then, I have visited church often.

It offers solace. I find peace there.

I find you in the silence between breaths, among the rows and rows of headstones commemorating the long departed. I can imagine you looking over me, looking out for me.

I love you, Raghu.

You are gone but you are always with me.

Yours, forever,

Divya

50

CHARITY

Charity misses Veer with a physical ache. As if she has misplaced a part of herself.

And although Mrs Kerridge says she has made the right decision, the other ladies nodding approvingly, it is scant comfort.

She wants to talk to Divya but how can she tell Divya her doubts? Her worries about Veer being different, that they might not be compatible, although when she was with him, it felt so very *right*. Her agonising that their children, if they have them, and she would *love* to have children with Veer, will be shunned?

As a fellow Indian, Divya would be hurt if Charity shared all this.

And Divya is going through a crisis of her own after losing the love of her life. Charity does not want to burden her friend with her own upset when Divya's love is never coming back.

But... Veer's absence is an aching, open wound, refusing to scab over, and she wonders increasingly, no matter what the matrons say, whether she has made a mistake.

She thought it would be simple again. That she could concentrate on Mammy and the boys. That she wouldn't feel torn always.

But her brothers ask after him.

They miss him and tell her so.

I do too, she wants to cry. *So very much.*

'It's not the same without him,' her brothers say.

'Why did you send him away, Charity?' Paddy asks. He, like everyone else on West India Dock Road and beyond, has heard the gossip. 'We thought you would get married.'

Connor, beside him, nods in agreement. Fergus is at his apprenticeship at the docks.

'Would you have liked that?' she asks, tasting salt in her mouth.

Both her brothers nod vigorously.

'We would love it. It's what we wanted, Fergus too. He told us so,' Paddy says.

'And most of all, he makes you happy, Charity,' Connor, who does not speak unless he feels it is very important, says. 'That's why we wanted you to marry him.'

She feels tears prick her eyes. Her brothers don't want a martyr. They want her to be happy just like she wants happiness for them. Loving Veer did not take away from Charity caring for her brothers and her parents like she had thought. Instead, it had allowed her to do so with good grace rather than resenting every minute of it, because she was happier.

But the realisation has come a little too late.

Veer is no longer at the lodging house in Bermondsey, she's heard.

He is gone and nobody knows where he is.

51

DIVYA

April 4, 1941

My darling Raghu,

You are no longer of this world and I am still trying to come to terms with that.

You changed me, fundamentally so.

I experienced the heady intoxication of love, and also utter, devastating loss.

Although it hurts more than anything, and I miss you with every breath, if I had to choose between having you in my life briefly to love and lose, and not knowing you at all, I would choose you every single time. Even knowing I would lose you, experience this colourless world without you in it after the glorious, heady, supercharged brightness of loving you, I would still choose to love you.

And now…

Oh, everything has changed yet again.

It is like that paperweight that Paddy had: every time you shook it, the scene inside changed.

This is how it's been since you came into my life.

It has changed.

For better.

For worse after I lost you.

And now…

I have been so very down the last few weeks. Since even before I received the telegram, for I somehow knew you were gone. There was a missing, a lack, an absence in my heart which beat for you.

I have gone through the motions, cooking, smiling, hosting, running the curry house.

Keeping busy.

But my heart has not been in it.

My heart has been yearning for you.

So I did not notice that I hadn't bled. That despite hardly being in the mood to eat, my clothes were getting snug.

And then last night, we were all in the Tube station when heavily pregnant Mrs Smith started to moan. 'The baby's coming. Help, it's decided to come now.'

Immediately, the women got to work, efficiently and calmly dealing with this emergency while the men looked horrified, edging away as far as possible, which wasn't far enough as the platform was packed full of people taking refuge from the raids.

Mrs Kerridge took charge, ordering the men to, 'stop your infernal games of cards and whatnot and entertain the young ones.'

The children, including Mrs Smith's girls, who were looking very worried, were taken in hand by Mr Brown and Mr Stone. 'Now then, we shall teach you how to play chess.'

Meanwhile, Mr Crosby took the young boys, Paddy and

Connor among them, who were getting inquisitive as to
what their sisters and aunts and mothers were up to, aside.
''Ere, lads, you'll want to know what 'appened when I was
bombed when bedding down with the spices and rum
down by the wharves.'

'He wasn't bombed as far as I know. He's making it all
up,' Mrs Neville said, snorting indignantly.

But his convoluted tale of heroism and near misses kept
the boys engrossed enough to ignore the huddle of
purposeful women all the same.

Babies were thrust none too ceremoniously upon Mr
Rosenbaum and Mr Lee.

Mr Rosenbaum looked perplexed by the infant in his
arms but Mr Lee smiled gently and started rocking the baby
he was in charge of while humming gently under his breath.

Taking his cue, Mr Rosenbaum did the same but his
humming was more of a deep-throated growl that fright-
ened the child he was holding to tears.

Mr Barney took it from him and cooed to it and the
bubba rewarded Mr Barney with a gummy smile.

The women meanwhile had created a makeshift wall
around Mrs Smith.

Mrs Rosenbaum, always prepared, supplied towels and
blankets to make Mrs Smith comfortable.

And once she was, the women gently guided her
through her contractions, telling her when to push.

To her credit, Mrs Smith did not make a sound, knowing
her girls were nearby, although she was in excruciating
agony.

Instead, she bit down on one of the towels while she
gripped my hand very hard and Mrs O'Riley's on the other
side.

It took nearly the whole night, but towards morning, just before the all-clear came through, her baby was born, his plaintive mewls drowned out by the siren and the rustles of those further down the platform and not involved in helping Mrs Smith, as they started gathering their belongings and standing up and stretching in preparation to leaving.

You would have thought there would be a great big celebration when the baby was successfully delivered but there was only a muted, 'Oh,' from Mrs Boon, who was poised to catch the bubba.

And from Mrs Kerridge, to whom the baby was passed to be wiped down, for she had been waiting with the towel in avid readiness, another distinctly uncomfortable, 'Ah.'

There wasn't the rousing cheer that should have accompanied the birth, especially given they had all assisted its arrival into the world. Instead, gasps from the women gathered beside and around Mrs Kerridge.

Mrs O'Riley and I exchanged worried looks; we were on either side of Mrs Smith, holding her hands, so hadn't had a glance at the baby yet.

Mrs Smith too was worried, for, although she could hear her infant crying, there was no accompanying joyous clamour. She queried, in an anxious voice, 'What's wrong? Is my bubba all right?'

In response, Mrs Kerridge silently handed her the child.

A lovely bonny, brown baby boy.

Yes. Brown.

Mrs Smith is white as they come and so is her husband.

In the Tube station, sheltering from air raids, we celebrated every little triumph.

But this, a new baby, whom we'd all helped to birth, was not celebrated.

There was no excitement, no happiness, no enthusiasm, apart from an exhausted Mrs Smith cooing over her babe, kissing him, clasping him to her chest, as tears of joy and tiredness fell down her eyes unchecked.

There was a shocked drawing in of breath from the other women as they set eyes upon the babe and then, they turned away from him and from Mrs Smith, the sight of his tiny, brown body nestled against his mother's pale chest.

Mrs Kerridge pursed her lips. Mrs Neville sucked her teeth as if she was chewing on something bitter.

You see, there had been a lot of gossip about Mrs Smith's pregnancy among the matrons of West India Dock Road when they were at the curry house which I couldn't help overhearing.

'Her husband has been away at the frontline for a few months longer than the duration of her pregnancy,' Mrs Kerridge had said severely.

'Unless she's miraculously conceived.' Mrs Neville had sniffed disapprovingly.

'Don't be catty,' Mrs Devlin had said. 'A child is a blessing.' Her face wistful. For she was all alone in the world, having lost her sons and her husband to the first war.

'Well her husband will have a shock, that's all I'm saying,' Mrs Neville tutted.

But nevertheless, whatever they thought of the matter, the women of West India Dock Road are essentially kind and good hearted and they had made a fuss of Mrs Smith and her girls and had come to her aid without question when she went into labour.

But this, a brown baby born to a white woman, was too much for them.

'He's beautiful,' I said.

Mrs Smith beamed at me gratefully.

The matrons gave the men the eye, when they hesitantly asked to have a look see, having picked up from the decidedly chilly atmosphere that something was wrong.

It was Mrs Smith's girls who said, crinkling their noses in bafflement even as they marvelled at their little brother, 'But Ma, 'e don't look nuffin like us.'

Mrs Smith was spared answering for the Tube station was emptying after the all-clear went, everyone trudging back up to check our abodes were still standing, Mr Rosenbaum gallantly helping Mrs Smith, her new bubba clasped to her bosom, up the stairs.

It was sometime during that night, as Mrs Smith clung on to me for dear life through her increasingly frequent and devastatingly painful contractions – she nearly tore a chunk off the towel – that it dawned on me, Raghu, why I was feeling sick in the mornings, why my clothes were tight, why I have not bled.

I think you took the fact that I needed something to remember you by to heart for…

Yes. You have left me a tangible memento.

Nothing short of a miracle, Raghu!

Now I see why my heart urged me so forcefully to visit you at Chalmer Grange, even though I worried that your feelings might have changed.

It was destiny. It was meant.

Oh Raghu, you do live on in me, and not only in my memories.

I am thrilled. I am ecstatic. I am excited. I am nervous.

I love you and I love this little being we have created together more than life itself.

Yours always,

Divya and baby

52

CHARITY

Charity is heartbroken as she sits beside her mother.

So much has happened.

So much lost.

This war has taken and taken and is still doing so. She hopes and prays that it will be over before her brothers are old enough to join. *Please. Not my brothers too.*

She does not know how those mothers and sisters and daughters and wives who've lost so many loved ones keep on keeping on.

Her father is gone.

'He is in heaven,' the nuns assure. 'Interceding with God on your behalf. You will be blessed.'

Charity does not feel blessed.

She found a good man, a man who loved and cherished her.

But she let him go.

'Your da,' her mammy says.

Charity startles. She did not realise her mother was awake.

'He was so handsome.' She takes a breath. Even talking

continuously tires her, more so since the smoke inhalation when trapped in the basement as their lodging house was bombed. 'But it was his kindness that I fell for.'

Charity does not recognise this version of her father.

'He was,' her mammy says gently, 'just like your man.'

'My man?' Charity looks at Mammy.

Her mother smiles softly at her. 'I know all that goes on, my heart.'

Her mother knows that Charity loves Veer. She called him, *your man.*

Even as Charity processes this, her mother says, 'He used to come and sit with me, chat to me. He treated me with respect. Listened to my opinions, asked for my advice. He told me how much he loved you.'

She takes a breath even as Charity marvels at her mother's revelation. 'He did?'

'Yes.' Mammy smiles tenderly at Charity. 'He would sit with your da too. Listen to him rant. He soothed him through his panic attacks. He is a good man.'

Her mammy gently raises a tremulous hand and wipes the tears Charity did not even realise she was shedding. They glisten on her fingers like precious jewels.

'I loved your da so much that I gave up what I thought of as my calling for him.' Mammy says, her voice wistful, gaze far away. 'And those first few years were wonderful. But too brief.' She sighs. 'The war changed him.' A pause, then, 'None of you got to see the man I loved. But I see him in all of you. You, Charity, with your loyalty, your love, your kindness and your great, big heart. Fergus with his idealistic determination. Connor with his mischief and his humour. And little Paddy's innocence.' Another longer pause. Then, 'Yes I know the war destroyed your father's innocence. But the Paddy he was before the war was naive and generous to a fault. A good man. And you have one of those.'

Mammy pats Charity's palm gently. 'A kind and good man is hard to find. There are precious few with the war taking all of our men. When you find one, you need to hold on to him. You don't know how many years you will get together. You must cherish them.' She takes a long breath.

Charity can see she is tiring. 'Mammy...'

Mammy holds her hand up, palm outward. She has more to say. 'Charity, love, appearances don't matter. Nothing matters in the end except what's inside.' Another long breath. Then, Mammy says haltingly, 'I was promised to God, and when I abandoned God for a mere man, people talked. They mocked.' Another pause for breath. 'When Paddy came back changed from the war, they said it was God's revenge.'

'I didn't know this.' Charity is shocked.

Mammy smiles tenderly at Charity. 'People will always talk, my love. But you must follow your heart. You have a good man in Veer. Keep him.'

'If... if we have children, they might be shunned and made fun of.' Charity shares her biggest fear with her mammy.

'Like I said, people will always mock. In any case, you don't want people in your life who revile your children because of their colouring. If they truly care for you, they will stand by you and your children. God made people of every colour and children are his gifts, his blessings to us.'

Charity tastes the sea in her mouth, feeling as if a great, big burden has been lifted off her chest. But then, her heart is heavy again for she remembers that Veer is... 'He's gone,' she cries.

'He's not gone,' her mother says. 'My Paddy is gone. Veer is here. Life is short and you don't know what's around the corner.' A pause for breath. 'So, my heart, wipe your tears and go tell him you love him.'

Charity sniffs even as she takes her mother's fragile hand in hers.

During the years of caring for Mammy, she's often felt like their roles have been reversed and she is the mother and Mammy the child.

She has sometimes resented it.

But now when she most needed her mother, without realising it, her mother has come through for her.

Charity was disheartened. Badly in need of direction.

When she had sat down beside her mother, she was feeling hopeless.

But now her mammy has given her the gift of hope.

She kisses her mother's hand.

'Thank you, Mammy,' she says.

'Go find him, my heart.' Mammy smiles. 'And before you do, pinch your cheeks to put some colour in them. He loves you anyway but there's no harm in looking your best.'

And Charity smiles through her tears.

She takes a breath.

And another.

In loving Veer and letting him go, she has come to understand that while it does not matter to her that Veer is of a different colour, she does care, far too much, for other people's opinions. She has always considered herself strong and independent-minded and she *is*, for the most part, but she has realised that she wavers when faced with personal decisions. She has learned that she has to allow others in, instead of doing everything herself and getting overwhelmed and exhausted.

She thought Veer helping her in the basement with Da was

a distraction which took her focus away from Da. But Da had liked Veer and Veer was able to soothe him, which Charity was grateful for. She would not have been able to handle Da by herself without getting hurt, as he was getting more and more agitated the longer the air raids went on.

And loving Veer did not mean she was neglecting her family; instead, she was better able to care for them, for she was happy in herself.

Charity was used to doing everything by herself. But she realises that she was tired and worn out and fed up and resentful. She was doing everything with bad grace, just because she had to. Then Veer came into her life. He took some of the burden from her, asked her to lean on him, and she did. She found that when they worked together, she enjoyed the chores she'd hated doing on her own. Veer turned her into a better version of herself. He made her happy. Her brothers had seen this. She has been looking after everyone but she needs someone who will look out for her and with whom she can share her worries, her thoughts, her life. This is what her brothers and her mother are trying to tell her. And Mammy has made her realise that she must listen to her heart, instead of being swayed by other people's opinions.

She will do as her mother says. She will find Veer. He might not be at the lodging house in Bermondsey but he couldn't have gone far, surely. She will not rest until she knows his whereabouts and then she will go to him. This man who was with her when her father died, holding her hand.

Who would talk to her parents, treat them like human beings, not invalids.

Who would comfort Da when he had one of his turns.

He is a good man.

Her man, she hopes, if he will still have her.

She will tell him she loves him.

I'm sorry, she will say. *I was swayed by what everyone said, and I am truly sorry.*

She hopes that it will be enough.

Please, she prays, *let it not be too late.*

53

DIVYA

April 18, 1941

My dearest Raghu,

Every day, I clock new changes in my body as our babe grows within.

Oh, the extraordinary, amazing miracle of it!

I wish you were here, to experience it with me.

I choose to believe that you are doing so, from wherever you are, in the next dimension, beyond the flimsy curtain that is all that separates earth-bound people from those who've moved on. And that you are just as thrilled, awed and blown away as I am.

Raghu, after you were gone, I did not want to go on.

I wanted to die, join you in the afterlife. I didn't care about the air raids and didn't want to take shelter from them.

But I did. For your voice in my ear telling me I must compelled me.

Now I know why.

I asked you for something of yours to remember you by while you were at war.

I was hoping for letters.

But you have given me a gift far beyond my wildest dreams.

We never talked about the future, marriage, family, children together.

When you died, I thought that was it. My dreams of a lifetime with you blown apart on a foreign battlefield.

But now, miraculously, magically, I do have a future which features you: your child in my womb.

I am scared, I will admit. To bring this babe into a world brought to its knees by war, on my own, without you.

Here, on West India Dock Road, I have been welcomed warmly into the fold, and am so very happy to have found my place. But all that will change, I fear...

For I am not married, and I will be having a child.

I love this babe so very much and so fiercely already. I will protect it with my all. But will it be at the cost of the community I have found here? My vocation, the curry house?

I am worried, nervous.

But I tell myself that I have been here before.

I was scared when I stood up for you even though everyone on West India Dock Road believed you had started the fire at the public house and killed those sailors.

But I did it anyway and emerged the stronger for it.

I was scared when I came to see you at Chalmer Grange. But thanks to that, we created a child together.

I am scared now.

It won't be easy, I know. I will most likely be ostracised. I will lose my hard-won place here on West India Dock Road with the people I love and have come to think of as family, this place that I have begun to call home.

But…

Loving you has transformed me from a naive girl into a strong woman.

And now, you have made me a mother.

I want this child.

Your legacy.

Something of you and me.

And I am going to have this child regardless of what is in store for me, for us.

Everyone talks about Mrs Smith behind her back.

Some have been foul to her face.

She is being treated differently already.

'Shame on you and your half-caste!' I heard someone hiss at Mrs Smith when I was going to Mr Lee's for groceries and she walked past. I turned round to glare at them, give them a piece of my mind, but they were gone.

I suspect it will be the same for me, if not worse.

I will become a pariah, perhaps.

It won't matter so much if they hurl abuse at me but what will hurt is if my child is shunned, targeted, treated differently.

I have considered going back to India. But even if I had the money for a passage back, which I don't, I cannot return until the war is over as the ships have all been requisitioned for army purposes.

And in any case, by running away, I will not escape. I will still be a single mother in India having to find my way, support my child.

I have decided that I will stay right here on West India Dock Road.

I have found my place and my community here.

Will they accept my child, born out of wedlock? Or will this be a step too far for them? Whatever it is, I will face it.

There will be people who will not want anything to do with me, no doubt.

But I also hope that there will be others who will accept me and my child.

Charity and her brothers, definitely.

And Mr Lee too. He stood by you when everyone else took against you because you were my friend.

As for Mr Stone, Mr Brown, Mrs Kerridge, Mrs Neville and the others on West India Dock Road whom I've come to care for… we shall see.

Your love has gifted me this child.

I am worried about the future but nevertheless, I feel blessed.

Yours, always,

Divya and baby

EPILOGUE
PADDY

His mammy is calling him home, her voice carrying all the way to where he lies, on the moist bed of sand beside the vast expanse of water, his head thrown to the wide-open sky, dreaming of sailing away on one of those big ships, carrying the exotic, alluring scent of foreign lands and mystic adventure.

He is weary to the bones.

Too tired to walk home, across the fields.

He longed to escape his beloved Ballinacurra. And he did, he remembers now. Took one of those very ships he'd long dreamed of sailing on. But when away, he missed home like a sore tooth, the pain sharp and prodding, always there.

He had adventures aplenty. He even fought a war.

Oh, the war. His friends, fellow mates, dead or dying in foreign soil and he...

He was a coward. When it mattered, he did not have the guts to do the brave thing. The right thing. He had run away to safety. Their dying eyes, the life force leaving them, begged him, pleaded with him, 'Don't leave us here.'

And yet, he did.

He will never forgive himself for it.

He abandoned them but he got to live his life.

His beloved Moira, whom he didn't treat well. Using her to forget what he had done. The doctor said no. Enough. No more babies. And yet he went to her, for in her arms, briefly he was able to forget.

And he broke her too.

He has a lot to account for when he enters the pearly gates. Will he do so?

'Yes,' Mammy whispers in his ear. 'You are already here, Paddy, with me and your da.'

Ah, but Heaven, it looks just like Ballinacurra. Lush fields. The river sparkling and glinting like the gleam in Moira's eyes, the sparkle on her face during their first days together, the glow when she saw him.

Heaven is home. Ballinacurra.

He has come home.

'Look, your friends are here,' Mammy says.

And he sees them. The soldiers he had abandoned.

'I'm sorry,' he says, afraid to look at them, face them, coward to the last.

'We understand,' they say and their voices are gentle and now he looks up.

They are not angry. They are smiling at him. And, wonder of wonders, they are not dying and limbless but whole. They are as he remembers them before war rendered them bloodied and broken. They are the enthusiastic youths who signed up alongside him, eager to fight for their country, for victory.

'We would have done the same, Paddy,' they say. 'We never blamed you. It's time you forgave yourself. You were but a boy. Just a few years older than your Fergus.'

He feels an easing of his heart, a lightness, the burden he has carried for years, falling away.

He is home. With his mammy and his da.

And yet...

Moira, the love of his life.

Fergus, Connor, Paddy and Charity. His beloved children.

He's left them behind. In a land once again being torn asunder by yet another war.

'They're all right,' Mammy whispers in his ear. 'Look.'

And he does.

They are surrounded by rubble, by loss, by devastation.

They are mourning him.

But...

'They have each other,' his mammy whispers.

And yes, he can see that they do.

Moira, Charity, Fergus, Paddy, Connor, consoled and looked after by the residents of West India Dock Road. Friends and neighbours who have become family. Broken by loss yet bolstering each other through their troubles.

His loved ones are not alone.

'They are never alone,' Mammy whispers. 'They have each other. And they have us.'

Mammy smiles tenderly at him. 'Moira will join you here soon. She can let go now Charity has someone to love and look out for her.'

And there is Charity, going up to a man, his dark skin glowing with goodness. Kindness. His eyes bright and soft with love. He puts his arm around Charity, Paddy's firstborn, whose tender shoulders are bent double with all she is carrying, the responsibility she hefts.

'Let go, Charity, love; let him ease your burden,' Paddy whispers.

As if she has heard his prompting, his daughter does just that, sinking into the embrace of the man she loves. And they kiss, gently, tenderly.

'They will be all right,' Mammy whispers.

And he sees that they will be, his children.

And his wife, his love, will be here soon.

'She is tired, she is ready,' Mammy whispers.

Mammy, Da and the other soldiers, his mates, they smile warmly, affectionately, at him.

'You're back home,' Mammy says gently. 'You rest now.'

And he does.

Finally, he does.

* * *

MORE FROM RENITA D'SILVA

Another book from Renita D'Silva, *The Secret Keeper*, is available to order now here:

https://mybook.to/SecretKeeperBackAd

ACKNOWLEDGEMENTS

I would like to thank my wonderful editor, Francesca Best – I don't know how I got so very lucky but I am beyond grateful to have you as my editor. THANK YOU for all you do.

Thank you to all the amazing team at Boldwood for helping make this book the very best it can possibly be, and for making it travel far and wide.

Thank you, Emily Reader, for your eagle eye and wonderful suggestions during copy edits for this book.

Thank you, Shirley Khan, for proofreading this book.

Thank you, Ben Wilson, for overseeing the production of the audio version of the book.

Thank you, Rachel Odendaal, Wendy Neale and all the marketing team for the amazing marketing campaign.

Many thanks to Kathryn Smith for ensuring copies of the book arrive with me in plenty of time for the launch.

Thank you to my lovely author friends, Angie Marsons, Sharon Maas, Debbie Rix, June Considine (aka Laura Elliot), whose friendship I am grateful for and lucky to have.

A huge thank you to my mother, Perdita Hilda D'Silva, who reads every word I write; who is encouraging and supportive and fun; who answers any questions I might have on any topic – finding out the answer, if she doesn't know it, in record time – who listens patiently to my doubts and who reminds me, gently, when I cry that I will never finish the book: 'I've heard this same refrain several times before.'

I am immensely grateful to my long-suffering family for willingly sharing me with characters who live only in my head. Love always.

And last, but not least, thank you, reader, for choosing this book.

AUTHOR'S NOTE

This is a work of fiction set around and incorporating real events.

The convalescent centre, Chalmer Grange, in Guildford is a product of my imagination.

The Poplar Hospital received a direct hit in 1941 and had to close for a short while but for the purposes of this story I have taken liberties with the truth, making it so that half the hospital was bombed in 1940 but nevertheless was still operating at full speed.

There were daytime air raids during the Blitz but the air raid in which Charity is caught when she goes searching for Fergus is entirely made up.

I apologise for any oversights or mistakes and hope they do not detract from your enjoyment of this book.

ALSO BY RENITA D'SILVA

Standalone Novels

The Secret Keeper

The West India Dock Road Series

New Arrivals on West India Dock Road

Wartime Comes to West India Dock Road

ABOUT THE AUTHOR

Renita D'Silva is an award-winning author of historical fiction novels. She grew up in the south of India and now lives in the UK.

For an exclusive story from the world of Renita D'Silva's West India Dock Road series, sign up to Renita's newsletter!

Follow Renita on social media here:

facebook.com/RenitaDSilvaBooks

x.com/RenitaDSilva

instagram.com/renita_dsilva

bookbub.com/profile/renita-d-silva

Letters from
the past

Discover page-turning
historical novels from
your favourite authors
and be transported
back in time

*Join our book club
Facebook group*

https://bit.ly/SixpenceGroup

*Sign up to our
newsletter*

https://bit.ly/LettersFrom
PastNews

Boldwood

Boldwood Books is an award-winning fiction publishing company seeking out the best stories from around the world.

Find out more at www.boldwoodbooks.com

Join our reader community for brilliant books, competitions and offers!

Follow us
@BoldwoodBooks
@TheBoldBookClub

Sign up to our weekly deals newsletter

https://bit.ly/BoldwoodBNewsletter

Made in the USA
Las Vegas, NV
15 July 2025

24952074R10177